Also by the Author

The Nightmare Man

IRONS IN THE FIRE

IRONS IN THE FIRE

THE CHRONICLES OF TALIS: BOOK I

ANTONIO URIAS

Copyright © 2015 Antonio Urias. All Rights Reserved.

Edited by Jake Logsdon

Cover design by James T. Egan, www.bookflydesign.com.

No part of this book may be reproduced in any form or by any electronic or mechanical means including information storage and retrieval systems, without permission in writing from the author. The only exception is by a reviewer, who may quote short excerpts in a review.

This book is a work of fiction. Names, characters, places, and incidents either are products of the author's imagination or are used fictitiously. Any resemblance to actual persons, living or dead, events, or locales is entirely coincidental.

ISBN-13: 978-1515281689

For my parents

Contents

Prologue — xiii

Part I. The City

1. Chapter One — 3
2. Chapter Two — 10
3. Chapter Three — 17
4. Chapter Four — 30
5. Chapter Five — 38
6. Chapter Six — 51

Part II. The Smoke and Mirrors Club

7. Chapter Seven — 69
8. Chapter Eight — 77
9. Chapter Nine — 85
10. Chapter Ten — 95

| 11. | Chapter Eleven | 112 |

Part III. The Turning Point

12.	Chapter Twelve	127
13.	Chapter Thirteen	136
14.	Chapter Fourteen	144
15.	Chapter Fifteen	152
16.	Chapter Sixteen	158
17.	Chapter Seventeen	172
18.	Chapter Eighteen	181

Part IV. The Victory Ball

19.	Chapter Nineteen	195
20.	Chapter Twenty	204
21.	Chapter Twenty-One	210

Part V. The Riots

22.	Chapter Twenty-Two	221
23.	Chapter Twenty-Three	231
24.	Chapter Twenty-Four	239
25.	Chapter Twenty-Five	251
26.	Chapter Twenty-Six	264

Part VI. The First Battle of Talis

27.	Chapter Twenty-Seven	277
28.	Chapter Twenty-Eight	283
29.	Chapter Twenty-Nine	292
30.	Chapter Thirty	305
	Epilogue	317
	About the Author	326

Prologue

The boy had light fingers and quick hands. Sergeant Obry almost hadn't noticed him. He watched the pickpocket as he weaved through the crowd and sidled up to an unsuspecting satyr. The boy lifted the faërie's wallet and gold watch too, for good measure. Then he was gone. No one else had noticed. Not that anyone would have cared. Even the boy probably didn't realize he had been seen. Sergeant Obry chuckled to himself at the thought.

The Rook Gate was crowded. Carriages and carts vied with omnibuses and trolleys, while pedestrians—human or otherwise—slipped in-between, heedless of the danger. It was easy for the boy to lose himself in the hustle and bustle.

Across the street, a cut-rate illusionist offered spells for a penny, but there was more trickery than magic in him. Probably a dropout from the local Wizarding College, Sergeant Obry thought, and he wondered how the illusionist had been permitted to ply his trade so close to the Gate. Someone had been paid under the table, no doubt, but it hadn't been him. A block over to the right, a monkey and his organ grinder churned out the same few songs over and over again, adding to the cacophony of noise—the clattering hooves, the rattling carriages, and the rumbling of the overhead train.

Obry's vision wasn't what it used to be, but he had a well-trained eye and the benefit of long experience. He found the pickpocket again, almost too easily. He never would have admitted it, but he was a little disappointed. He had expected better. The boy had made his way across the street into the shadow of the great wall that encircled the Old Quarter, all that remained of the original City of Talis.

One of the oldest of the Twelve Great Cities, Talis was second only to the capital in wealth and prestige. It straddled both sides of the river and over the centuries had risen into a multi-tiered hodgepodge of crumbling rooftops and smoke-stained spires. There was a thriving population of nymphs, hobgoblins, fauns, pixies, and all manner of faërie creatures, largely segregated in their own Quarter. It was safer for all concerned.

Obry found it difficult, sometimes, to pin down what precisely constituted a faërie. It had become a catchall term for any creature or being that came from beyond the Twelve Cities, from the Lands of Faërie. There were few true fairies or fey among them, and in Obry's experience most of them had been born in the Cities themselves, until recently at least.

Shaking himself from his thoughts, Obry turned his attention back to the boy. He had chosen a human this time, a dandy, all frills and powders. Obry sighed; as amusing as the pickpocket's antics were, it was no longer any of his business.

He glanced down. The paperwork all seemed to be in order. He stamped the permits with the Official City Seal of Talis, and returned them.

"Have a nice day," Obry said.

Prologue

The family didn't reply. The father took the papers without a word, while the mother and her children avoided his gaze. Strange bird-faced creatures, they kept their heads down as they passed beneath the armed guards and continued through the Gate.

Obry turned and craned his neck upward. A cyclops loomed above him in an ill-fitting coat and tails.

"Papers please," Obry said, stifling another sigh. Sometimes it was hard to remember that he had requested this assignment, put in the transfer request himself. He had spent forty years on the streets, patrolling the Faërie Quarter, spying in bars, doing Commandant Hessing's dirty work, but he was older now. He was tired. Hessing had understood. The Commandant was an old bastard himself, but he made a point of rewarding loyalty, and had personally arranged Obry's new post.

He stamped the cyclops' permit and waved him through. The cyclops gave him what could have been a polite nod. Obry returned it. The Rook Gate was the most secure checkpoint in the city. Armed guards lined the wall, and there were specially trained sniffer dogs, their three heads alert for the slightest whiff of magic. It was an easy assignment, free from excitement, a way station on the road to retirement and a chance to line his pockets. He and Johanna wouldn't be able to live comfortably on a policeman's pension alone.

Obry frowned. For a moment he thought he'd heard a faint whistling, but a quick glance at the crowd revealed no whistlers. He shook it off and nodded to the waiting faërie, a minotaur in a top hat. His papers were not in order, but the fifty-pound note concealed among them certainly was. Obry pocketed the money subtly and stamped the minotaur's papers.

Prologue

"Have a nice day," he said again with a little more cheer in his voice. The minotaur gave him a secret smile.

Unlike many of his colleagues, Obry didn't mind working with faëries and monsters. Some of them were almost human and he was even friendly with a few of them, or as friendly as their kind could be. There were more of them now than ever before. Refugees of every manner and shape were flooding into the city daily. None of those Obry had spoken to had been willing or able to explain what they were running from, but they were all filled with a nameless dread.

Talis was starting to creak under the strain, and while he wasn't much given to politics, Obry was of the opinion that they could avoid a lot of unpleasantness if Parliament and the Duke just granted passed the Faërie Rights legislation. Not equal rights, of course. His Ma, Gods rest her soul, would have turned over in her grave, but a few gradually implemented rights to calm them down and help civilize them wouldn't be amiss. They weren't living in the Faërie Lands any longer, but there was no reason they couldn't adapt.

Obry stamped an air sprite's papers absently. The whistling was back again, closer now. He thought of asking one of the nearby guards, but they didn't seem to have heard anything. Obry wasn't fond of them anyway. The puffed-up bastards would only laugh and call him 'Grandpa.' Obry had confronted rampaging manticores and goblins, even faced down a witch one terrible night, armed only with a cudgel. Let the idiots laugh, with their rifles and shiny bayonets.

Obry barely even skimmed over the next permit. The whistling was getting louder now. It was distracting, and worse, it was making him nervous. Something was wrong. A train had just

Prologue

rumbled through the rooftops and screeched to a halt at the new platform high above the street. That could have been it, but Obry knew it wasn't. It had been a whistle not a shriek. People and faëries were descending from the platform into the already crowded streets. Obry caught sight of the boy again as he headed down a side alley, almost dancing through the masses, picking pockets left and right, but that wasn't what he was looking for. His eyes darted through the throng, desperately.

Obry finally spotted him—a little hobgoblin man in a shabby coat, with a whistle still on his lips. Their eyes met for a long moment, and then the figure smiled mischievously and nodded toward the Gate. Obry followed his gaze, but saw nothing. When he turned back, the hobgoblin was gone, vanished into the crowd. Obry was genuinely worried now. He studied the Gate more closely, wrought from iron and designed especially to keep the faëries at bay. Still nothing. Unless…

There. Nestled in a shady corner flush against the wall was a small brown paper package wrapped in string. In an instant Obry knew, without being told, what was inside. His instincts were screaming the answer, but he couldn't understand how the hobgoblin could have gotten close enough to plant the package, right under the guards' watching eyes. It shouldn't have been possible. The guard dogs would have smelled the telltale scent of magic. But that didn't matter now. Obry leapt to his feet, a warning on his lips. He was too late.

Sergeant Obry was killed instantly. There was a terrible flash, a blinding and burning. The whole world seemed to tremble with the force of the blast. Every window within a mile's radius shook and shattered. There was nothing now but dust and death, and the screams, so many screams. A world of mangled

Prologue

corpses—humans and faëries were buried beneath masonry and shrapnel, their parts mixed together until you couldn't tell human from griffin or minotaur.

There was a crater where the Rook Gate had once stood, a gaping, smoking gash in the ancient wall. The fire was everywhere. A plume of dense acrid smoke rose into the sky and coated the remains in ash. Worse were the survivors, some no less mangled than the dead. Their voices filled the air, their cries and pleas in a thousand tongues, some not even remotely human, all in pain.

The city responded slowly, as if in a stupor. Policemen poured in from all across town, to dig through the rubble. Ambulances and fire engines came wailing, as fast as their horses and unicorns could carry them. Others came too—onlookers, volunteers, and scavengers—to pick over the dead and dying.

Amidst the chaos, the little hobgoblin man in a shabby coat made his way untouched and unnoticed through the ruins of Worst Street, away from the fire and death, whistling an old Merman Ballad to himself, as he went.

Part I

The City

I

CHAPTER ONE

Her name was Countess Antoinette Wyman-Straus, and she had the documents to prove it. Very good documents they were too, printed on official paper, with the proper seals and signatures, all in order, all correct. They were fake, of course, as fake as her smile, and Mr. Covét ought to know. He had forged them himself.

Covét was an elderly faun with a severe white beard dressed in an old-fashioned frockcoat, expensive and well cared for, but decades out of style. The Countess could feel his eyes on her as she finished perusing the documents. They were quite satisfactory; but then, Covét had come highly recommended, although she had been forced to endure his constant unfriendly glances when he thought she wasn't looking.

"These are flawless," she said.

Covét sneered at the compliment. "Did you have any doubts?"

"None at all." She smiled apologetically, her proper little smile, but he wasn't paying attention, pointedly staring over her shoulder. The awkwardness lingered, and Covét showed no sign of breaking it.

"You don't like humans very much, do you, Mr. Covét?" she asked at length, reaching into her coat.

"No, I don't," he replied, but took her money nonetheless. He couldn't afford to be too particular when it came to clients, especially those who could pay.

"£1500," she said, "as agreed."

He lived in a ramshackle apartment above a print shop in the Faërie Quarter writing invectives and editorials for an anti-human rag, and supplemented his income with forgeries for his mostly human clients. It was only a meager living and it showed. The furniture was tattered and dusty. The wallpaper was cracked and peeling and the books were faded and well worn. They were everywhere. Every available wall space was covered in shelves, and there was a whole shelf of ancient tales containing everything from *The One-Eyed King of Huor* to *The God-Eater* and *The Tripartite King*. More books were piled on the floor, in chairs, or propping up tables. Only his workspace was pristine. It needed to be.

"Appearances can be deceptive," the Countess said. "Perhaps I'm not as human as you think. Perhaps I'm something a little more."

Covét glanced up from counting the money and gave her a once-over. She was younger than he'd thought—mid-twenties, perhaps younger, perhaps older. Human ages could be tricky, and she *was* human. There was no doubt of that, with her long coat and big red hat. Disgustingly, fashionably human.

"Ah," he said. "You're one of those. You think we can't do it alone; think that we need humans to help us, that we'll latch ourselves gratefully onto the first friendly face." He sneered. "You're not the only one to make that mistake. These days every human with a guilty conscience claims a faërie relative. Ten or twelve times removed, of course."

She blinked at the vitriol in his voice, and what it implied. Someone else was making unwanted overtures in the faërie community. That was useful information, and so too was his response, and the speed with which he had dismissed her claim. She said nothing.

"Well," Covét continued, "aren't you a woman of many facets—a criminal and a faërie sympathizer."

"I am not a criminal," she said, her voice level.

Covét snorted. For someone so cultured, it was a surprisingly animalistic sound. "In my experience, the only humans who come to old fauns like me for help are criminals."

He moved to the window and peered down through the curtains, his hooves clomping softly on the rug.

"Take a look, Countess," he said.

She collected her identity papers and joined him at the window. It took her a moment to see what he was pointing at, but only a moment. There were six of them, loitering across the street. One appeared to be in a drunken stupor outside a tavern. Another was panhandling in rags and tatters, and a third leaned against a telegraph pole assiduously reading the newspaper.

"Hessing's jackboots," said Covét. "Spying for the Duke." They were all too casual, carefully not watching the third floor apartment, exactly as they had been trained to not watch. And they weren't all human. There was a bull-faced man with sharp teeth, and hiding on the far corner, a fairy of the fey fluttered on its dragonfly wings and a sphinx curled up, seemingly asleep, but with one eye open.

"Traitors," Covét spat, then stopped himself, remembering the Countess. "I wonder which one of us they're watching for." He glanced at the Countess slyly. "Shall we find out?"

*

They descended the narrow stairwell together. The air was close and stale, and there was barely space for two to walk abreast. The Countess went first, silently, keenly aware of Mr. Covét's breathing on her neck and the stamping of his hooves. She forced herself to maintain an even pace; she would not rush, or, more importantly, let him see her rush.

They passed a hag on the stairs with a long, crooked nose and spindly fingers, struggling with a bushel of groceries under each arm. She narrowed her eyes at the Countess and muttered to herself disapprovingly in her own tongue. The Countess idly wondered if those had been groceries or ingredients for hexes and spells. Not that it mattered. Not to her. Finally, they emerged out onto the street.

After the claustrophobia of the stairs, the Countess stretched and took a deep breath. She immediately swallowed back a dry retch. The city stank of sweat and soot, of manure, and other things. The old stories spoke only of wonder; they never mentioned the stench. Faëries and other monstrous creatures were inhuman and they smelled like it. She had forgotten that in her need for open air. She would have to control herself better in the future.

The Countess turned back to Mr. Covét, who was watching her with a knowing, bitter smile. She had lost ground there, a childish mistake. Composing herself, she held out a hand to shake. "Pleasure doing business with you," she said.

Mr. Covét studied her for a long moment, glanced subtly across the street at their secret observers. Her hand didn't waver. He shrugged and then shook it. Covét's grasp was firm and he stared into her eyes, more curious than before, but still bitter. They parted ways with exaggerated politeness and headed in opposite directions.

Most of the spies contrived to follow Covét—the ones they could see, anyway—but two trailed after her. It was almost absurdly obvious, if you knew to look, but she wasn't laughing. While she had been shaking the faun's hand, the Countess had caught sight of a hobgoblin in an overcoat from the corner of her eye, but when she turned, he was gone and she couldn't find him again. She was sure there were other spies who had escaped her notice, and that was not a comforting thought.

Still, the Duke, or Hessing, or whoever had sent those spies, clearly considered Covét the greater threat, an understandable error. She allowed herself to relax, but only slightly. It had been a long, strenuous few days, spent hiding in carts and stowing away on riverboats, but she was here at last, in Talis. She had prepared so long for this moment, too long. There were dangers all around, but she welcomed them. It was better than the endless lifetime of waiting that had preceded it.

A primly dressed young woman emerged from the crowd and took her place half a step behind the Countess. It was delicately handled. She appeared from one moment to the next, as if she had always been there.

"How did it go, my lady?" she asked.

"Mr. Covét was exactly as you described, Elise," the Countess said. "Sullen but competent."

"I'm glad," Elise said with a pleased smile. The Countess gave her a tight nod, but her eyes flickered to the panhandler and the drunk who were following them. Elise didn't turn, but she knew immediately where the Countess was looking.

"I see them." Her hand strayed to her waist, where she had a knife secreted in her bustle, sharp and deadly. "Shall I handle them, my lady?"

Although they had only met the night before, the Countess knew that beneath her dress, Elise had a thin, wiry strength, and the Countess had no doubt that her prim and proper companion could handle the spies easily.

"Best not to draw too much attention to ourselves," said the Countess. "Not yet. Let them see what they will see."

"Yes, my lady."

As they continued down the street, the crowd seemed to part around them, almost unconsciously. Men, women, and faëries found themselves stepping out of the way as if by happenstance. Elise kept her head down, but she was not surprised. For her part, the Countess was too preoccupied to notice, but if she had, it would have worried her. She should have had more control than that. It had been beaten into her for years. Control was paramount, especially for someone like her. She had been ordered to abstain from magic as much as possible, but a day in the city and already she was slipping.

Covét had been more difficult than she had expected, even with Elise's warning; and if he was indicative of the general sentiment in the Faërie Quarter, she might have to adjust her tactics. She could be flexible. She had to be. All in service to her glorious, all-consuming purpose. She could feel it always, burning inside her, influencing her thoughts, twisting her, nudging her down the right path for its fulfillment.

"Is everything prepared for the Ritual?" the Countess asked.

"Jules is gathering the last of the ingredients. It is a delicate matter," said Elise.

"I want to perform the Ritual as soon as possible. There's no time to waste."

"My brother knows that."

"Good."

The Purpose had been passed to her by her mother, as a legacy and an infection. Three generations had toiled beneath its auspices, and had sacrificed everything. Elise and her brother had helped prepare the way and she was grateful, but the Countess knew with terrible, vivid certainty that her purpose was hers alone. The real work had only just begun.

CHAPTER TWO

It was a cold, gray day. The Commandant of Police shivered beneath his fur coat and rubbed his hands together. Baron Hessing was a man of vast abdominal contour but the chill had reached down to his bones. He exhaled and his breath misted in the air. There was a terrible pit in his stomach, a sickly gnawing that wouldn't go away. He wasn't ready for another funeral, not so soon after his son's.

There was a flurry of hats, as the pallbearers began lowering the bodies into the ground. There had been one hundred and eleven police and guardsmen on duty that day. One hundred and five were being consigned to the earth. Some of the boxes were empty, however, as some of the body parts had been too scrambled to be identified.

They had been fresh-faced boys, most of them. Hessing barely knew them, but there were a few old timers among the dead, Sergeant Obry for one. That had been a blow. He had kept his head down and his mouth shut for decades, and Hessing appreciated the loyalty. He shook his head. He was getting sentimental in his old age, but Obry was one of the few Hessing had ever truly trusted, and now he was gone. There would have to be a reckoning for that.

Hessing noticed Obry's widow at the front with the other family members. She had a quiet, round-faced beauty that lingered amidst the drab mourners. He had forgotten her name—Joyce maybe, or Johanna. He used to be able to remember everyone's name within moments. He was losing his touch. Mrs. Obry was flanked by two of the oldest veterans on the force—Inspector Erkel and Sergeant Lund. They had both been very close with Obry, ever since the incident with the witch almost forty years ago. They had also kept their silence and been well rewarded for their allegiance.

Hessing turned away to watch the crowd warily. No faëries had been permitted to attend. The funeral was a strictly human affair. With most of the city's elite, even the Duke and Duchess, present to show their respects, Hessing and his men had worried that the gathering might prove an irresistible target to the bomber or bombers. However, the funeral seemed to pass without incident. As the last of the caskets was laid to rest, the crowd began to disperse and headed back toward the city.

The Duke and Duchess lingered and offered their condolences to the grieving families. They shook hands with dignitaries in the crowd with practiced ease. Hessing admired their technique. Everything he knew about politics he had learned from watching them. It had been a lifelong education.

The Duke spoke softly with Mrs. Obry, then turned and found Hessing. He left his wife to console the remaining widows and orphans. She had more patience for it.

"Your grace." Hessing bowed as he approached.

Lord Edward Clesinger, the Seventh Duke of Talis, was a thin man, gaunt and graying with a sharp nose and a firm gaze. He nodded to Hessing.

"We appear to have escaped without incident," he said.

"Yes, your grace," Hessing said. "But I won't relax until everyone is safely back in Talis." The graveyard was on a hill across the river, outside the city walls. "We make a very tempting target."

"Yes," said the Duke, "I suppose we do." They shared a grimly amused smile.

The Duke and Hessing were friends, more or less. Certainly, it was as close as either of them had ever gotten to true friendship. They had a shared history and shared expectations. Hessing had been the Duke's most able and loyal servant for decades. In return, the Duke had made Hessing, raised him from nothing and given him power and a title to go with it. Hessing was constantly aware of the debt, even more so in recent months. It hung over their every conversation.

"We're under siege," the Duke said. "The attack was too public. The other Cities will be watching us."

"I'll handle it," said Hessing.

"Yes." The Duke agreed. "I have faith in you." He glanced at the lines of fresh graves. "You lost a lot of good men."

"Yes, your grace."

"I'm sure you and the others are eager to get your revenge."

Hessing said nothing. He already knew what the Duke was going to say.

"Keep your men in line. We need the bomber or bombers alive. They need to be punished publicly with the full force of the law."

"I understand."

They stood in companionable silence until the Duke's wife, Lady Anne, at last moved to join them. They had said all that needed to be said.

"Theodore," the Duchess said and leaned up to kiss Hessing's cheek. She was still as beautiful as ever. "It's a terrible thing. Did you know many of them well?"

"Some better than others," said Hessing.

"I'm sorry," she said. "And so soon after..." she trailed off awkwardly. "How's Olivia doing?" she asked after a moment.

"As well as can be expected," Hessing replied shortly. His wife was not a pleasant topic of conversation. No one had seen her in weeks. The Duchess reached out and squeezed his arm reassuringly.

"Let her know that I'm thinking of her."

"Thank you, my lady. I will."

She gave him a sad smile. "It's time," she said to her husband. "We should head back."

The Duke nodded. "Join us?" he asked Hessing.

"Thank you, your grace, but I still have my own obligations here."

"Of course. Remember what I said."

"We'll capture them alive," Hessing said. "But no guarantees that they'll be unharmed."

"Understood. Alive and aware. That's all I ask."

Then the Duke and Duchess were gone, leaving Hessing alone with his thoughts and the gnawing in his gut. He hated funerals.

*

Mrs. Obry hadn't cried yet, and least not when anyone was looking, but the laughter was gone from her eyes. In its place was something brittle. She had struggled to maintain her composure during the ceremony, and Erkel and Lund's solid presence behind her had been a comfort, if a hollow one. She'd known them for years, since they were constables with her husband, though they had all advanced since then, Erkel most of all.

Obry had taught Erkel and Lund almost everything they knew about policing. They had even fought a witch together once, and Erkel had the hex scars on his back to prove it. None of them had ever spoken to her about that night, not even Obry. It wasn't a secret. It was a silence. She knew all his secrets and most of Erkel and Lund's. None of them had ever been able to keep anything from her. But that night was different. Magic could have that effect.

The pallbearers had finished their work and the gravediggers had taken their place. Each shovelful of dirt took her husband farther and farther away. She couldn't say his name anymore, not even in her own head. It was strange. She felt oddly cold, distant, as though her grief was not her own. She shivered. Behind her, she could feel Lund make an abortive step toward her. He had been very kind these last few weeks.

Another policeman was coming over. It took her a moment to remember his name. Inspector Cambor had mostly kept to his own circle, but he was of an age with Obry and the others.

"Mrs. Obry," he said. "We're all terribly sorry for your loss."

"Thank you, Inspector."

"And I want to assure you that we will catch who did this. You have my word."

She glanced back at Erkel and Lund, who nodded. "Thank you," she said to Cambor. "I'm sure you will."

Cambor had noted the glance, but said nothing. Now was not the time or place. He knew that Erkel and Lund wanted the case and were shamelessly lobbying the Commandant. He knew too that Mrs. Obry was supporting them, but Hessing had given the Rook Gate Bombing investigation to Cambor and hadn't shown any sign of changing his mind.

"I'll do my best to keep you informed," he said and reached out his hand. After a moment, Mrs. Obry shook it.

"I would appreciate that, Inspector Cambor," she said.

A patrolman came running up to Erkel, panting and out of breath. "Sir," he managed.

"Take your time, son," Erkel said.

"Thank you, sir." The young man sagged. He had gotten there as fast as he could.

"Not that much time," Erkel said after a moment.

"Sorry, sir." The patrolman stood up straight. "There's been another murder," he said. "They think it's the Ripper."

Erkel and Lund exchanged glances, immediately alert. "Where?"

"On Mervyn Street."

Erkel turned to Mrs. Obry. "I'm sorry, Johanna," he said. "I don't know if we'll be able to make it to the wake later."

She waved his apology away. "Don't worry," she said. "I know how it goes."

"Yes," he said. "I suppose you do." Then he took off for the waiting police carriages. Lund lingered for a few moments.

Mrs. Obry nodded to him. "Go," she said. "I'll be fine."

He hesitated for a moment then followed Erkel, as fast as his legs could carry him. Mrs. Obry watched him for a moment, then turned back to her husband's grave. She wouldn't cry, not yet—perhaps not ever.

3

CHAPTER THREE

Covét slipped into a darkened alleyway and slumped against the wall for a moment, breathing heavily. He wasn't as young as he used to be. He had left these sorts of escapades behind him decades ago. He was an academic now, albeit disgraced; a letter writer, but he had a few hidden talents left. He knew how to evade a tail, though it hadn't been easy.

He had tried to lose his pursuers in the clamor of Main Street, but they had proved unexpectedly stubborn. The humans he evaded quickly. There were parts of the Quarter where they dared not go, and he had managed to lose the sphinx and the pixie not long after in the labyrinth of winding nameless streets. He had lived in the Faërie Quarter all his life. He knew these streets like the back of his hand. Few knew them better. Oddly it was the bull-faced man who had proved the most persistent, but Covét was finally free of him. He could relax for a moment and catch his breath.

A shrill whistle startled him. His heart thundered and he turned. A familiar figure in a familiar coat emerged from the shadows and stood watching him from the mouth of the street. Covét exhaled slowly, his heartbeat still racing.

"Mr. Tarr," he said. "You startled me."

The hobgoblin did not apologize. Instead, he grinned unrepentantly. "You did well," Mr. Tarr said, "giving Hessing's boys the slip."

Covét grimaced. "I can still be nimble when I need to be."

"Yes," Mr. Tarr said with a grin. "And you enjoyed it, too. Just like the old days." He chuckled. It wasn't entirely friendly.

Covét frowned but didn't deny it. There was more truth in Mr. Tarr's words than he cared to admit. After a moment, a thought occurred to him. "How did you know I was here?" he asked.

"I've been shadowing you since the apartment."

"What? Are you trying to get caught?" Covét straightened up and glared at the hobgoblin sharply. "Every policeman in the city is after you. What if they'd seen you?"

Mr. Tarr waved the concern away. "Them? I've been following you for the past hour. If you didn't notice me, what chance would the police have?"

Covét sighed. "You're far too reckless for your own good," he said.

"I know what I am, and I know what they are." Mr. Tarr shrugged. "It's the woman that concerns me."

"The woman?" Covét frowned. "You mean the Countess? Or whoever she is?"

"Yes," said Mr. Tarr, "the Countess, or whoever she is. She saw me on the street earlier when you were shaking hands. It was just for a moment, but that's enough. Usually no one can see me if I don't want them to." He paused to let that sink in, and it was worth pondering. Covét knew from personal experience just how elusive the hobgoblin could be. It was in his nature.

"She wasn't even trying," Mr. Tarr said. "She just saw me, and I know of only one other person who has ever managed it so easily." Mr. Tarr met Covét's gaze and nodded. They both knew exactly who he meant, and it didn't bode well.

"You're not implying..."

"I'm not implying anything," said Mr. Tarr. "Just stating facts."

Covét grimaced then shook the thoughts away. They had more immediately pressing issues. "We should head out," he said, "or we'll be late."

Mr. Tarr looked up at him and shrugged. "Hazard of the business," he said. "Besides, I doubt the others would have appreciated our punctuality. If we'd been on time, we would have lead Hessing's spies right to their doorstep. Better to be late in these circumstances."

Covét conceded the point gracefully, but the Countess was preying on his mind, and he still thought Mr. Tarr putting himself in the way of the police had been far too rash. He had probably been laughing to himself the whole way, too, as he followed the police following Covét. It was the kind of thing he would find amusing. That was why no one ever fully trusted him. The hobgoblin was useful, but always too mischievous for his own good, too much the anarchist. It was commonly known in their circles that Mr. Tarr didn't much care about the fire, so long as he was the one who lit the flames. Almost as many faëries as humans had died in the bombing. Not everyone had forgiven the hobgoblin for that. For his part, Covét preferred to think about the flames as little as possible these days. He was far more interested in what would rise from the ashes, assuming there was anything left.

They exited the alley and took another winding street, far from the noise and the crowds. Covét glanced around. Everything was a dark, grimy gray. Thick brick walls rose above them into great gothic windows, all barred shut. The houses seemed to tilt, leaning haphazardly outward, back toward the way they came. Covét was not deterred. He could hear the murmur of laughter and hushed conversation ahead.

The grim, claustrophobic alleyways opened abruptly into a little enclave, an oasis in the heart of the city. Daylight shone down, brightening the soot-stained houses considerably. Covét breathed more easily. He was not fond of enclosed spaces. Across the street, nestled in this cul-de-sac surrounded by a labyrinth of backstreets and dead ends, sat a bustling tavern and coffeehouse. Covét regarded it warmly. It had not always been so out of the way.

The Thirsty Goblin was once the most popular tavern in the Quarter. Centrally located, generations of faëries had drowned their sorrows behind its doors. As the times changed and the faëries began thinking less of their sorrows and more of action, the owner had renamed it the Café Goblot and it had begun attracting a different clientele. At around the same time, the twisting labyrinth had started growing up around it, collecting side-streets and blind alleys when no one was looking, until it had been all but swallowed. Covét had drunk at the tavern and sipped coffee at the café, but even he could not pinpoint when it had gone from main street to enclave.

Perhaps the owner had hired a down-on-his-luck magician from the College or made a deal with other, less savory, characters. There was one, at least, who had performed such enchantments before; the Smoke and Mirrors Club was rumored to be even more difficult to find than the café. Or perhaps the furtive secretiveness of the patrons had seeped into the city and had twisted reality, pulling the streets around them like a veil. Such things were known to happen in Talis, especially in places where a witch had died or battles had been fought. Magic always left its scars on the city.

*

They entered the café. It was filled with merchants, shopkeepers, and a smattering of writers and artists—all of them faëries, of course. They looked up from their newspapers and card games. Covét knew many of them and they greeted him with a nod. Most of them passed over Mr. Tarr without comment, but a handful spared him a dark glance. The rumors about him had been swirling. The eight-armed proprietor gestured them to the back quickly, hoping to avoid anything more than vague suspicion. Covét obliged and dragged Mr. Tarr with him. The hobgoblin seemed more amused than anything.

They passed through the backroom and down a narrow, curving flight of stairs to the cellar. There were five doors waiting for them. Mr. Tarr turned to Covét. It was his job to remember these things. The faun counted them out.

"Second one to the left," he said. Mr. Tarr nodded and strode up to the door. He knocked rapidly, seven times in a concentric pattern. After a moment, a small hatch swung open, and a giant eyeball peered out. It swung left, right, and then down, searching.

"Password?" a voice rumbled from inside. Covét leaned forward and spoke a single word. It was a relic from the ancient forgotten tongue, older even than the Witches. Its true meaning was lost and fragmented, but the others said it meant 'freedom' and that was good enough.

There was a long pause; then the door creaked inward, and a stooping cyclops bent down to usher them inside.

The room was small and cramped. Benches and chairs had been lined up in rows against the wall to form a makeshift auditorium. There were no windows and the candles and lamps flickered uncertainly. Faëries of every denomination were present—gnomes and jinn, goblins and sprites, fairies and manticores. Some gnarled and wizened, others radiant and strange. It was a grand assemblage of hooves and scales and horns. Covét and Tarr were the last to arrive.

The usual suspects were all present. On one side sat Anselm, his face expressionless. He was a free homunculus, half the height of a normal human but perfectly proportioned. Necromancers and alchemists had produced hundreds of his kind and sold them as laborers and servants. Anselm had been among the first to gain his freedom. Human-made, homunculi were generally distrusted by pure faëries in Covét's experience. Anselm was the exception. At his side was the ever-faithful Droz, a birdman with the sharp nose of a vulture. They watched as Covét and Mr. Tarr took their seats. Droz's gaze was pointed and deadly, but Anselm was as unreadable as ever.

A few seats down from them sat the headless Mr. Brunet. He was the only one present not born in the Twelve Cities. Before his head was taken, he had been a monstrous human from Deeper Faërie where the concentration of magic and power had twisted his ancestors into something new and strange. To his right was

Heinrich, a well-dressed troll with a bowler hat resting on his lap. Covét had always found him to be reasonably intelligent if a trifle naïve, and unlike many of the others Covét did not begrudge the troll's human business connections. That would have been hypocritical of him, given the faun's own side dealings.

In front of this assembly stood the Hon. Charles Raske, Esq. The youngest son of a Baron, he had recently made a name for himself by winning an important and widely talked about case and was attempting to capitalize on his success. His wife, Evá, sat in the front row, demure and encouraging. They were the only humans there. Covét and Mr. Tarr slipped into their seats against the wall. They didn't seem to have missed anything important. Raske was trying to rally the faërie leaders to his political banner. It was going about as well as could be expected.

"You need my help," Raske said. He was a red-haired man dressed in a coat that was a size too big for him. "After the bombings and the murders, the mood in the city has turned ugly. You all know that. Even as we speak, powerful men are lobbying Parliament for stringent measures. You need a strong voice to speak up for you, a human voice, my voice."

"Yours?" Heinrich said, softly; but when a troll talked, everyone listened. "It's true the mood has turned against us, but I've spoken personally with the Duke and Duchess…"

"Regular visitor, are you?" Droz interrupted sharply. There was a rustle of angry feathers. "Lunch meeting? Tea and scones?"

The troll straightened to his full and impressive height. "As it happens," he said primly, "I have a number of business interests."

"Yes." Droz sneered. "We know. Very profitable, I'm sure."

"That's enough." Anselm was leaning forward; his half-formed patchwork features were fully alert. He placed a calming hand on

Droz's shoulder. "Not now." His eyes flickered to the humans who were both watching the interplay with interest. Droz subsided reluctantly. In the flickering lamplight, his shadow had grown wings.

Anselm gave Heinrich an apologetic nod, anxious to prevent an argument. Covét watched them with interest as well. Heinrich was secretly bankrolling the Dissident Movement. Anselm and Droz's dreams of freedom and vengeance were reliant on the troll's good will. After a moment, Heinrich returned Anselm's nod slowly and then continued. "As I was saying, I have been personally assured that no punitive actions will be taken by the government. They are hunting for the bomber, nothing more."

Covét glanced at Mr. Tarr, who grinned wickedly.

"Since when do Hessing's men show restraint?" asked Brunet. He had lost his head to a drunken inspector who had been testing a rumor. It had long been said that monstrous humans could regrow their lost limbs. Inspector Vorn and a number of his men had decided to see if Brunet's head would grow back. It had not.

"Promises mean nothing," Brunet finished. His voice echoed hollowly from his chest. No one knew how he was still alive, let alone how he could speak, but there was magic in his blood.

"They do if the Commandant orders it," Heinrich said."Or else." There were nods at that. Hessing kept tight control over his men when he wanted to, and he never disobeyed the Duke. His loyalty was infamous.

Heinrich turned back to Raske. "And as for human voices," he said, "the Duchess has been our staunchest ally for decades—she has organized societies, donated generously and helped pass legislation. What do we need you for?"

"What do we need any human for?" asked another voice from the back.

"You can't force the system to change, not on your own. You may not like it, but you need us." Raske's face was coated in sweat. He looked down at his wife, who gave him a tight, encouraging smile. He took a deep breath and rallied. They had expected resistance.

"And you're right, the Duchess has been a good and loyal friend to you in the past, but what has that friendship gotten you? She has only ever offered you crumbs to keep you happy. I am offering substantial change, now. Not in a decade or a century, but now!" He was starting to get back into the rhythm of it. He and his wife had practiced the speech for weeks.

"I have in my hands a draft of the Faërie Voting Act granting every faërie in this city and its dominions the right to vote." A murmur ran through the assembly. The Duchess had always balked at such a step. "You can all read it and make any suggestions you feel are warranted, but I promise that if I am elected, my very first act will be to put this bill before Parliament. I'm not saying it will be easy. They'll fight us tooth and nail, but my friends and I are willing to fight, and we will win." He paused to take a breath.

"And in return?" Anselm asked softly.

"Endorse me," said Raske. "Privately, and you'll see what force and vigor I can bring to this."

"Privately," said Droz.

"Excuse me?"

"You want us to endorse you privately. You've come here in secret to peddle for our support. Are you ashamed?" The room started to protest. "Or do you think the voters would abandon you, if they knew?" Angry shouts broke out. Everyone was talking over one another.

"Wait!" Raske called into the sudden noise. "Wait!"

Anselm held up a single finger, and the clamor subsided, slowly like chastened children. "We invited him," said Anselm. "Let the human speak."

Raske took that as a show of support and nodded gratefully. From the look on her face, his wife knew better.

"You have the numbers," Raske continued. "I don't just want your support behind closed doors. I need you. All of you. Bring your people to my upcoming rally. Demonstrate on my behalf. Let everyone know what I am offering. Make our enemies quake, and show our friends what your support can do. Together we can change the face of this city."

"You want us to be your private little army," Droz said sneering.

"I wouldn't have put it like that."

"And that's all you want?"

Raske hesitated. "Not exactly," he said. "When the Act passes, faëries will become the single largest voting bloc in the city, and they will largely vote as you tell them."

"You want us to vote for you," Heinrich said. It was simple enough. He'd made a thousand similar deals with a thousand different humans, all as greedy as each other. The faëries started muttering to each other again.

"Yes," said Raske. "Among other things."

"Ah." Anselm leaned forward. This was the true price at last. "Such as?"

"The succession."

A hush fell over the room. Even Anselm was taken aback. The Duke was not getting any younger, and he and his wife had never produced an heir. No one spoke about it in public, of course, but the whispers had begun. In backrooms and parlors across the city, questions were being asked, lines being drawn. The Faërie Quarter was not immune. They had all wondered, not that they could have affected the outcome, until now.

Covét was begrudgingly impressed. Someone had put a great deal of thought into this—Raske or whoever was behind him. Faërie Rights had never garnered much support on its own, but whoever controlled the faërie votes could control Parliament, and whoever controlled Parliament would control the succession. There would be many who saw the value in that, many who might otherwise have opposed the Act. It was a clever plan. It might even work.

The moderates were starting to look swayed. They could do the political calculations as well as Covét, and had reached the same conclusion. Heinrich appeared more conflicted than the rest, but then, he had tied himself most strongly to the Duchess' party, even as he financed the regime's most radical opponents. Covét had known the troll for years and had never quite managed to figure him out.

Anselm and his followers watched with stern disapproving eyes. They had given up on legislative solutions long ago and adopted more dangerous methods. They had a plan, and Mr. Tarr's bombing had been only the first stage. They weren't about to let Raske and Parliamentary politics stop them now. They were committed. In truth, Covét found them as laughable as the moderates. Droz with his impatience and purity of purpose; Brunet on his course of vengeance; even Anselm with his deceptive calm and hidden well of bitterness. They all believed they were the first to think such thoughts. They were living in a dream and their plans would come to naught, like their predecessors before them.

Covét had sat in this very room, when the Thirsty Goblin was still the Thirsty Goblin, and made plans no less violent and radical then their own. His fellow plotters were long gone now, exiled or executed, and Covét no longer believed in any solution at all, but he despised hypocrisy and naked ambition. He had no desire to be a prop for one person's career or, worse, a tool for human politics. It was disgusting.

"Humans," Covét muttered to himself.

Mr. Tarr checked his pocket watch and shrugged. "Did you expect anything less?"

"You're leaving?"

"I have more important things to do than watch this." He stood slowly. "It's pointless anyway."

"I suppose it is," said Covét, "but you still have to make your report."

"I'm sure I don't know what you mean."

"You're seeing Him," said Covét. It was not a question. "You made a deal with Mr. Nix."

"You know I can't tell you that," Mr. Tarr replied, and that was true, in more ways than one. Even in a city full of secrets, Mr. Nix was unusually ferocious in keeping his own.

Mr. Tarr made a mocking bow, and then slipped out the way they had come. No one noticed the hobgoblin leave, as they were too busy shouting and muttering to themselves; *almost* no one. Evá Raske turned back to her husband after a moment, frowning. She thought she'd seen someone, but it was nothing, probably. Then she schooled her expression into a loving, reassuring mask.

Her husband was doing fairly well so far, but he was going to need all the support he could get.

CHAPTER FOUR

Inspector Erkel watched the photographer and his assistant struggle with their lumbering, newfangled monstrosity. They arranged the tripod's legs slowly, and carefully adjusted the dials on the camera. There was something mesmerizing about the process, but in his opinion it was more trouble than it was worth—time consuming and finicky. He preferred good old-fashioned police work. It was simpler, cleaner.

Around them, policemen bustled about their business, marking out the length of the room, sketching, and taking notes. Like Erkel, many of them had just come from the funeral, and like him, many of them would have preferred to be elsewhere. A pair of constables with a black bag and a stretcher were waiting patiently by the door, while two more constables of a particularly burly bent stood guard outside.

The camera was finally arranged to the photographer's satisfaction and he slipped his head under the black cloth. He raised his finger from beneath the dark enclosure and his assistant lit the powder. There was a flash. Erkel was temporarily blinded. That was the other reason he didn't like the cameras, and this photographer in particular never gave a warning.

Erkel tried to blink the spots out of his eyes. He was doing his best not to look at the body. One poor fellow had already been forced to run from the room. Erkel had no sympathy for the boy. You needed a strong stomach in this line of work and it was better he learn now instead of later. Erkel's reticence had a more prosaic motive. He didn't want the case. He didn't want to be involved, and as soon as he looked at the body, as soon as he examined it, he'd be trapped.

"They were right," Sergeant Lund said as he approached. "It does look like the others." He was an easy-going man, but keen-eyed and weathered. Erkel trusted Lund's instincts, but he wished they had pointed in a different direction.

"Yes," Erkel agreed, but he still didn't look down. Lund understood. He knew Erkel better than most, and shared his motives. Faëries died all the time. They would rather be investigating the Rook Gate Bombing. They would rather have vengeance.

Obry had been eradicated in an instant. Painless, the coroner said, but what would he know. They hadn't even found the body, only pieces and stray limbs. It had been left to Erkel and Lund to tell the old man's widow. Sitting at her kitchen table, Erkel had promised to find the bomber and make him or it pay. He owed him that much and more, so much more. The hex scar on his back still stung when he thought of it, and it would have been much worse if Obry hadn't been there.

Lund had stayed behind with Mrs. Obry and comforted her long after the inspector had left. Erkel had kept his comments to himself, although he hadn't failed to notice how attentive Lund had been at the funeral. He might need to have a word with Lund about that soon. People would talk, but that was a problem for another day. They had promised Mrs. Obry that they'd avenge her husband's murder, but instead, they were here in an abandoned lodging house on Mervyn Street, babysitting a faërie murder. What a waste, even if Lund was right and it was the Ripper. At any other time this would have been the case of their careers. Erkel would have stabbed his own mother in the back for a chance to solve it, but things were different now, since the bombing.

A sudden commotion interrupted Erkel's musings. He stepped gingerly over the body and went to the window. The glass was so dirty and fogged that he could barely see down into the street, but a crowd had gathered outside the house, and it was growing. Humans and faëries had peered up curiously at first, but now they were getting restive, shouting at each other. Somehow they already knew what had happened. The few policemen he had left downstairs were hard pressed to keep them back. Erkel sighed. He could feel a headache forming. They were going to need reinforcements. Worse than the brewing mob, however, was the handful of men standing to one side. They had sharp eyes, notepads, and a photographer of their own—newspapermen. Someone had talked. There would be hell to pay for that.

A sudden shout broke through the noise and, with a thundering of hooves, a black carriage with a family crescent inlayed in silver charged through the crowd and pulled up in front of the house. Erkel recognized it immediately. It was Baron Hessing's personal coach. The Commandant of Police had deigned to come in person, straight from the funeral. He must have been certain this was the Ripper; and worse, that meant he had assigned Erkel personally. Maneuvering his way off the case would be more difficult than ever, if not impossible. Erkel leaned his head against the glass for a moment. The cold soothed the ache briefly as he mustered his arguments. He had promised.

Below, the Baron descended from the carriage with an exuberant wave to the crowd and extended a gracious nod to the reporters. He was a canny operator with a store of well-practiced cunning. Erkel wouldn't put it past him to have contacted the newspapers himself. They would need all the good press they could muster after the debacle of the past few months. But even as he doffed his hat, Hessing was having a whispered conversation with a patrolman that sent him scampering for reinforcements. Like his master, the Duke, Hessing was always playing more games than one. With a final almost-bow to the crowd, he turned and entered the building. He left them momentarily stunned, but it would pass and his presence would even raise more questions, especially among the reporters.

Erkel could hear Hessing barreling up the stairs, greeting everyone loudly by name and asking after their mothers, or sisters, or wives. It was important for him to know these things and be seen to know them. It was a talent that he had slowly cultivated. Everyone appreciated the effort, but Erkel wasn't sure he got everyone's name right anymore.

"Our lord and master," Lund muttered. Erkel gave him a half-smile.

"Careful," he said, "even in jest. The Duke might not appreciate that comment."

"The Duke doesn't pay half as well."

"True enough." With all the bribes and backroom deals, anyone Hessing favored stood to become a very wealthy man, and over the years Erkel and Lund had been very favored.

Hessing barged into the room and he continued his greeting ritual, giving everyone a firm handshake and an exuberant greeting.

"Sir," Erkel said with a respectful nod. Hessing returned it with the expression he reserved for his most trusted subordinates. Erkel hadn't seen him in weeks. He had glimpsed him at the funeral but only from a distance. Up close, Hessing seemed more tired than Erkel remembered. For all his characteristic whirlwind energy, there was a sadness to Hessing these days, a worn-out tightness about the eyes, even before the bombings. They had all heard the rumors about his son.

Erkel had met young Gregor Hessing once or twice, and had found him to be a clever if often sickly and solemn child, forever overshadowed by his father. Erkel hadn't been surprised when the young man died, but then the stories had started. Unable to deny his curiosity, Lund had taken the coroner out for a few drinks. The man had been tightlipped, even with more than a few pints in him. No one willingly betrayed Hessing's secrets, not if they valued their life, but Lund had learned a great deal from the gaps in the coroner's story, and Erkel had contacts of his own. There was something peculiar about Gregor's death, but Erkel couldn't quite put his finger on it, and perhaps that was for the best. Knowing too many of Hessing's secrets could be exceedingly dangerous.

"Inspector," Hessing said. "Shall we?" He leaned over the body, forcing Erkel to join him and look down at last.

Before them lay a dismembered, bloodstained horror. The corpse had been expertly carved open. Its insides were spewed upon the floor, and its features mangled beyond all recognition. In life it had been a she, young, and not entirely human.

There were too many limbs. Erkel counted at least seven, and the blood was thick and black. She had been one of the monstrous humans from Deeper Faërie perhaps, where the magical forces had shaped strange, enchanted beings. Hessing examined the body dispassionately for almost a quarter of an hour. He peered at every cut and laceration and lifted limbs. He had been a detective once himself and knew his business. Finally, he stood, bloodstained and grim.

"It's him," he muttered.

"The Ripper?" Erkel asked.

"Yes," Hessing said. "There can be no doubt now. I had my suspicions, of course. And I was right." He sighed. "With the press baying for our blood, we'll need answers and soon. That's why I put you on the case. You're reliable, Erkel. You get results."

"Thank you, sir." Erkel knew it was futile now, but he had to try. He cleared his throat. "But about that, sir, I was hoping that I might be reassigned to the Bombing Case. I know Inspector Cambor is quite capable, but..."

"The Bombing?" Hessing studied him seriously. Lund moved to flank the inspector. "I see." Hessing glanced between them. "Obry was a good man," he said.

"Yes, sir," Erkel and Lund chorused.

"You want revenge. I understand that. We all do, but I need you here, both of you. Cambor doesn't know the Faërie Quarter like you do, and I need answers. I am sorry." His expression was suitably contrite, and Erkel believed it was genuine, mostly.

"I just want to be there when you catch him," Erkel said. There was no changing Hessing's mind, but he might agree to this. "Whoever he might be."

Hessing nodded slowly. "I think that can be arranged," he said."For both of you."

"Thank you, sir," said Lund.

Hessing placed a reassuring hand on their shoulders. "Don't thank me," he ordered, "just find who did this. Solve the murders for me, and soon. That's all the thanks I need." Then he was gone. Erkel and Lund shared a rueful glance, but, in truth, that had gone better than expected.

*

Baron Hessing lumbered slowly down the stairs. The gnawing in his stomach had grown. This was a nightmare—six murders, each more gruesome than the last. If it had just been faëries, the papers would have let it rest. The Faërie Quarter was filled with all manner of monsters. Prevailing opinion said let them kill each other, especially in the aftermath of the bombing, but there had been human victims too, and that was a different matter.

The press only knew about three of them so far, but they were already baying for his blood, circling hungrily. After all the effort he had spent cultivating them, the years of groveling and pandering, this was his reward. He knew he should go talk to them, do his song and dance routine, give them a choice quote and dangle a few crumbs, but he was too tired for that, tired and drained. There would be time later. He would make the time.

Erkel and Lund were effective and, most importantly, loyal. He had bought them long ago, bound them to him, and he would need that loyalty in the coming weeks. They would go by the book, make sure no one could say they hadn't done their duty, but neither of them cared much for faëries. And, as expected, they both had their eye the other major case. They would be distracted but able, which should be enough to buy him some time, time for Hessing's personal inquiries. He had his own private suspicions, and the latest victim had crystallized them. He would need to be very careful now. The eyes of the city and beyond would be on him.

The Duke would not be pleased.

CHAPTER FIVE

Lord Edward stood at the window peering down at the city. He had been master of the city for forty years, and he ruled it with genial ruthlessness and subterfuge. Behind him in his study a small army of servants and secretaries stood patiently at attention, dwarfed by the high, vaulted ceilings that were lined with paintings and sculptures. They knew their master and his moods. Lord Edward was given to fits of melancholy and would sometimes spend hours watching the people as they made their way across the Square. He knew his city, knew its sights, its sounds, and its moods, and the mood was turning ugly. He didn't need an army of sycophants and spies to tell him that. He could see it taking shape with his own eyes.

In Auberon Square below, the evening strollers promenaded in all their finery beneath the looming ducal stronghold and past the

Parliamentary Dome. At the center of the square rose a stature of Lord Frederic the Liberator who had helped end the Rule of the Witches and had freed the Crescent from their tyranny. The First Duke of Talis stood in all his transcendent, marble glory, with his arms outstretched toward a better tomorrow.

It was a colorful menagerie—men in coats and tails, ladies in their bustles and most feathery of hats, soldiers in their uniforms with polished epaulets. The great, the good, and the middling all walked the promenade together eager to show themselves at their best, hoping to catch a glimpse of a dignitary: a cabinet minister, perhaps, or a ducal prefect.

Even faëries of a certain class could not resist the allure of being seen. Centaurs with monocles, trolls in top hats, even true fairies with their wings peeking through their coats and dresses all flocked to Auberon Square to prove to anyone and everyone watching that they too belonged here. After all, it was named after one of their kind and the name had remained even after the Fall of the Witches. Nevertheless, it was a brave but ill-advised show of defiance on their part, especially today. Tensions were running high after the funeral. The soldiers watched them warily, their hands straying to their swords and guns. The women glared from beneath their fine hats. One gentleman spat at a centaur as he passed. No one dared bother the trolls, of course, but there was no question that they were not welcome either. It had become a common sight of late. But no matter their differences, they all, humans and faëries alike, scurried past the Ducal Mansion, averting their eyes with farcical displays of nonchalance. Behind the tall wrought-iron gates, soldiers and triple-headed dogs patrolled back and forth, their teeth bared and bayonets fixed.

The Ducal Mansion itself was a formidable sight. A sprawling soot-stained grotesquery of pointed arches and pillars, of high walls and vast gardens, it had been built at the height of Witchling Rule as a monument to their undying power. It was a palace and a fortress holding many secrets—hidden passages and lost rooms, deep secret places marinated in old magic and old ambitions. Even after almost two centuries, the Dukes had not fathomed all its mysteries or penetrated all its dangers.

There were those who still whispered that the last ruling witch had cursed the mansion's foundations with her dying breath, and that the buildings themselves, the very walls, sought vengeance against the usurpers. Eight generations of Dukes had lived there in defiance of the rumored curse as a symbol of their fearlessness and strength. However, over the years they had hired an unusual number of magicians and curse breakers from across the Twelve Cities, and their official insistence that the Second Duke of Talis' untimely death beneath a piece of fallen masonry had been entirely natural had struck many at the time as being somewhat desperate. The Witches were long gone, however, and the current Duke feared no curses. He had more than enough to worry about already.

Lord Edward turned away from the window at last. He had seen what he needed to see, and there was work to do. A side door swung open and a weedy-looking young man entered with a bow, passing a telegram to one of the secretaries. The secretary glanced at it and turned toward the Duke's desk, but he waved him over with a gesture. The Duke read the telegram through twice and sighed. He had been hoping for better news from the Capital, but he wasn't surprised.

Lord Edward folded the telegram into his pocket and returned to his great mahogany desk. A servant quickly closed the curtains behind him. The study was nearly a hundred feet long and thirty feet wide. Lord Edward sat at the far end of the room. A giant portrait of his illustrious ancestor, Lord Frederic, loomed above him with a grim expression, as he returned to work. He poured over papers, reports, and dossiers with a practiced eye, signing orders, scribbling notes. He was intimately familiar with the paperwork of government. Occasionally he sent secretaries scurrying back and forth on various errands, but he barely even spared them a glance.

There was an untouched glass of whiskey at his side. He had his valet pour it over an hour ago, but had forgotten almost immediately. He was in full evening dress, although his tie had come undone at some point, and his ornamental sash and Ducal insignia were strewn on a chair, waiting. He was supposed to be preparing for dinner. The guests had arrived almost an hour ago. He had seen their carriages out the window, but he could afford to leave them in his wife's capable hands for a little while longer. He had more pressing concerns at the moment.

Something had to be done. Next year would be the bicentennial of the Overthrow of the Witches. That could be a useful rallying point, but the current situation required more immediate solutions. He could feel his control of the city eroding—more and more events were eluding his grasp. It had been building for months, years even. The scene outside was only the latest incident. They were growing more frequent. He wasn't desperate; Lord Edward had never known true desperation, not even as a child when the mob came, but he was worried. These days he was always worried.

The door flew open abruptly. The secretaries turned in alarm. No one would dare disturb the Duke, but Lord Edward continued scribbling away, unperturbed. He knew who it was. There was only one person in the city who could enter his presence unannounced, and after all these years, he knew the sound of her footsteps.

"You didn't tell me," Lady Anne snapped without preamble. She marched down the long room, resplendent in pearls and satin. Her feet thudded angrily on the thick fitted carpet. The Duke looked up at that, questioningly, but remained silent.

"About the envoy," she said in reply to his unasked question. "I had to find out from one of our guests. The Honorable Mr. Clarke took great pleasure in telling me, even more so when he realized I had no idea what he was talking about."

The Duke put his pen down deliberately. "Leave us," he said softly. The assembled secretaries wasted no time scurrying for the door, as quickly as propriety allowed. While they left, the Duke raised the forgotten whiskey to his lips, and took a long sip.

"You have to tell me these things, Edward," she said once they were gone. "We can't afford to look weak, not now."

"I only found out yesterday, myself," he said. "Which is worrisome in itself."

"All the more reason to tell me. I have relatives at court."

"Yes," the Duke agreed. "Relatives who told you nothing." He handed her the telegram from his pocket. She perused it silently.

"You asked my cousin without even mentioning it to me?"

"For all the good it did us." The Duke was unapologetic. "He couldn't find anything."

"Are you blaming him now?"

"I'm not blaming anyone," the Duke said. "The Emperor is perfectly capable of keeping secrets." He sighed. "I meant to tell you, but it slipped my mind."

"An Imperial Envoy slipped your mind?" Standing over him, she poured every ounce of condescension she could into her voice.

The Duke bore her disdain with the ease of practice. "There were other matters to attend to—the building projects, the bombings, the murders." He took another sip. "And you were busy with your Associations. I can't always remember what you know."

"I see." Lady Anne was not appeased, but he wasn't lying. She swallowed her anger. They had guests waiting, and she was nothing if not pragmatic. "This isn't over." There would be time to argue later.

"I know."

She sank into one of the plush chairs. "Good. Then I suppose the real question is: why now?"

The Duke nodded. "And why so suddenly? The Victory Ball is in a few days, but that doesn't feel right. Next year is the bicentennial. This year is just another Ball, and the Emperor hasn't bothered sending an official representative, let alone an envoy in over a decade."

"Do you think he knows?" she asked.

"That we're in trouble? That we have plans for the Ball? Of course he knows. The Emperor is young but clever. Still, I don't see why that would worry him."

"No," she agreed. Their plans were ambitious but local, certainly not threatening to the Emperor of the Twelve Cities. In the face of mounting tensions, reminding everyone of a time when humans and faëries had stood united against the Witches seemed opportune. The Ball was the lynchpin. "Perhaps he wants to observe our progress," she offered.

"Then why wait until the last minute, and why keep it secret at court? That doesn't make sense. Not yet."

"There's another possibility," she said slowly. His face tightened.

"I know," he said. "But the Emperor has never interfered in matters of ducal succession before."

"But there's always been an heir before." He stiffened but said nothing. It was his greatest failure. The silence lingered for a moment.

"Well," she said, clearing her throat, "we shall just have to show this envoy that the faërie tensions are nothing to worry about, and put on a united front, starting with our guests."

He blinked. "Ah yes," he said, "we mustn't forget about our guests." He rose slowly and began to straighten his tie. "Speaking of Mr. Clarke, his new friend Raske went into the Faërie Quarter today, where Hessing's spies promptly lost him."

"That's suggestive," she said.

"Very," he agreed sharply. "But suggestive of what? He is a blatant rabble-rouser. What does he think he's playing at? The faëries would never trust him."

"Don't be so sure, Edward," Lady Anne said. "He lacks tact, but that could appeal to some of them. And for all his rabble-rousing, I doubt he would do anything too radical, not with Clarke backing him."

"Depends on what you mean by radical," the Duke said. "There are rumors of a Faërie Rights Act."

"I don't consider the vote too radical," she said. "I'd even call it necessary."

"My wife, the faërie sympathizer," he said. They shared a wry smile "In some ways, my dear, you are still a dilettante and a moralizer, and while that can sometimes be an issue, at least you come by your opinions honestly—which is more than we can say for Mr. Raske and Mr. Clarke."

"That's what I love about you, Edward," she replied. "There's not a patronizing bone in your body." She reached up and adjusted his sash. "It's not as if you haven't made good use of my sympathies. After all, I sometimes think you only married me because you found my views politically useful."

"Your money had something to do with it," he said thoughtfully.

"Money always has something to do with it." She waved her hand dismissively. "But remember: whatever Raske is up to, whatever the Emperor is planning, we will weather this storm as we have weathered all the others. None of them are a match for you."

"For us," said the Duke, and arm in arm they headed out to greet their guests.

*

The unmarked carriage pulled up outside Hessing's house. Dr. Trefusis emerged wearing a long coat and a concerned expression. Lady Olivia watched the doctor from her window. He was just a boy, really, but he was her husband's creature, bought and paid for, just like all the others. She was sure of it. She wrapped herself tightly in her nightgown. Her husband had locked her in her room, and stationed one of his manservants outside the door. She would have to endure the doctor's attentions and relentless sympathy as best she could. She had no choice.

Dr. Trefusis straightened his tie and knocked on the door. He had been called away from his dinner, but he was well compensated for his convenience and discretion. Besides, it was unwise to refuse a summons from the infamous Commandant of Police, no matter the hour.

The door opened and Trefusis was ushered in by the butler, Lemann.

"This way, sir," said the butler. Thin and lean compared to his master, he led the doctor to the central vaulted staircase. The Hessing House was a veritable fortress of thick walls, strong locks, and barred windows. Borderline illegal charms and spells were branded into the very foundations. Hessing had taken no chances and had spared no expense. Along with his Barony, the Duke had made Hessing a very wealthy man, and with that wealth came a great many enemies. Trefusis had been there many times now, but he couldn't help but swallow nervously.

The Baron was waiting for him outside Lady Olivia's bedroom. One of his servants was standing guard behind him.

"Good evening, doctor," he said.

"Sir." Trefusis fought to keep his hands from fidgeting. In person, Hessing was a terrifying boar of a man.

"My wife had another fit tonight," Hessing said.

"So I was given to understand," said Trefusis. "These bouts of melancholy are to be expected in the circumstances. Grief can be a very powerful and unpredictable thing."

"It's not the melancholy that worries me," Hessing said.

"No," Trefusis agreed. He remembered the first night quite clearly. He had been one of the five doctors summoned, and by far the most junior. He remembered her violence and her screams. It had taken the five of them plus a number of Hessing's people to subdue her, and her outbursts had continued sporadically since then. Trefusis was the only one still on retainer. The others had been dismissed and paid for their silence. For some reason Lady

Olivia seemed to respond best to him, possibly because he reminded her of her son.

"This can't continue," Hessing said.

"Is she taking her medicine?"

"I'm not sure. I considered slipping it in her food, but she eats so little these days."

"I understand." Trefusis hesitated. "Perhaps it might be best if I went in alone."

"Very well," Hessing said after a moment. At his nod, the door was unlocked. "But leave it open behind you."

"Yes, sir."

Trefusis entered cautiously. He found Lady Olivia lying in bed with a vacant expression on her face. She seemed to see right through him, as if he wasn't even there.

"My lady," he said.

She frowned. "Doctor," she said, "back so soon?" Her speech was slurred and distant.

"Your husband was worried."

She made no reply. He tried again. "How are you feeling?"

"Tired," she said. "So very tired."

He took her arm gently to check her pulse. Steady if a little weak. "Have you been taking the medicine I gave you?"

"Yes," she said. She could see her husband hovering in the doorway.

"Good," said Trefusis. He opened his bag and pulled out a number of vials. "You just need a little rest, that's all."

He went over to the dressing table. The previous bottles were sitting there, mostly empty. She was telling the truth. He poured her a glass of water then mixed in a few careful drops, just enough to make her sleep. She seemed calm enough already, though he noticed the broken vase on the floor. The servants hadn't cleaned it up yet, afraid of her, perhaps—or maybe Hessing had wanted him to see.

Trefusis returned to her bedside and handed her the glass. "Drink this," he said with a soft smile.

"Thank you, doctor," she patted his hand. "You're always so very kind." She glanced behind him blearily. "I think my husband wishes to speak with you."

He turned, and sure enough Hessing was standing there expectantly.

"Good night, my lady," he said.

"Good night, Dr. Trefusis." Her eyes were already starting to close.

He took the empty glass from her and set it down at the bedside. He joined Hessing outside and they talked in quiet whispers. When finally the murmurs subsided and they were gone, Lady Olivia opened her eyes.

They were perfectly clear and alert.

*

The troll checked his pocket watch for the third time in as many minutes. Heinrich felt conspicuous in his coat and tails, especially in the Faërie Quarter, but they had told him to be on this particular corner at this particular time. They were late, however, and worse, they were going to make him late as well. He had more important things to do than wait at their convenience.

"Heinrich!" He turned. Two figures emerged to join him: Anselm and Droz, his ever-present shadow.

"Anselm," Heinrich greeted.

"Were you followed?" Droz asked.

"Were you?" the troll responded.

Droz frowned. "My loyalty is not in question."

"No one's loyalty is in doubt," Anselm said. "We're all on the same side here."

"Are we?" Droz muttered, but fell silent under Anselm's glare.

"You're heading to the Mansion?" Anselm asked.

"Yes. At the Duchess' invitation. I should be there already."

"At your mistress' beck and call," Droz said.

"That's enough," said Anselm. "Heinrich is exactly where we need him to be."

The troll nodded gratefully, sparing Droz a dark look. The birdman's suspicions were becoming tiresome. "It's to be a relatively small affair," he said. "A good chance to see their mood in light of recent events, although my invitation itself is a sign that the Duke and Duchess don't want to escalate matters."

"Or they're trying to lull us into a false sense of security," said Droz.

"Perhaps," said Anselm. "Either way it means they're not prepared to act. We can use that. Who else will be there, do you know?"

"Some local dignitaries, businessmen, a few members of Parliament. That should give me an opportunity to test the depth of Raske's support."

"You think he's genuine?" Anselm asked.

Heinrich shrugged. "Too early to tell."

"Or too late," said Droz.

Heinrich glared at him. "Promise me you won't do anything rash until we're sure. If we can get the vote without further bloodshed, this could be a golden opportunity."

"I promise," said Anselm. "Nothing rash."

"Good," Heinrich said. "Now it's time I left; don't want to be late. I'll report back as soon as I can."

They watched the troll lumber back toward his waiting carriage.

"Are we really going to stop everything at his say-so?" Droz demanded as soon as the troll was out of earshot. "He's suspect at best, and a traitor at worst."

"No," said Anselm. "We're not stopping anything."

"Then you lied to him."

"I promised that I wouldn't do anything rash and I meant it, but we've been planning the next stage for months. There's nothing rash about that."

"He's not going to like it."

"If we succeed, we won't have to care about what he likes anymore. Money or no money."

"And if we fail?"

"Then we'll all be dead," said Anselm. "Including him."

CHAPTER SIX

The Countess luxuriated in the bath. The water was scalding and scented with perfumes and oils to relax the muscles and purify the body. The Ritual Invocation of the City was a physical and mental ordeal beyond anything she had previously attempted. These preparations and purifications were almost as important as the invocation itself, especially if she intended to survive the experience.

She had performed similar if lesser rituals before, all designed to lead her to this—the pivot point of danger and power on the jagged edge of magic. In the great hot springs high in the mountains, she had been keenly, viscerally aware of the risks. In the hotel's surroundings it was easier to forget, to be lulled into a false sense of security.

The hotel suite was the picture of decadence and splendor. The

Countess felt provincial, as if she was playing dress up with her fancy clothes and her stolen title. There was a casual opulence in every chair, every furnishing. She had never experienced such luxury, and that stung with a bitterness that, for once, was mostly her own. Her true title was far grander than anything the Twelve Cities could muster, and yet she had been raised in squalor, exiled and forgotten, while these humans grew ever richer and more prosperous.

She emerged, dripping, from the bath. It was nearly time. Elise was waiting with a towel at the ready. This was a new and welcome deference. The Countess was not accustomed to servants, or to the quality of devotion that Elise and her brother, Jules, had shown. She was the vessel of her sisters' hopes, their will made flesh, but they had seldom treated her as more than a weapon to be forged, sharpened, and aimed. Their devotion was to her purpose, not to her person. Her great aunt Aenora firmly believed that she would have been better suited to be that vessel. She was not alone in that belief, and Aenora had never let her niece forget it, not for a moment. There was no deference at home, only hope and thwarted ambition.

The Countess wrapped her robe around her, enjoying the touch of it. She was already half in another world, her mind and body hovering in between realities. She felt soft, relaxed, and ready, as if in a vivid dream.

The Countess practically floated into the main room of the suite, Elise trailing behind her. Jules was crouching over the floor, looking awkward in his stolen bellboy's uniform. Sharp-faced and lean, he glanced up at their arrival and blinked at the sight of the Countess. There was little left to the imagination. Jules turned away quickly, red-faced and flustered, and contrived to look everywhere but back at the Countess.

He had been busy while she cleansed and purified herself. While masquerading as a porter, he had smuggled a number of packages into the suite containing the ingredients for the Invocation. Collecting and assembling them had been bloody, difficult work. It had taken weeks, and he had started long before the Countess arrived. Elise had helped where she could, but the more mystical tasks were his specialty. He had a clear interest, although he lacked the requisite Talent to cast spells of his own. Preparing the invocation was a dream come true and he had approached the task with enthusiasm.

He had carefully measured out the room, scribbling occult calculations in his notebook, before tearing out a piece of the carpet at the very center and placing a giant map of the city in its place. He surrounded the map with a number of signs and sigils in the proscribed runic pattern.

"You've done well," the Countess said, examining his handiwork. He had clearly studied the old texts. His rune work was precise and his preparations were exact. They needed to be. One symbol out of place could be catastrophic. Magicians were known to practice their patterns and sigils for years before channeling even the slightest drop of power through them. The Countess did not have that luxury.

"Thank you, my lady," Jules said.

"Where did you learn this?"

"Your great aunt cultivated my interests. Lady Ae..."

"Do not say the name!" the Countess interrupted quickly. "Not here, not yet. The city has too many ears and until the invocation is complete, we don't know who's listening."

"I'm sorry, my lady," he said. "She was very kind to me."

"And you've proved worthy of her kindness."

He blushed and stood. Elise gave him a sidelong glance and he looked away.

The Countess paid no attention to the byplay. She knew the effect she had on him. It was of no concern. Her great aunt's interest in nurturing him and his sister was more troubling, but she would have to ponder the implications later.

She turned her attention to the three chalices resting on the table, one filled with blood, another with oil, and the third with water all consecrated and mixed with herbs. Traditionally, the blood was meant to be spilled by the supplicant's own hand, but the spirit she was invoking would not care. She knew that, instinctually.

"Will you be needing anything else?" Elise asked.

"No," the Countess replied. "That will be all."

Elise curtseyed and turned to leave, but noticed her brother lingering. She elbowed him sharply and dragged him out behind her, whispering angrily.

The Countess watched them go. They were no younger than she was and in some ways far more experienced, but she felt older. For all their willing devotion, this was her path to walk, her purpose to fulfill, her invocation to perform.

*

The Duke and Duchess always served a magnificent table. The meal had started with a basilisk soup and they had moved on to a selection of oysters, anchovies, shrimp, and sardines. Even Heinrich, a proud gourmet, was impressed. He took a sip of wine, careful as always not to crush the crystal glass in his hand, and glanced around at the others. It was a modest gathering by Ducal standards, only fifteen guests, but they had been chosen with great care—a patchwork collection of faëries, politicians, merchants, and a handful of minor aristocrats.

Heinrich was clustered with the faërie contingent at the Duchess' end of the table. There was Krist, an elderly krampus with graying muttonchops, who was wearing his old uniform and displaying a new, specially minted medal. He looked distinctly uncomfortable sitting between a siren and one of the muses. They were both leading members of the faërie literati and had recently been commissioned to write an opera commemorating of the Witches' Overthrow. It should be ready next year in time for the Bicentennial. Heinrich had personally suggested them to the Duchess. It was a great, if calculated, honor.

To the Duke's right sat the Chancellor of the Wizarding College, Grand Master Undur. A fastidious, sober man dressed in the long coat and ornate collar of his Order, Undur fiercely promoted the College's interests. Lord Edward had little magical talents of his own, but the Grand Master never let him forget that the Duke's own illustrious ancestor had been one of the founders, especially when discussing budgetary matters, as he was now.

Across from him sat Mr. Lloyd Pullman, the skeletal Chair of the Parliamentary Budgetary Committee with a stranglehold on the Centre Party. Then there was the Hon. Mr. Antony Clarke, his rotund counterpart in the Unity Party. Together they utterly dominated Parliament and were among the Duke's most ardent and dangerous critics. They were listening to Undur intently. It was unwise to be impolite to a magician, especially one with the Grand Master's reputation.

"I hoped," Undur was saying, "that Parliament might reconsider the Psychic Communications Project."

"The telepathic training program?" Pullman asked.

"Yes." Undur nodded. "It would be a tremendous leap forward, and some of the other Cities are already developing their own pilot programs."

"They are?" Pullman glanced at Clarke, who shrugged as he scarfed down an oyster.

"Yes," the Duke interjected. "Argen and Ort have both begun selecting candidates."

"Interesting," Clarke said. "But perhaps, Grand Master, you should direct your question to Lord Edward. After all, it's his little building projects that are taking up most of the budget."

The Duke smiled tightly. "Those little projects, as you call them, are for the good of the city. The roads and trains were in desperate need of repair. Our city was falling apart around us," he said. "We must prepare for the future even as we remember the past."

"I agree completely," said Pullman. "We must all certainly prepare for the future no matter what it might hold." There was a sudden hush at that. Everyone present knew exactly what he was referring to—the succession. Heinrich took note. It appeared that Raske had been, at least partially, telling the truth.

"I see the Commandant is not with us tonight," Pullman said after a moment. Around him, the other guests slowly began eating again. "No doubt he's busy."

"Or hiding," Clarke added with a smirk. "He hasn't been particularly popular of late."

"I assure you," the Duke said, "that Baron Hessing is doing everything he can to deal with the situation."

"I'm sure he is," Pullman said. "And that is the crux of the matter. Perhaps, the murders and the bombings are finally more than he can handle."

The Duke narrowed his eyes. "Baron Hessing has my full confidence."

"You've always had a blind spot where he is concerned," Clarke said. "You show commendable loyalty, but not everyone in the city shares your faith."

One of the margraves leaned forward. He was a burly soldier from the Borderland on the edge of the Protected Crescent. He was rarely in the city but he had a great deal of influence within the Dukedom.

"Perhaps," the margrave said, "we should not judge the Commandant too harshly. Faërie brutality can be difficult to handle." His eyes lingered on Heinrich for a moment.

The troll delicately wiped his mouth. "I feel I should remind you that many of the Ripper's victims have been faëries, and that over half of those killed at the Rook Gate Bombing were as well." Beside him, the muse nodded.

"I lost four sisters," she said. "And I assure you that I want the perpetrator caught as much as anyone here."

"Of course you do, my dear," Clarke interjected quickly. Pullman nodded beside him. "And on behalf of everyone here, please accept our sincere condolences on your loss."

Heinrich glanced at the Duchess, who was narrowing her eyes at Clarke and Pullman. They were encroaching shamelessly on her territory, like Raske before them.

"I believe we can speak for ourselves," she said.

"Do you mean you aren't sympathetic?" Pullman asked.

"I mean nothing of the sort," the Duchess snapped. "That's why the Duke and I have already set up a fund for the faërie victims. Perhaps you and Mr. Clarke would care to make a donation."

Neither of them spared the muse a second glance, but Heinrich noticed that she seemed increasingly uncomfortable. All the faëries did.

Grand Master Undur cleared his throat. "Now, now," he said. "Murder and death are not suitable dinner topics. We're all friends here."

"Indeed we are," said the Duke. The corners of his mouth twisted. It was blatantly untrue, but no one dared contradict him or the magician.

"Personally," Undur continued, turning to the muse, "I enjoyed your recent premiere at the Opera House."

"Thank you," she said, embarrassed. "I thought it was one of my weaker efforts."

"Not at all," Undur replied expansively. "It was fascinating—the lyrics, the score, even the inclusion of subtle magical notes. Marvelous."

Heinrich watched them, amused but wary. Undur had deflected the tension effectively, if not altogether subtly, but in his own way he was spoiling for a fight just as much as the rest. It was no secret that Undur had always wanted to test his powers against faërie magic, but he was too much of a gentleman to provoke any conflict directly.

The servants emerged from the shadows to remove the plates as unobtrusively as possible. It was time for the third course. Heinrich glanced around. The servants were all faëries. That too had been calculated. The Duke had many human servants and footmen as well, but he was sending a message—to Heinrich, to Clarke and Pullman, to the margraves. He and the Duchess were walking a delicate, narrow path. There were undercurrents of fear and malice everywhere.

Heinrich reached for another glass of wine. The dinner party wasn't going well.

*

At last the Countess was ready to begin the Invocation. She had checked and double-checked Jules' calculations and sigilwork. He had a true gift. Everything was as it should be, not a mark out of place. He had no magic of his own, but there were alternatives. No wonder her great aunt had encouraged him; she would have to do the same, if she survived.

She took a deep breath and centered herself. Then she reached out and held up the first chalice. It was filled with the blood of human and faëries, joined in death willingly and unwillingly. She spoke a few words over them, a dedication and a consecration, and then poured it out onto the runes below. The blood pooled outward, tracing the sigils and patterns onto the map. There was a great rush of energy, palpable but invisible. She heard the voices of the dead murmuring in the quiet places of her mind, before bursting outward into the streets below.

Next she took up the second chalice and poured out the water, taken from the River of Talis. It sizzled and bubbled when it met the blood. The room began to turn around her, but she forced it steady. There was still one more offering. Finally, she emptied the oil over the troubled mixture. It calmed immediately and a sweet, dreamy scent filled the room.

The Countess gazed down at her work. The blood, water, and oil had stained the map with a great spiraling pattern. For a true adept, the ritual was merely a prop, the signs and sigils merely symbols, but symbols held power, especially for Elise and Jules.

Their belief was an ingredient as well, the final ingredient. They believed in her purpose and her worthiness, and if they required these accouterments to channel that belief then so be it.

The Countess knew the exact moment her offerings had been accepted. It was as if every street, every avenue, every block, every building, brick and window was looking at her. Everyone with even a modicum of awareness would have felt it on some level, but she knew it was meant only for her. The city had become a giant eye made of architecture, space and light, and she was standing on its pupil. She had woken the city, attracted the crushing, curious weight of its attention.

She stepped barefoot into the circle. The canvas crinkled. She felt an immediate rush of power and awareness coursing eagerly up from the soles of her feet. That was only a taste of what was to come. She sat in the center and closed her eyes. Her body had been purified. The way had been prepared.

It was time to say hello.

*

Dessert had just been served when Lord Edward rose at the head of the table. Conversation slowly died down and all eyes turned toward him.

The Duke waited until the conversations had all ceased, and then raised his glass in a toast toward the krampus. "To Captain Krist," he said. "In recognition of his service in the Goblin Wars." At the other end of the table, the Duchess echoed him. The others followed suit with varying degrees of enthusiasm.

Heinrich and the other two faëries present were naturally the most effusive, although the troll couldn't help but feel a twinge of cynicism. The Goblin Wars had ended almost thirty years ago, and Krist's rank was an affectation. No faërie had ever risen above a sergeant's rank. Heinrich was more interested in the others' reactions, especially after the earlier tensions.

Grand Master Undur raised his glass politely, and Heinrich thought he might have glimpsed a half smile hidden beneath Undur's well-trimmed beard. The Grand Master's views on Faërie Rights had always been deliberately vague. As a magician, he seemed to consider himself above, or perhaps beyond, the fray. Beside him, Clarke and Pullman were more overtly enthusiastic. The Duke had deliberately waited and had stolen a march on them.

"That's most kind of you, your grace," said Clarke.

"It's about time our faërie brothers received their due." Pullman added with an earnest nod. It was obviously false. Neither of them had ever heard of Krist before tonight, or had ever made the slightest gesture toward faërie veterans, but the fact that they were making the effort spoke volumes to Heinrich. Some of the other guests, mostly minor aristocrats, were less sanguine.

"That's all well and good," the margrave said. "But more and more faëries are pouring into the Crescent from the mountains, creatures we've never seen before. Something has to be done—even your pet Brigadier, Kronberger, agrees. We're not going to give them all a medal, I hope." He glared down at Krist's end of the table.

"No one is suggesting anything of the sort," said the Duke.

"No one seems to be suggesting anything at all. They bomb the city and you invite them to dinner as if nothing had changed."

"We need to be careful," the Duchess said, "not to tar everyone with the same brush. Talis has the largest faërie population apart from the Capital. They aren't all murderers and bombers. Most of them are businessmen and artists, and, as we've already been reminded tonight, some of them have suffered as well."

"It is exactly that permissive attitude that has allowed them to carry out these acts of violence."

"We are in the Protected Crescent," said the Duke. "Bordered on all sides by the mountains and rivers with an ocean at our back. Generations have sheltered here from the dangers of Deeper Faërie. We should at least make an effort to continue that tradition. Even the Witches never turned anyone away."

"That may be so," the margrave said, "but I'm the one 'protecting' the Crescent, and there doesn't seem to be any clear strategy. Some of the other Dukes are closing their borders, while you're maintaining an open policy. The Emperor needs to take charge of the situation. It's not sustainable. What does he think he's doing?"

"Perhaps you should ask the Imperial Envoy when he arrives tomorrow," Clarke suggested innocently.

The room fell eerily silent and an uneasy murmur rumbled through the party. The Duke glared at Clarke and held up a calming hand.

"It's true," he said. "The Emperor is sending us an envoy, Borchard-Márai, no doubt simply to observe our progress. Nothing to worry about." Some of the sharper guests eyed the Duke and Duchess thoughtfully at that. Neither of them were getting any younger and the succession was on everyone's mind. Sending not just an envoy, but one of his own cousins implied that the Emperor had more on his mind than simply observing.

"The Emperor has always been a friend to Talis," the Duke continued.

It was feeble and they all knew it. Borchard-Márai had already garnered a reputation for doing the Emperor's dirty work. Imperial policy was shifting, everyone at the table could feel it, but no one was sure which direction it would turn, or what was behind it.

Clarke and Pullman were looking particularly smug to Heinrich's eye. The evening was theirs. They had sown the seeds of doubt. Whatever their plan truly was, it seemed to be proceeding apace. Anselm would have to be informed, and about the envoy as well. That was news, and might convince him to abandon his plans for the moment.

Suddenly, Undur paled and his hands began to shake. He fell back in his seat breathing heavily. His glass slipped from his fingers and crashed to the ground in a shattering of crystal and wine.

The Duke was at his side in an instant. "Grand Master?" he asked, reaching out an arm to steady him. Undur lurched as if caught in some great wind, but said nothing.

As everyone focused on the ailing Undur, Heinrich noticed from the corner of his eye that the muse was slumped forward too, and was trembling slightly.

"Something," she murmured as if in a daze, "something vast with a thousand eyes and ears is...waking...watching..."

No one except Heinrich appeared to have heard her, but there was a strange current in the air—a wrongness, or an awareness. Heinrich was ill-equipped to describe it, but all the faëries could feel it, even the servants, though none of them as much as the muse, or as deeply as the magician.

It passed as suddenly as it had begun. Undur came back to himself and sat up quickly. He ran a hand through his beard and sighed. "Thank you," he said. "I'm quite alright, your grace." He didn't look it. He was still pale and there was a peculiar tightness around his eyes. "Probably just a bout of indigestion."

No one believed him for a moment, least of all Heinrich. "Are you alright?" he whispered to the muse.

She stared at him for a long moment, almost as if she couldn't understand the question. "No," she said at last. "None of us are."

A chill ran through the troll. There was a pall laying over the guests—a vague sense of unease. The Duke and Duchess shared a worried look across the long table. Nothing was going according to plan.

*

The Countess reached down into herself, through her feet into the parchment and beyond out into the city. She moved passed the streets and the architecture, past the people and ideas, past the light and the sound. There were many cities layered on top of each other. She saw them all dimly. No two were alike and yet they were all Talis.

Some were vast and sprawling. More than mere geography, they cast their shadows across the years. The Talis of the Dukes was a fairly young city, barely two centuries old, precarious and delicately balanced. It was trying to be the fulcrum of a thousand different Talises, human and faërie alike, and it was failing. The Countess could see the cracks in its foundation.

It had been born from the ashes of the Witches' Talis, that two-thousand-year behemoth that had sunk its claws and spells deep into the city. The Countess smiled to see it. The Dukes had tried to erase it, and write over it, but that Talis was still close to the surface, jutting out everywhere. All the other cities stumbled over it, even the first, the dimmest and most distant of them all, the Talis of its beginning.

That beleaguered outpost of humanity clinging to the riverside had been a desperate, desolate place, less of a city and more a collection of hovels and a handful of humans, trapped in the Faërie Lands, alone with the wonder and terror.

The Countess felt it, felt the ancient desperation, knew the humans' names, tasted their fear. For a moment those long-ago hovel walls were as real as her hotel suite. She knew them all intimately. She saw them, just as she saw a doctor at that very moment walking down Founder's Row without a second thought. Little was left of that original Talis—a handful of street names and a bronze plaque where the first hovel was believed to have stood. The Countess knew now that, in truth, it had been half a mile away, but that didn't matter. It was a legend, a story the city told itself; or the humans told themselves, at least.

There were smaller private Talises, as well. The doctor strolling down Founder's Row had a Talis of his own. It was a small place, inhabiting only a few streets and houses. It was a human city, a city of sickness wrapped in wealth, that kept to itself.

Talis was all of those cities and none of them. They were tendrils of its being—its heart, its lungs, its mind. The Countess could pass from city to city like moving from thought to thought. It was exhilarating. She reached out and greeted the city.

The City replied.

Part II

The Smoke and Mirrors Club

7

CHAPTER SEVEN

Hessing had lain awake tossing and turning for hours. There was no comfort in the night, no rest, no quiet, only aches and doubts. The dark thoughts and memories gnawed at him constantly, but during the day Hessing was able to distract himself. He deliberately cultivated a never-ending rush of noise and activity. He was always busy, always shouting, almost never still. But in the evenings when he went to bed, he was alone with his night thoughts and they would devour him whole. There was no escape.

He could barely remember the last time he'd been blessed by a quiet night's sleep. It had been years, perhaps, but recently it was worse than ever. He longed to rest, but these days he never managed more than a few hours a night. Even the little sleep he got was plagued by dreams. He could never remember them exactly, but he knew Gregor was always there. Sometimes as he'd found him on that terrible night, other times as the solemn boy he had been. He would speak, but Hessing could never remember what he said. It always left him unsettled, or worse, far worse.

Outside, Hessing heard the city bells begin to ring. It was morning at last. He gathered his bulk and lumbered blearily to his feet before the first bell had finished ringing. He had survived another night. Lemann entered with a discrete knock and practiced timing. He knew exactly when his master was ready for him.

Lemann went about his business in silence. He laid out Hessing's shirt, pants, waistcoat, uniform, and cuff links neatly on the bed, and began to dress him. Their routine used to be filled with loud voices and Hessing's booming laughter. He was not a naturally talkative man by nature, but he had taught himself to be professionally gregarious. He still made a point to know the names of all his servants, just as he knew all his policemen and their families, but he had found it harder since Gregor to put on his accustomed humor. Lemann understood, better than most. He had been with Hessing for decades, had known Gregor as a boy, and mourned him in his own way.

Fully dressed, Hessing descended for breakfast. He wasn't looking forward to the day, but it was better than staying here. The Hessing House was a place of quiet now, a place of long, lingering silences and emptiness. That was how he preferred it for the most part, but there were more rooms than Hessing knew what to do with, especially after Gregor. His wife, Olivia, had decorated it in all the trappings of wealth and power—paintings and artwork from across the Crescent, Goblin pottery, and artifacts from deep in the Faërie Lands.

As he reached the bottom of the stairs, he could hear the early morning bustle coming from the street, but amidst the usual sounds of the city there a rising murmur of angry voices.

"Another crowd, Lemann?" He asked.

"Yes, sir," the butler replied. "And a rather unhappy one." Hessing nodded. That went without saying. The crowds outside his house were seldom gathered in celebration.

"Any particular reason?"

"I wouldn't like to say, sir." Lemann shrugged apologetically. "It's all in the newspapers."

"Ah, of course." Hessing could feel the beginnings of a headache, a dull roar at the back of his skull, but he steeled himself and entered the dining room. Olivia was already there, dressed all in black.

He went to serve himself his usual breakfast of kippers and eggs, and took his accustomed seat at the head of the table. They ate in utter silence save for the clinking of cutlery, and the tinkling of teacups. Hessing opened his mouth once or twice to speak, but closed it hopelessly. There were things he wanted to tell her, answers he owed her, but he wasn't sure how to start. The words wouldn't come. She ignored him pointedly, and his eyes kept straying to the third empty place setting across from her, as if their son would appear at any moment.

Hessing wasn't sure what was worse, this bitter silence or the hysterics that had preceded it. She had screamed and railed the night before, and even thrown a centuries-old goblin vase at his head. Dr. Trefusis had come to administer his opiates, but she had calmed down by then. He claimed she was taking her medicine, and she certainly seemed quieter, but Hessing wasn't so sure. He knew his wife. She had a sly, mistrustful turn of mind and had accused him weeks ago of bribing the doctors. She hadn't mentioned it since then, but he knew she hadn't forgotten and she hadn't forgiven.

The butler interrupted his thoughts with a discrete cough and handed him the morning paper, fresh off the presses and neatly creased and folded. The headlines were not encouraging—Rook Gate Bomber Still At Large! Ripper Strikes Again! Parliament Calls For Hessing's Resignation!

He was used to opposition, calls for his dismissal, outright hatred even, but it felt different this time. The mood was different. Hessing was worn-out and, for once, the papers weren't wrong. The investigations were stalling, and worse, the Duke knew it. The situation was deteriorating rapidly.

Outside the murmur of the crowd had risen to a dull roar. Hessing went to the window and peered out. A carriage had pulled up outside the house, forcing its way through the throng. He checked his pocket watch. The coachman was as punctual as ever.

"Time for me to go, my dear," he said. He leaned down to kiss his wife on the cheek. She remained motionless, staring straight ahead. She didn't like to be touched, but he did so anyway. It was a petty revenge and he regretted it instantly, but he had been fond of that vase. He tried to apologize, but he couldn't, not for this, not for anything. He left her to her breakfast. This was not a happy house; not, he noted, if only to himself, that it ever had been.

Lemann was waiting with his hat and coat.

"Perhaps you should send for an escort, sir," he said.

Hessing scoffed. "That rabble can't hurt me."

"With respect, sir, yes it can."

"Thank you for your concern, Mr. Lemann." Hessing gave him

a wry smile. "But I'd rather face the crowd out there than her indoors. I know how to handle them."

"No comment, sir."

Hessing patted the butler on the shoulder. "Very wise of you," he said.

The crowd gave a dangerous bellow when he emerged from the house. He could feel the force of their anger like a blow to the face. Lemann had not been exaggerating. There were humans and faëries shouting and waving their fists and talons in between glaring at each other. Hessing was amused that despite their tensions, at least there was one thing they could still agree on—hating him. He'd never been a unifying force before. It was oddly flattering.

As he descended down the front steps, the crowd surged forward, but he was not cowed. He glared back at them with a sneer on his face, daring them to attack. There was a reason he was the Duke's most feared and able servant. The crowd stumbled to a halt. There was death in his eyes and confidence. Whatever else he was inside the house, out here he was the Commandant of Police.

"That's enough!" he shouted. "I've seen your faces now." His eyes were running over everyone, fixing them with his terrible attention. Each member of the crowd felt that he was glaring specifically at them and a chill ran down their backs at the thought.

"Go to work," he continued. "Forget this nonsense, and I will forget you."

The crowd wavered then stilled again, this time staring upward. Hessing frowned and followed their gaze.

A giant white and gold airship floated over the city, glinting in the morning sun. Even Hessing could not quite contain his awe at the sight—an Imperial Airship, one of only seven in the world. It was a grand monument to human ingenuity. The political implications did not escape him, however. Airships were reserved for important court officials. Something was happening, and for once he had no idea what it was.

"Move along," he said turning back to the crowd. They scattered. A couple of humans pushed a faërie out of the way, and a fight almost broke out, but after a few worried glances at Hessing, the two parties separated. They circled each other warily but left peaceably, spitting curses.

Hessing paid no attention to the fracas. He had more important matters on his mind. On top of the bombings, murders, and calls for his head, now he would have to deal with whatever the airship imported.

He climbed into the coach. "Drive," he said. He needed to get to Headquarters. The Duke would be sending for him shortly, and hopefully Hessing would have some progress to report by then.

*

Police Headquarters was a crumbling cathedral to law and order. The arches sloped above into a distant, vaulted ceiling. Iron struts had been added here and there to reinforce the structure, and lanterns hung low from recently added metal beams. Gargoyles lined the walls at regular intervals gazing down with rictus faces. Erkel had always found something vaguely sinister about gargoyles that never moved. It was unnatural, especially in Talis. They were rumored to be ancient prisoners, encased in stone by the Witches as a warning and a consecration, and even after all these years, Erkel didn't know if it was true. He didn't want to know. They were grotesque enough as it was.

Daylight streamed in from the high, narrow windows. Lund returned from the break room with two mugs of coffee. He placed them down on Erkel's desk, careful not to disturb the papers. They had been there all night, pouring over coroners' reports and pictures from the crime scenes. Their desks were a mess of files and folders and a handful of scribbled ideas. They had nothing. No leads, only a matching pair of headaches and a gnawing frustration. To add to their bitterness, they hadn't been alone for their all-night vigil. Inspector Cambor and his bombing taskforce had been there as well. They were both feeling the pressure, but where Erkel had only a single sergeant, Cambor had half a dozen men.

Erkel and Lund had been forced to listen to them all night, laughing and joking, and worst of all, making progress. They sent baleful glares at the others, but Cambor and his men didn't even seem to notice. One of them, a keen young man barely old enough to shave, had found references to a strange whistling in one of the survivor's statements. It had sent them scurrying through the other reports, and sure enough, there were multiple accounts not just at the gate but throughout the city. Erkel had to admit that it was good police work. Cambor had chosen his team well, but it should have been their case—his and Lund's.

Inspector Cambor crossed the room to join them. "Erkel," he said. "Sergeant." They gave him a sullen nod, uncertain if he had come over to gloat or to share. Erkel doubted that he knew, himself. Cambor was a sour, contradictory man.

"I know you were close to Obry. We all were," Cambor hastened to add. They said nothing. He scowled self-consciously. "I just wanted to say that we're making progress."

"We heard," said Erkel.

"We'll catch this whistler..." Cambor waved his hand back toward the others.

Erkel and Lund exchanged glances and smiled.

"What?" he demanded.

"Don't you know who he is?" Erkel asked lightly.

"Always whistling," Lund added, "with a fondness for fire..."

Cambor blinked. Suddenly the answer was obvious. "The hobgoblin!" he said. "Of course! Why didn't I think of that?"

Erkel and Lund regarded him smugly. They'd recognized the hobgoblin as soon as the whistling was mentioned.

Cambor's eyes snapped back and took in their expressions sullenly. "And what do you have?" he demanded, rummaging through their papers. "Nothing! Maybe you should spend more time on your own case, instead of sticking your nose into mine!"

He stormed off, but as he went, he shouted at one of his men to fetch Mr. Tarr's file.

Erkel and Lund glared at his back.

"We gave him that," Lund muttered.

Erkel held up a restraining hand. "Let it go," he said. "For now."

The front doors swung open and more policemen began to stream inside. Inspector Vorn was at their head. He glanced from Erkel to Cambor and back again, shaking his head. He never burned the midnight oil if he could help it, and he usually could. But he had something else on his mind.

"Have you seen the airship?" he asked.

CHAPTER EIGHT

Mr. Tarr made his way down the cobblestone streets toward the riverfront. It was early in the morning and sun was barely peeking over the horizon. As he approached the docks, the smell reached him first, wafting on the breeze. It was followed shortly by the great cacophony of noise and commerce—the rumble of caskets being rolled down gangways, the creaking of ships, shouted orders, and sea shanties.

When he turned the corner, he was confronted at last by a forest of masts and sails rising above the water in a tangle of ships and steamers of every size and description. They had plundered the Faërie Lands, and returned to disgorge their spoils. On the shore, Mr. Tarr slipped unseen between the porters and carters, whistling his favorite tune. Clerks in dapper suits and well-oiled mustaches peered up from their records; sailors giddily ashore at last sang, and drank, and wandered; ship's captains passing bribes to customs men, who glanced around guiltily. A few of them caught a note or two of Mr. Tarr's whistling and searched in vain, but he was nowhere to be seen, and his tune was soon lost in the clamor.

The docks were the lifeblood of the city, its beating maritime heart, and Mr. Tarr hated it, all of it—the noise, the smell, the pandemonium. There was no true chaos here. Beneath the sound and fury there was order and business, human business. And everywhere there were soldiers.

This was not Mr. Tarr's world, but there was another, below the docks, in the in-between places. Beyond the hulking, grime-encrusted warehouses, where not even the leanest, hungriest laborers ventured, lived the scavengers and finfolk. There were bone-pickers and mermen, selkies and mud-larks, nymphs and dredgermen. They were the Peoples of the Water. Once they had dwelt in splendor and plenty in distant oceans, rivers, and lakes, but now they lived in squalor, feeding off human detritus. Mr. Tarr knew them well, knew their broken pride, their simmering hate, and their eerie kindness. They had something that belonged to him.

He reached a secluded part of the waterfront past a rotting wharf and glanced around—no one was watching. He whistled the final notes of his song and then sat down cross-legged at the shore and waited. He watched the ships pass and the waves roll back and forth. They would come in their own time. He had all day. He could be patient.

Finally, a head rose from the water, followed by another and another. They were mermen with long, sharp teeth and bulbous eyes. They hovered in the water, watching. In their hands they carried tridents and spears. Mr. Tarr stood respectfully. It was an honor guard of sorts and the People of the Water were sticklers for the old forms. When they had determined that the coast was clear, the final figure emerged from the river. It was a great golden sea lion with the face of a bearded man. He crawled ashore slowly on his flippers and studied Mr. Tarr for a moment.

"We meet again, hobgoblin," he said in a deep, melodious voice. "My sister wishes to speak to you."

"And I with her."

The sea lion nodded.

"Very well." His mouth contorted, opening impossibly wide. A head emerged from that mouth and then shoulders, arms, and legs. It was a young woman—a human woman—with dark hair and the ocean in her eyes. She stood before him, naked and dripping. Behind her lay her shedded brother's skin glistening in the sun. In her hands she held a box. She had kept it safe inside him.

It was a small box, perhaps six inches in diameter. There were no keyholes, no hinges, no openings of any kind. Its surface was a smooth, solid black, but it shimmered sometimes in the light, illuminated with strange patterns. Even Mr. Tarr could feel a vague unease oozing out from it, polluting the air around them with an indescribable wrongness.

"Greetings, hobgoblin," the young woman said, her voice as melodious as her brother's. Behind her the mermen and merrows kept watch, and there were others—spirits that lived in the foam and the waves, mud-larks crawling in the sand and muck—all the water dwellers had sent a representative.

"I am Lira," she continued, "and I speak for the Finfolk and the Water Dwellers."

"Greetings," he replied. "I speak for the Faërie Land Dwellers of Talis."

"We have kept it safe for you," she said holding the box forward. "My sisters sang it from the Deep. The mermen guarded it with their tridents, and the undines spelled it down to sleep. It is yours now, Mr. Tarr. Do with it as you must."

"Thank you." He reached out and took the box from her, carefully. There was power inside, a danger even he respected. "The others will be pleased." He paused. "Mr. Nix will be pleased as well."

The selkie nodded solemnly. That was worth more than all the merchant's wealth in the world and they both knew it. "We will remember that."

"And He will remember you, when the time comes."

"When?" She asked. "We are ready now. The mermen and merrows sharpen their spears; the nymphs prepare their war songs. The humans pollute our waters every day; we cannot wait much longer."

"Soon," said Mr. Tarr. "Very soon. Thanks to you." He nodded toward the box. There were great plans for that box and what was inside. There had always been factions, dissidents, and Mr. Tarr had known them all, had gone with whoever promised action—vicious Droz and coiled Anselm, vengeful Brunet or bitter Covét. But lately there had been a clarity of purpose, a driving force that promised chaos beyond Mr. Tarr's wildest imaginings. He had pledged himself to that purpose and the anarchy it would sow.

The selkie maiden nodded, her errand complete, and began to crawl back inside her brother's skin. Mr. Tarr watched, fascinated. The siblings were an odd pair, born of the river queen and a selkie man. She shoved herself back inside, legs first. Mr. Tarr started to leave.

"Wait, hobgoblin," came a voice. "There is something else." He turned back. The sea lion had been restored and stretched himself to his full height. "Two nights ago a woman smuggled herself down the river in a raft. The humans did not see her, as they do not see you. But we are the People of the Water. This is our domain. We miss nothing."

"A woman?" Mr. Tarr asked. His mind turned to the woman who had caught a glimpse of him on the street outside Covét's apartment, the so-called Countess. "Was she human?"

The sea lion paused and pondered. "We do not know," he said. "She smelt of land and air, and of magic."

"Interesting," said Mr. Tarr. "Very interesting." He nodded his thanks, and took his leave.

Whoever the woman was, she was starting to show up all over the city, with alarming frequency. She had the potential to change things drastically. He considered warning Anselm and the others, but shrugged. It would be more fun this way.

He whistled happily to himself.

*

Anselm made his way alone to a large house in the most fashionable part of the Faërie Quarter. It was almost the size of the block, and the mark of new money clung to it. The architecture was grandiose and the decorations more than a little excessive. A maid with resentful eyes let the homunculus in immediately through the servant's entrance. She was human. Anselm slipped her a fifty-pound note and followed her inside. It always gave him a thrill to see humans in service to faëries after a lifetime of the reverse. She led him to a small, dark room at the rear of the house.

Heinrich was seated in his dressing gown, smoking a cigar. The maid exited discretely.

The troll lumbered to his feet as soon as she was gone. "What are you doing here?" he demanded. "You could have been seen!"

"I wasn't," Anselm said. "Except by your girl there, and we can handle that, if you think she might be a problem."

Heinrich waved that away. "I told you never to visit me at home. How did you even get in?"

"No doors are closed to me in the Faërie Quarter."

"Apparently not even human ones." Heinrich frowned. He had worried that Anselm might have spies on his faërie staff, not his human one. "Why are you here?"

"For your report. I was expecting it sooner."

Heinrich bristled. "I don't answer to you."

"I misspoke." Anselm held up a pacifying hand. "But I would like to hear your thoughts on last night's dinner. That is why you went, is it not?"

Heinrich nodded. He couldn't deny it. This had been his chance to make a contribution to the cause, although he had his own motives. It was a delicate game he was playing, nearly as delicate as the Duke and Duchess' efforts.

Anselm made himself comfortable in one of Heinrich's plush chairs. "Then tell me," he said. "Tell me everything."

Heinrich sat slowly and mustered his arguments. This was his last best chance to make his case.

"I believe the Duke and Duchess are sincere," he said, "but distracted."

"They're always distracted by something," said Anselm. "That's their modus operandi. And what of Raske?"

Heinrich frowned. "I'm not sure. The threat seems to be real.

The Duke was very careful of Clarke and Pullman and they were circling him, falling over themselves to show their faërie sympathies. There were definite undercurrents. And if it is true, then we could play them all against each other."

Anselm said nothing, his face carefully blank.

"I just need a little more time," Heinrich said.

"There is no more time. The Victory Ball is tomorrow."

"There has to be another way."

"Not for me," Anselm said. "I'm not going to twiddle my thumbs while you play at politics."

"I'm not playing."

"That's all you've ever done. Now you have to choose a side."

Heinrich glared. Beneath the veneer of civility, Anselm was a sanctimonious, ungrateful bastard. Heinrich had pulled the homunculus from obscurity, paid his debts, and introduced him to like-minded faëries. Anselm owed him.

"I have chosen," Heinrich said through gritted teeth. "You know that."

Anselm rose. "I'll see myself out."

"I haven't finished my report."

"It doesn't matter. I learned what I needed to," said Anselm. "You've lost your nerve, Heinrich, now that the end is in sight. If you find it again, you know where I am."

Heinrich waited until the homunculus was almost at the door. "An Imperial Envoy is arriving today," he said. Anselm halted. "One of the Emperor's cousins, Borchard-Márai."

Anselm turned. "How do you know that?"

"Clarke and Pullman couldn't wait to tell everyone last night."

"I'm sure," Anselm muttered. He was lost in thought. "This is perfect."

Heinrich frowned. "Making a direct move against the Emperor would be suicide," he said.

"Thank you for the concern," Anselm said. "But you play your games, and I'll play mine." He left Heinrich alone to his thoughts.

The troll had made no mention of the muse's words, or the Grand Master's peculiar collapse. Heinrich believed that in the end, that would be more important than a thousand Imperial Envoys. It was better to keep that secret for now. Anselm was set on a dangerous path, and whatever happened, Heinrich was determined to have a place in the new order. If something magical truly was stirring, he would find a way to exploit it with or without Anselm and the others.

CHAPTER NINE

Elise and Jules entered the hotel suite warily. The air was heavy with magic. A vast presence seemed to have imprinted itself upon the room. Nothing was out of place, but it was as if every piece of furniture, every item, every particle of dust had been lifted, imbued with some strange force, and then returned to exactly where it was before. It made their skin crawl and tingle from the outside in.

The Countess was lying naked and motionless on top of the map, surrounded by the ritual paraphernalia. Elise was at her side in a moment, but Jules hesitated, perhaps from embarrassment, or perhaps a prudent sense of caution. Rituals were sensitive things.

"Is she alive?" he asked.

Elise felt for a pulse. Nothing. She moved her hand over the

Countess' mouth. They waited for a long, dreadful moment, before Elise let out a sigh of relief.

"She's breathing."

Jules closed his eyes and gave a brief prayer of thanks. "Good," he said.

"Don't just stand there," Elise snapped. "Make yourself useful. Fetch her robe and then start a fire. She's terribly cold."

Jules hastened to obey. They half-carried the Countess into a chair by the fireplace and wrapped her in her robe. While Elise tended to her, Jules began stoking the fire. Soon he had a sizable blaze roaring.

"She's in no shape to see him," Elise said.

Jules looked up. "There's no choice," he said. "The appointment is tonight and Mr. Nix doesn't give second chances."

"I know that, but look at her," said Elise. "She's barely alive."

"The invocation would have killed you or me within seconds. She's strong."

"Strong enough to treat with Nix?"

Jules had no answer for that. "You know what she is," he said instead. "Have faith."

"Faith," she repeated. "Is that what you have?" He looked away, unable to meet her eyes.

The Countess stirred in her chair. "What are you two arguing about?" she asked. Her voice seemed to come from a long way away, as if she'd forgotten how to speak, or had only just remembered that speech was even a possibility.

"Nothing," Elise said. "Don't worry about it. You need to rest." She was hovering over the Countess, wringing her hands, unsure what to do with herself.

The Countess shifted with a tired sigh. She turned to Jules, who still hadn't moved from the fire.

"What are you arguing about?" she asked again.

He glanced at his sister for a moment. She shook her head, and he frowned. The Countess had a right to know.

"Don't lie," the Countess said. Something moved behind her eyes, and peered out at him with terrible intention. She was more than the Countess. She was Purpose wrapped in flesh and thought, and she would have obedience. Her beauty compelled it, and her will demanded it.

"We've arranged a meeting with Mr. Nix, as you requested," Jules said."He'll be waiting for you tonight, at the Smoke and Mirrors Club."

"You can't go," Elise said. "You're still weak."

The Countess turned her terrible, purpose-filled eyes on Elise. After a moment, she blinked and crumpled under the pressure.

"He's too dangerous," she offered feebly.

"So am I," the Countess said, but she was already folding back into herself. There was nothing in her eyes now but the Countess."Where's the Club?" she asked.

Jules winced. "I'm not sure. Only those with an invitation can find it." He removed an envelope from his jacket. "The satyr gave me this. They're your instructions."

The Countess took the envelope. "I needed to walk the city anyway. It's the final stage of the Invocation." She frowned. "My instructions?"

"The Club must be approached by a particular path or you'll never find it."

"Ah," said the Countess. "Don't stray off the path. I

understand. It's more common in forest enchantments, but he's adapted it to the city. That's impressive magic."

"He's powerful," Jules agreed.

"Mr. Nix is not to be taken lightly," Elise interjected. "No one knows what he really is."

"Not here, perhaps," the Countess said. "But we know him of old. My great aunt told me all about him."

Elise and Jules were unconvinced.

"I doubt even the Five Tribes know everything about him," Jules said. He believed in the Countess, but in his opinion, her confidence was excessive.

"We know enough," the Countess said. "And the City will tell me more, if I need it. It's already begun speaking to me, calling to me."

Elise and Jules exchanged worried glances. The Countess smiled at them fondly.

"I appreciate your concern," she said. "But I have to do this. It is my purpose and I have trained for it my entire life." She stood slowly. Her limbs protested, and her legs quavered, but she steadied herself and stood tall and proud. "I have much to do," she said. "It's time I got dressed."

She headed to the bedroom, each step more solid and assured than the last. Elise and Jules watched her, ready to leap to her aid, but they weren't needed.

"And you doubted her," Jules said once she was out of sight.

Elise frowned. "You can't see past your little infatuation."

"I'm not the one whose emotions are compromising my judgment."

Elise looked down at that. As much as she wanted to deny it, it was true. "She's not like the others," Elise said after a moment. "She's...kind."

"Yes," Jules agreed. "But you know our orders, if she fails."

Elise glanced back at her brother sharply. "I do."

"Good."

The Countess reemerged from the bedroom fully dressed with her customary red hat in hand.

"You read the instructions?" Elise managed to ask.

The Countess glanced between them, curiously. "Yes," she said. "And I have them with me, just in case."

"Did you want us to accompany you?" Jules asked. "Just in case?"

"You're sweet," said the Countess, "but I must walk the path alone. And it's probably best that I perform the final stage of the invocation free from distractions."

Jules nodded. "Good luck," he said.

"And be careful," Elise added.

"Thank you," said the Countess. "Both of you." Then she was gone.

Elise waited until the door was closed before grabbing her hat and coat.

"She said not to follow her," Jules said.

"No," Elise corrected. "She said not to accompany her. There's nothing to stop a brother and sister from taking a nice little walk, is there?"

Jules blinked. "Not a thing," he said. "And if we should happen to see a young woman in a red hat..."

"What a remarkable coincidence."

They shared a conspiratorial grin and were out the door within moments, both heavily armed and determined. They both had a great deal invested in the Countess' success, and neither of them wanted to contemplate what they'd have to do if she failed.

*

Hessing sat alone in his office overlooking the main bullpen. He leafed aimlessly through the reports on his desk. For him, policing mostly consisted of paperwork these days. It was dull and monotonous and his eyes skimmed over them, barely reading the words. He had other things on his mind. The Duke would be summoning him soon and he wouldn't be pleased. Still, even a dressing down from the Duke would be preferable to home.

He had hoped to find some respite at work, but Headquarters was haunted as well. He saw the pity in his men's faces when they spoke to him. Some of the old guard tried to hide it and spare his feelings, but in its own way that was just as damaging. He was not that fragile, at least he didn't think so. And then there were the rumors about his son. Though he'd done his best to cover up what had really happened, the stories still spread—half-truths and lies mostly, but enough to haunt him. There was no peace here. Even Erkel had started snooping around the coroner.

Hessing went to the balcony and gazed down at the policemen below—vultures, all of them. Inspector Vorn was holding court over a number of younger officers. He was too ambitious for his own good. His brand of policemanship relied more on brawn than brains, but he was popular with the men. Erkel and Cambor looked over at him from their desks, then shared a disgusted glance. Those two had never been fond of each other, especially now with Erkel sniffing around Cambor's case, but they despised Vorn more. Hessing sighed. He didn't have the time or the energy for their petty rivalries, but he was the only one who could keep them all in line.

His harried-looking secretary burst in clutching a telegram. "Forgive me, sir, but it's urgent..."

Hessing turned and held up a hand to stop her. "The Duke wants to see me," he said.

"Yes, sir. Immediately."

"Thank you, Ms. Lane."

"Sir." She paused. "How did you know?"

He gave her a severe glance and she backed away with a barely audible squeak. Reports of his omnipotence needed to be carefully nurtured. It was one of his greatest assets.

"Cambor!" He barked down into the bullpen. "Erkel! In my office, now!"

They rushed up the stairs as quickly as they could and entered diffidently. There was a brief squabble at the door, which Hessing pretended to ignore.

Erkel entered first and Cambor followed with narrowed eyes, perhaps irritated that the other inspector had arrived first, perhaps simply annoyed at his presence. They could be oddly childish sometimes.

"The Duke wants to see me immediately," Hessing said. "I need you two to bring me up to speed quickly. Erkel, you go first."

The inspectors frowned at each other and Erkel sighed. "I'm afraid I have nothing to report, sir."

"Nothing?"

"Well," Erkel said with a grimace, "not entirely. We believe the murders are part of a ritual of some sort." Hessing nodded encouragingly. He had reached the same conclusion weeks ago.

"Unfortunately," Erkel continued, "no one at the Wizarding College will speak with us, and frankly, arcane magical rituals are not my area of expertise."

"No," Hessing agreed. The Colleges kept tight control over magical knowledge. Despite his contacts, Hessing had difficulty procuring even a handful of magical texts and grimoires. He was not surprised at Erkel's lack of success. It had given him time for his own inquiries. Not that he truly needed to investigate. He knew he was right, and he knew what that meant—more trouble.

"And you?" Hessing turned to Cambor. He was a sour man, but he got results. Hessing had placed him in charge of the Bombing case hoping he would resolve the matter quickly, but so far Hessing had been greatly disappointed.

Cambor also grimaced. "There's been some progress, sir," he said. "But to proceed any further…" He hesitated. "I may need to consult the Oracle."

"I see." Hessing raised his eyebrows. "The Duke won't like that. That's even more difficult than getting the magicians to talk, and twice as confusing."

"I know, sir."

Hessing sighed. "You two are coming with me to the Duke," he said. "You can finish briefing me in the carriage."

"Yes, sir." They looked distinctly uncomfortable at the thought, but hastened to obey. Despite their personal animosity, they were both of the old guard. Their loyalty to him was absolute. That could be useful. Magicians and the Oracle in one day. The Duke wouldn't thank him for that mess, especially not with an envoy already knocking. He would need a way to deflect attention and, possibly, blame. Cambor and Erkel would have to suffice.

*

The *HMS Beatrice* had arrived at dawn, passing solemnly over the city. It was an experimental airship, specially chartered for imperial service, and had made the twelve-hour journey from the capital in only five hours. The *Beatrice* touched down in one of the gardens within the Duke's grounds. A landing area had been hastily constructed over night, and a few of the Duchess' favorite begonias had been sacrificed in the name of progress and diplomacy.

The airship door swung open and Henri Borchard-Márai, Imperial Envoy for His Serene & Imperial Majesty Gregory III, emerged, sauntering down the gangplank. The Duke and Duchess welcomed him with as much early-morning pomp as they could muster on such short notice. At the Duke's nod, the soldiers snapped to attention. The envoy received their salutes gracefully. He had well-polished manners and a well-oiled mustache, and was resplendent in imperial white. He said that he had come to convey the Emperor's well wishes at this time of remembrance and celebration. The Duke didn't believe it any more now than he had the previous night.

The envoy's arrival was a power play of some kind, perhaps the Chancellor and his faction at court testing their strength. Count Olivér de Grimvard had spent years circling the Cities, attempting to centralize power and undermine the ruling Dukes. This would not be the first time he had tried to interfere in Talis, but the choice of Borchard-Márai indicated that the Emperor had taken an active role. This was more than just an unofficial spying mission, casting a friendly or unfriendly eye over the city. There were wheels within wheels. As if the Duke didn't have enough to worry about already.

The morning passed in a careful array of polite conversation and politic laughter. Borchard-Márai professed himself highly impressed with the Ducal Mansion and its grounds.

"An excellent example of Middle Period Witchling

Architecture," he said grandly. "Equal to even the Imperial Palace."

"You're too kind," the Duke said. "I've seen the Palace many times, it puts my family's estate to shame."

"Not at all," the envoy replied. He didn't even blink at the mention of the Duke's family. Lord Edward and Lady Anne had been baiting him all morning, but he gave no sign of noticing and avoided even the most oblique reference to the succession. His reputation for cunning and discretion appeared to be well earned.

A servant arrived interrupting them with a polite bow, and whispered in the Duke's ear. Lord Edward nodded.

"You'll have to excuse me," he said. "A matter has arisen that requires my attention."

"Of course, Lord Edward," Borchard-Márai said. "You have a city to run. I quite understand."

"Thank you," said the Duke, "and now I shall leave you in my wife's capable hands." He departed, sending his wife an apologetic look. She still hadn't forgiven him for his secrecy, and this would not help matters.

Lady Anne kept her smile firmly in place and took the envoy by the arm. "Not to worry," she said. "We won't let my husband's absence spoil our fun, will we?"

"Certainly not." Borchard-Márai matched her practiced smile for practiced smile. "I'm sure we can find something to entertain us."

The Duke left them in the garden, the sound of their laughter following him. He hoped that Hessing had some progress to report, for both their sakes.

CHAPTER TEN

Baron Hessing and the two inspectors stood waiting in the Duke's study. Erkel and Cambor glanced about in awe, dwarfed by the high ceilings and lavish furnishings. They had met the Duke before from afar, but never in close quarters and never in the Mansion.

"Do not speak unless you are spoken to," Hessing ordered, drawing their attention back to him. "Do not contradict me, and do not offer your opinions unless I ask for them." He glared. "And do not allow your petty feud to interfere."

"Yes, sir," Cambor said. Erkel nodded a moment later, but said nothing.

They waited a few more minutes in awkward silence. Cambor fidgeted with his uniform, while Erkel counted the number of statues in the room. He had reached twenty-four when the doors swung open and the Duke burst in, trailing servants.

"Theodore," he said in greeting as he made the long walk to his desk.

"Your grace," Hessing said and bowed. The other two followed suit. "This is Inspector Cambor and Inspector Erkel. They are in charge of the Rook Gate and Ripper cases, respectively."

The Duke shook their hands firmly. "I'd say it was a pleasure, but that remains to be seen." He took his seat and with a wave of his hand ordered Hessing to sit. The inspectors remained standing, flanking him.

"Tell me you have good news," said the Duke.

Hessing sighed. " There has been some progress. The culprit in the Rook Gate Bombing has been tentatively identified as a known anarchist, a hobgoblin called Mr. Tarr."

"You have a name." The Duke sat forward. "Excellent."

"Inspector Cambor has done good work."

"It would seem so," the Duke agreed. "But why didn't I read about it in this morning's paper? Where is this Mr. Tarr now?"

"Still in the city, we believe."

"In the city," the Duke repeated sharply. "Talis has a population of a little over six million humans and faëries, and you think this Tarr might be one of them?"

"Sir..." Inspector Cambor started, unable to help himself despite his promise. Hessing scowled at him, while the Duke spared him an incredulous glance. He stopped short under the combined weight of their glares. Beside him, Erkel hid his glee as best he could. It wasn't difficult when he thought about the state of his own investigation.

"He's been spotted in the Quarter," Hessing continued after a moment, "and by the Docks, but never directly. Hobgoblins can be slippery buggers when they want to be."

"Then find him," the Duke ordered. "Round up any known associates, make them talk. You should have more than enough spies for the task. Root him out. The Victory Ball is imminent. We can't have a lunatic hobgoblin running around."

"No, sir. And to that end..." Hessing hesitated.

"Yes?"

"We would like permission to consult the Oracle."

"The Oracle?"

"You did promise the papers that you would use every resource at your disposal."

"I didn't mean her." The Duke sighed. "Even if I consent, there's no guarantee she'll help."

"I know." Hessing waited.

"No," the Duke said at last. "It's far too risky. I will not involve that woman unless there's absolutely no other choice. I don't trust her." He scowled. "She lies."

Erkel and Cambor started at that. "But that's impossible..." Cambor started again before he could stop himself, but quickly fell silent.

"Find the hobgoblin another way." The Duke's voice brokered no argument.

"Yes, your grace," Hessing said.

"And the Ripper?"

"There are now six confirmed murders—three human and three faërie."

"Six? The one on Mervyn Street?" Hessing nodded. "You're certain?"

"Yes, sir."

"I see," said the Duke. "And?"

"I'm afraid there are no suspects at the moment," said Hessing. "Not real ones."

"Not even ones you're holding back."

"No, sir."

"Human or faërie?"

"We don't know."

"What do you know?" the Duke demanded.

Hessing hid a grimace. This was treacherous ground. "Perhaps it would be best if the inspector filled you in on the details himself."

The Duke raised an eyebrow but nodded. "Very well."

Erkel licked his lips nervously. He felt as though he had been thrown to the wolves.

"Your grace," he began, then took a deep breath. He could do this. He had been a policeman for most of his life. He knew how to give a report. Let them make of it what they would.

"Organs were removed, your grace, from each of the victims—the lung, heart, stomach, liver, kidney, and intestines. We believe it might be in preparation for a rite or ritual. This is, apparently, a magically auspicious time. But none of the usual suspects would be bold enough for this. We're keeping an eye on them nonetheless. We've also put out feelers, to see if any new players have arrived recently. No one with the requisite amount of power could have entered the city entirely without notice."

The Duke nodded. "Very thorough, Inspector Erkel. Have you been to see the magicians?"

"Not yet, your grace." Erkel carefully didn't mention that the magicians had denied him an audience. He didn't think it would have been politic to mention, but something must have shown on his face.

"I see," said the Duke. "They are an insular lot, but they can be useful when they choose to be. I'll have one of my secretaries arrange an interview. The Grand Master owes me a favor."

"Thank you, your grace." Erkel hadn't expected anything so proactive.

"Gentlemen," the Duke said, "I appreciate your efforts and I have great faith in your success."

"Thank you, your grace," Cambor and Erkel said.

The Duke nodded and dismissed them with a gesture. They bowed and retreated. Hessing remained behind. When they were gone, the Duke rose and went to the drinks cabinet.

"Drink?" he asked as he poured.

"A little early in the day for me, sir."

The Duke placed a glass down in front of Hessing with a clank. "Drink," he repeated. This time it was not a question. Hessing obeyed.

"You saw the papers?" asked the Duke.

"Just the *Chronicle*."

"It's worse this time."

"I know, sir," said Hessing.

"Parliament wants to force your resignation. They were drafting a referendum to that effect, just this morning."

"That bad?"

"Yes," said the Duke. "This isn't a stunt. They mean it this time, and they may even have the votes." He took a long sip. "I've ruled this city for almost sixty years, and you've been with me all that time. You're my man, Theodore. I made you, and I will stand with you as I always have, despite the papers and the politicians."

"Thank you, Edward," Hessing said and meant it. He owed everything to the Duke's friendship.

"But in return I need results," the Duke continued. "Provide them. Soon."

"I will."

"Good. That will be all." Hessing hesitated. "Was there something else?" the Duke asked.

"I wish you'd reconsider."

"About the Oracle? You know what she's like."

"No," said Hessing. "I remember her all too well. I meant the Victory Ball."

The Duke leaned back with a frustrated sigh. "Not this again. You bring it up every year."

"It would be easier to protect you if we moved the Ball from the Armory to a more secure location: the Mansion, or City Hall even."

"A more secure location?" The Duke was incredulous. "It's an armory."

"It *was* an armory, your grace." Hessing corrected. "Now it's a museum."

"You worry too much. The walls are nine feet thick, for Gods' sake!"

"And we have a bomber on the loose, who left the Rook Gate a smoldering ruin. Walls are not enough. The Armory is too isolated, too far from the Mansion. I can only do so much..."

The Duke held up a hand to stop him. "I understand your concerns," he said. "But I can't move the Ball and you know it."

"With respect, your grace, yes you can."

"It would look like cowardice."

No," said Hessing, "it would look like prudence."

The Duke laughed softly. "You're only saying that because you're trying to convince me." He shook his head. "The Armory is where the Lord Frederick started his rebellion. It's an integral part of the legend."

"Yes, your grace."

The Duke nodded. "I appreciate your concern," he said. "That'll be all."

Hessing left with a bow. He had tried, but now he had another meeting to attend.

*

The Countess followed her instructions to the letter. Jules and his sister had been adamant on that point. Her path had been chosen for her and all forms of transportation—the cabs, trolleys, and even the vast looming network of trains—had been expressly prohibited. She had been forced to walk a winding circuitous route that doubled back on itself several times and took her through five separate checkpoints. She had smiled a shy little smile at the sergeants, who for their part had stood up a little straighter, as they waved her through. Each time her papers had managed to pass inspection, the fruits of Mr. Covét's labor.

The twists and turns in her route would have seemed frustratingly haphazard to most people, but the Countess could sense the meaning and intentions behind every bend and curve. There was a pattern to her movements, occult and obscure, and all the more powerful for it. She absently admired the ingenuity and craftsmanship, but her attention was focused elsewhere—inside and out.

She was opening her mind, stretching her consciousness out into the world. She was just starting to get the lay of the land, and hear the City's song, however faintly. Talis was alive, as all cities were. Generations of witches, humans, and faëries had lived and died there, giving birth to a slumbering thing of dreams and architecture, of hopes and petty, fragile lives.

This was the final and, in many ways, the most difficult stage of the Invocation. Waking the City had taken sacrifice but now the merging had begun, the union between her and the City. It was a delicate process, fraught with dangers. Even the most trained and disciplined mind could be overwhelmed by the deluge of sensations and awareness, and have their sense of self lost forever, scattered into the streets.

The Countess was better prepared than most. She was accustomed to sharing her being with something not her own. The Purpose had burrowed deep inside and carved out a home for itself within her. It remained to be seen if it would share her with the City, or if she would be crushed between them and hollowed out. As she walked through the streets, the Countess was confident, perhaps more than was warranted. She could feel the soul of the City—the locus magicus—reaching out to her in ways she could not fully understand, not yet, but as she walked she understood more and more.

She saw the City reflected in the faces and people around her, thin and portly, winged and horned. She could feel its thoughts reaching out of the ground as she tread on the City's cobblestone skin. She could hear it calling out in the babble of human tongues and faërie dialects, in shouted conversations and in a flower girl hawking her wares. There was a rhythm to it, a song half-heard and only partially understood. It sang of history and cycles, of magic and myth. It told her about those following her—spies for Hessing on one side and those for the dissidents on the other. The

Countess' very presence had ruffled a few feathers, some of them literal.

She could sense others fumbling in the dark. Learned, narrow minds groped half-blindly from across the river, wielding their incipient understandings like a cudgel. It took her a moment to realize who they were—the magicians. She would have to tread more carefully. They might be blind, but they had other senses, and would be able to find her, if they only knew to look.

She swerved out of the way suddenly and barely avoided colliding with a drunken man as he stumbled down the street muttering to himself. The near collision pulled her back into the present moment, the present street. The Countess saw a homeless man in rags holding a sign with anti-faërie slurs, and an old hag pushing a cart keeping her head down to avoid the baleful stares. She could feel the City's unease churning all around her. It was burrowing beneath her skin, clawing at her.

At the far corner, she saw the drunk talking with the flower girl in hushed tones. The sense of unease deepened. Whatever she was saying, it wasn't to his liking. He struck her suddenly and sent her and her flower cart crashing to the ground. Then he stumbled away, laughing. No one stopped him. No one helped her. The pair of policemen watching across the street didn't even stir. A few faëries—a minotaur, a dog-face man, and a sprite, made no move to help, but seethed in anger and fear. The flower girl was a proper fairy with her little wings discreetly hidden, but not invisible.

Where the others hesitated, the Countess saw an opportunity. She had already made an impression on those watching eyes; it was time to mold that impression. She walked deliberately to the young fairy's side and offered her hand. The flower girl disdained her assistance and rose to her feet unaided. Her wings flapped slightly to help, but she forced them under control. The Countess shrugged, taking the girl's hostility in stride.

"Very well," she said in a calm clear voice. "Then I should like to buy a flower. A rose, I think."

The flower girl studied her with narrowed eyes, searching for any sign of mockery. Finding none, she pulled out a single rose.

"That'll be a penny, miss," she said, unable to keep a note of suspicion from her voice, but a penny was a penny.

The Countess smiled and paid. Then she continued walking, keeping her pace deliberate. Her pursuers had changed their tactics. One of the dissidents—the dog-faced man—was shadowing her more closely now.

A small, rowdy group passed, laughing loudly. They brushed past the Countess and forced the dog-faced man to stand aside and avoid trouble. When they were gone, he attempted to follow the Countess at an appropriate distance, but she was gone. He stopped, startled.

The street was empty. He frowned. She couldn't have simply vanished. Not so quickly. He turned and almost yelped in surprise. The Countess was standing behind him, smiling benignly.

"Good evening," she said. "I want you to take a message to your leaders."

"Excuse me?" asked the dog-faced man.

"You heard me. I believe we should come to some arrangement. Especially if they're going to have me followed everywhere."

"I don't know what you mean," he started, but she interrupted him. She spoke a single word, the ancient eldritch word for 'freedom.' He blinked in shock. They had chosen the password only the other day. She couldn't possibly have learned it already, unless they had a spy in their midst.

"Should I knock on the wall as well?" The Countess asked. "It's seven times, I believe. Or perhaps you would prefer to hear a riddle. Something to do with roses?" She waved her newly purchased flower.

"How do you know the protocols?"

"You would be surprised by the things I know," she said. "Now give your leaders my message. I believe we can be of some use to each other."

The dog-faced man sputtered but nodded.

"Excellent," she replied. "Now perhaps you could deliver my message, while the air sprite hiding in the alleyway accompanies me to the Club. I have a meeting to attend."

*

The Wizarding College was nestled among the hills on the far side of the river. Few of the uninitiated had ever been permitted past its high stone walls and spell-locked gates and onto the campus. It was a place of mystery, of secrets and learning, and of power. The magicians guarded its secrets jealously.

The guards at the outer wall checked Erkel and Lund's identity papers three times before they were satisfied, and read over their letter of introduction twice. Erkel and Lund eyed each other uncomfortably. Even the Ducal Mansion had less stringent security measures. Their appointment with Grand Master Undur had been set for 5:30 in the afternoon precisely, and magicians were very particular regarding punctuality, except when it came to their own. Erkel glanced at his watch. They only had ten minutes.

Finally, a long-faced student with sullen eyes arrived to escort them inside. He reread the letter himself and regarded Erkel and Lund with naked disdain.

"Under normal circumstances," he said, "the uninitiated would be blindfolded before proceeding any further."

Erkel tilted his head but said nothing. It was unnecessary.

The student sighed. "But the Duke seems to have convinced the Grand Master that you are trustworthy." He clearly had his own opinion about the matter.

"Thank you, mister..." Lund trailed off questioningly. The student pointedly ignored him. It was a foolish question to ask a magician. Names had power, especially for magicians, and Lund knew it. He had simply wanted to tease the smug young man, and judging by his expression, Lund had succeeded.

"I suppose you two had better follow me," said the nameless student.

He led them through the gate and onto the campus. The central courtyard was bordered on all sides by a number of great halls and arcades. On the far side was the library rotunda containing the second largest collection of magical texts in the Crescent.

It was a pleasant evening, but no one was loitering on the grass. Students of all ages walked quickly across the lawn, or along the arcades. They kept their heads down, and their were arms laden with books. Magicians and adepts were interspersed among them with their sashes and collars of rank. A few of them gave the visitors suspicious glances, but for the most part they all went about their business.

In these hallowed, cloistered halls there was an atmosphere of dangerous knowledge and furtiveness. Erkel could feel it pressing against him. The very air seemed to throb with secrets. Lund could feel it as well. For the past two centuries more magic had been performed within these few acres than anywhere else for a hundred miles. Even the city with all its faërie inhabitants could not match the College for the pure concentration of magical energy. It was bound to leave a mark. Erkel was not comforted by the thought.

Grand Master Undur's office was on the second floor in the rotunda. Erkel and Lund passed through the long reading room and up the marble stairs in silence. There was a palpable, oppressive hush in the air. Students and magicians were bent at their work, surrounded by piles of books.

They stopped outside Undur's office and the student knocked. Erkel checked his watch—5:30 precisely. He glanced at Lund, who grinned slightly. They were perfectly punctual, after all.

"Enter," a voice called from inside, and the doors creaked open of their own accord.

"The policemen, sir," said the student.

Grand Master Undur rose to greet them. "Welcome, gentlemen," he said, inscrutable behind his white beard. "You may wait outside." He nodded to the student, who left without another word.

"Thank you for seeing us, sir," said Erkel.

"Not at all, Inspector. Anything for Lord Edward. Please, have a seat."

Undur's office was filled with magical instruments and tomes of every description. There was a giant orrery in one corner, and another was filled with a number of brass-polished contraptions, the purpose of which Erkel could not even begin to imagine. There was no clutter, however. Erkel was filled with the certain knowledge that everything in Undur's office was in its proper place. There was a system, an order. He sat down slowly.

Grand Master Undur crossed his fingers and set them down on the polished oak desk. "Now," he said, "how may I be of assistance? And please, be concise."

Lund turned to Erkel who removed a file from his coat. "I take it you are familiar with the recent wave of murders, sir."

"Only what I've read in the papers."

"The papers only tell part of the story."

"I assumed as much." Undur tilted his head curiously. "And you're here to fill in the blanks for me. Why?"

Erkel grimaced. "We believe the crimes might be magical in nature."

"I see. Motive or method?"

"Motive." Erkel shook his head. "The wounds were made with surgical implements."

"Surgical?" Undur frowned. "Are you certain? Magical crimes are usually carried out with magical weapons—ceremonial daggers, for example. It's not strictly necessary, of course, but it is a common misconception, even among my students."

"No," Lund spoke for the first time. "We've seen more than enough of those to know the difference. It was definitely surgical tools."

"Then whoever you're looking for is either a rank amateur or an adept of the highest level." He paused. "Or there's nothing magical about it at all, and you're wasting our time."

"I don't think so," said Erkel. He removed a few pictures from the file and handed them to Undur. "The brutality of the mutilations hid their purpose for some time."

Undur accepted the pictures and pulled out a pair of reading spectacles. "Which was?" he asked.

"The removal of organs, one from each body."

Undur remained impassive. He studied the photographs carefully, seemingly unperturbed by the horror before him. "These organs," he said. " The heart and lungs?"

"Yes," said Erkel. "And the stomach, liver, and kidney. There is a purpose here, that much I can see."

"There certainly is." Undur nodded. "Were the bodies displayed in any particular way?"

"Only as you see." Erkel pointed at the photographs.

"But they were discovered," said Lund, "on the third, sixth, seventh, ninth, eleventh, and thirteenth of this month."

"Ah." Undur tossed his glasses on the desk and leaned back. "An occult number sequence. I can see why you came to me," he said, rubbing his face. "And the stars are in alignment this month."

"Yes," Erkel said noncommittally, but something must have shown in his voice.

Undur smirked. "But I suppose anyone with an almanac could have told you that."

Erkel smiled apologetically. "I may have consulted a few already."

"Very wise," Undur said. "But I'm sure you're more interested in what this Ripper is doing."

"That would be useful."

Undur sighed. "There are two possibilities," he said. "Either it's an invocation of some kind, or it's a resurrection spell."

Erkel blinked. "Necromancy?" he asked.

"Yes."

"And which do you think it is?"

"Invocations are rare and exceedingly dangerous to the practitioner. I'm afraid it's probably necromancy," said Undur.

"But there are hundreds of back-alley necromancers," Lund said. "Half of them are from your College."

"I'll pretend I didn't hear that."

Erkel frowned at Lund. "What my sergeant is trying to say is that necromancy is not unheard of in the city, and it doesn't usually involve organ snatching."

"No, it wouldn't," said Undur. He stood and retrieved a leather-bound tome from one of the shelves. "But there are degrees," he continued. "The street-corner necromancy you're familiar with is the simplest and least effective method. It is clumsy and limited. The body must be relatively undamaged and only recently deceased." He paused. "Or so I've read."

"Of course," Erkel said.

"I'll pretend I didn't hear that," said Lund, who shrugged when Erkel threw him a look.

Undur cleared his throat. "There are other, more dangerous methods, and this is one of them, one of the oldest."

"So, what does that mean?"

"It means that you're looking for someone with access to ancient knowledge and a magical practitioner of great power."

"How much power?"

"More than anyone I know of," said Undur. He hesitated. "More than me."

"I see," said Erkel. That was a terrifying thought.

"I'm sorry I couldn't be any more helpful."

"Not at all," Erkel said rising. "You've given us a great deal to think about. Thank you for your time." He gestured for Lund to join him.

"Inspector," Undur called as they reached the door.

"Yes, Grand Master?"

"Be careful. There hasn't been power like this in Talis since the Witches."

11

CHAPTER ELEVEN

It had taken her most of the afternoon and into the evening, but at last the Countess had arrived. Across the street loomed a five-story edifice of balconies and ornate columns nestled between a series of drab little shops—butchers, drapers, and tinkers. Humans and faëries were carved into the arched doorway in discretely obscene poses, and above them, bathing the street in red, hung a blinking neon sign. It read: *The Smoke & Mirrors Club*.

The Countess could hear the sounds of music and raucous laughter drifting across the thoroughfare. Despite the name, the Smoke & Mirrors Club appeared to be extravagantly conspicuous, but as the Countess watched, humans and faëries passed beneath the Club's walls, seemingly unaware, even as they were illuminated in red and the laughter from inside washed over them unheard. They continued about their business, some stopping at the shops on either side, but none of them by glance or gesture made the slightest sign that they had noticed the Club's presence. It was as if the building itself did not exist. Not everyone was blind, however. A few went right up to the door unerringly. The crowd parted before them absently, and paid them no more mind than they had the building itself. They too had become invisible; that was the power of the Smoke & Mirrors Club.

It was known throughout the city. There were rumors about the Club everywhere—a place of debauchery and sanctuary, but it was by invitation only. If six patrons were asked to locate it on a map, they would have pointed to as many places: in the Faërie Quarter, on Main Street, even across the river. It was in many places and in none, but there was only one Club, and it could only be seen if you knew the way.

The Smoke & Mirrors Club was always open to those who followed their instructions. This was not like the haphazard concealment of the Thirsty Goblin. There was skill here, precision and intent. The Countess admired that. She could feel its architect waiting inside, an obscure presence, opaque even with her new awareness. It was the proprietor, Mr. Nix, the one she had come to see.

The city had taken on a different character at night. It was an evening carnival of noise and bustle, of assignations and rendezvous, but beneath it all there was a savage, darker tinge. Lamplighters with their ladders and polls made their slow way down the streets, leaving a string of artificial lights behind them.

People's shadows took on strange, deformed shapes in the lamplight. Their faces were sharper, and they moved quicker, with a wilder gleam in their eyes. The Countess watched a young man pursuing a woman down the street, catching her eye and winking when she turned. She passed goat-faced men in topcoats and monocles and bird-faced women in fashionable dresses. In the artificial light, the glances between humans and faëries were fiercer, and around them the policemen were out in force. There was a watchful, nervous frenzy in the air.

The Countess could feel Elise and Jules lurking in the shadows, her devoted protectors. They too were different in the night, cloaked in secrets and riddled through with something treacherous. She took a deep breath and pulled back into herself. There would be time to unravel that later. She couldn't afford to let anything slip. Not here. Not tonight. She crossed the road toward the roaring, laughing, drunken hubbub. There was no turning back now.

Neither passes nor permits were required at the Smoke & Mirrors Club. Despite the tensions, all were welcome regardless of species or inclination, provided they had an invitation. Lawyers, taxmen, gentlemen and roustabouts all mingled freely with hobgoblins, fauns and pixies. Nymphs in green satin trousers and crimson sashes wove their way through the crowd selling cigarettes, and hinting at other less savory pleasures. On stage, Éponine La Roux was dancing up a storm, working the assembled masses into a frenzy, her dragonfly-wings fluttering behind her.

The Countess was expected. A satyr in a tux approached her almost immediately. She had hoped for a moment to observe and gather herself, but there was no time. The satyr weaved his way nimbly through the tangle of hypocrisy and debauchery. The Countess simply waded in after him. The dancers parted before like a wave, scarcely aware they were doing so. The satyr led her backstage through a side door. A minotaur was leaning against

Irons in the Fire

the wall smoking a cigar. Behind him was a faded poster: Votes for Faëries Now.

They went down into the bowels of the building, past the staging areas and dressing rooms. This was the inner sanctum, the most secret part of the most secret building in all of Talis. Finally, they came to a pair of heavy metal doors. The Countess could feel the spells and enchantments etched into the doorframe, but it was nothing compared to the looming, terrible absence behind the door. The City was full of secrets. It whispered them to her. If she wished to know, it would have told her the history of every wooden beam, every brick, and every stone in the house. It could have told her the life stories of the workers, bricklayers, and masons, who had labored in its construction. That storehouse of lives and knowledge bubbled around her. It was a constant effort to hold back the deluge, but beyond that door there was nothing, only silence.

"He wishes to see you alone," the satyr said and gestured.

The Countess nodded. "Thank you."

The satyr remained silent, waiting. She closed her eyes for a moment, armed herself with Purpose, armored herself with the City, and wrapped the Countess' identity around herself so tightly that no could ever find her True Name. She was ready.

Mr. Nix was waiting for her inside. This was the moment she had been waiting for, the moment she had been dreading.

The doors clanged shut behind her.

*

Back in the dance hall, the Smoke & Mirrors Club was in full swing. Humans and faëries of all denominations were laughing and drinking with reckless abandon. Outside, the city might be coming apart at the seams, but inside the Club everything was still alright, so long as the drinks flowed generously and no one stopped to think even for a moment. There was an edginess in the laughter, however, and the voices were louder, too loud. In the far corner, Mr. Clarke was enjoying the attentions of several chorus girls, their false giggles cutting through the haze, the smoke and the noise. Everyone was trying desperately to put the escalating tensions out of their minds.

Erkel and Lund were ensconced at their usual table. No one of any consequence, except perhaps the Duke, could escape the lure of the Club. The policemen were no different. A few faëries threw them dirty looks, but they were lost in the revelry. Erkel and Lund were too preoccupied to notice.

"Drowning your sorrows?" Erkel asked after a long pause. "Or finding courage in a bottle?"

Lund started and glanced up from his glass. "Don't start that again," he said.

"Start? I haven't said anything."

"Yes," Lund agreed. "That's the point. I know you too well. You've been not saying it, very loudly."

Erkel tried to look innocent but failed miserably.

"Fine." Lund sighed. "Say your piece."

Erkel took a long sip. "It's none of my business," he said, "but are you sure you know what you're doing?"

"I'm not doing anything," said Lund.

"You've been to see her twice."

"Can't I visit an old friend's widow?" Lund asked, but his poker face was no better than Erkel's, and there was a tinge of red in his cheeks.

"You're not just visiting," said Erkel. "And I'm not the only one who's noticed. People are starting to talk. Obry's only been in the ground a few days."

"There's nothing to tell."

"Yet," Erkel said.

"I don't even know if she'd have me," said Obry.

"Oh, I wouldn't worry about that," Erkel said with the hint of a smirk.

Lund suddenly found his glass very interesting. "What are we going to do about the case?" he asked.

Erkel lost his smirk immediately. "I'm not sure."

"Did you believe Undur?"

"I don't know. Resurrection and witches—not my favorite combination of words."

"Witches," said Lund, "or something worse."

"I can't imagine," Erkel said. "One witch was more than enough for my lifetime."

"And mine." They fell silent for a moment in shared memory. They never talked about that night, but they remembered. Lund recovered first.

"We need to do something, though, witch or no witch. Six murders, almost a month on the case..."

"I know," Erkel said. "You weren't there but when I saw the Duke, he definitely wasn't happy."

"Not surprising."

"And I think Hessing was setting me up to take the fall."

Lund blinked. "Are you sure? He's never done that sort of thing before." Erkel gave him an incredulous glance. "Well," Lund said, correcting himself, "not with us, anyway."

"The pressure's different this time," said Erkel. "But no, I'm not sure. Hessing's up to something, but that doesn't mean anything."

Lund sighed. "If our neck's on the line…"

"My neck," said Erkel. "I don't think you're in trouble."

"Please," said Lund skeptically. "Cambor and Vorn have never liked me, and if you're gone just how long do you think I'd last?"

Erkel nodded. He couldn't disagree. Hessing's good will would only go so far.

"But what if it is witches?" asked Lund. "Or something just as bad?"

"Then we're in trouble," Erkel said. "Because even if the Duke allowed it, I doubt Undur would get up from behind his desk to help and then where would we be without magic of our own?"

"I don't know. The old boy had some fight in him. He just might help, but only if he thought he could win."

Erkel snorted. "And what would be the odds of that?"

"Slim." Around them the Club roared and laughed and sang with reckless abandon, but it couldn't drown out their thoughts.

"There's always another option," said Lund.

"Oh?"

"Everyone wants us to catch someone, so we catch someone or something. There are plenty of faëries who consume organs, and who's to say that it wasn't one of them?"

Erkel gave a humorless smile. "Yes," he said. "I wondered when you'd suggest that."

"It's not like we haven't done it before."

"Not with this much scrutiny, especially if they're already looking to make me the scapegoat." Erkel sighed. "And not with the magical connection."

"Did you tell him?"

"I put the report on his desk. Whether he read it or not…"

"Maybe you can ask him." Lund nodded to the door. Hessing had arrived.

They weren't the only ones to notice his appearance. A sudden hush fell on the crowd, as they eyed him nervously. After a moment the band started up again; Éponine La Roux began to croon, and slowly the noise and laughter resumed. Hessing was a regular visitor, after all. There was nothing to worry about, not in the Smoke & Mirrors Club.

Erkel and Lund gave him a respectful nod. Hessing looked surprised to see them but returned it after a moment. He looked unusually tired, even jittery.

"I don't think he wants to talk," said Erkel.

"No," Lund agreed. "Have you noticed how worn out he looks lately?"

"Hardly surprising, considering his son."

"Poor bastard," said Lund and neither of them were sure whether he meant the father or the son.

"Another round?" Lund asked.

Erkel frowned. There was something nagging at the back of his mind, but he couldn't quite place it. "Yes," he said. "Another round."

*

The satyr, immaculate as ever in his tux, led Hessing to a table in the back. He hadn't expected to see Erkel and Lund here, tonight of all nights. It was probably a coincidence, of course, but it was far too convenient for comfort. He had read the report on their meeting with the Grand Master. Erkel was very thorough, even if he hadn't wanted the case. Undur had confirmed his worst suspicions. The murders were part of a resurrection ritual carried out by a magical practitioner of extraordinary power. Undur had suggested a witch, but there were other powers in the world. Erkel and Lund knew that, although their personal histories might blind them for a time. Hessing lived in hope.

He sank slowly into the velvet seat, as if in a dream.

"Mr. Nix will send for you as soon as he's ready, sir," said the satyr.

"Thank you," Hessing said absently.

"Would you care for anything while you wait?" asked the satyr politely.

"Whiskey on the rocks."

"Yes, sir." The satyr bowed and left as unobtrusively as he had arrived.

Hessing stared down at the velvet tablecloth with unseeing eyes. He could feel Clarke watching him from the far corner. The minister was his most bitter parliamentary opponent, but Hessing paid him no heed. There was an unwritten and unspoken rule in the Club—nothing that happened here could be used against you. Everyone had too many secrets. No one knew what would happen if they broke the rule, and no one wanted to be the first to find out.

"Here you are, sir." A nymph was standing over him. She placed his glass down in front of him and left the bottle. "Compliments of the house," she said.

"Thank you," he said, his mind elsewhere. He felt apart, distant from the hubbub. Not even the fairy dancers onstage, with their high-kicking legs and fluttering wings made any impression. It was all drowned out by the thrumming of his heart, and the churning of his doubts, around and around.

His wife still hadn't forgiven him and she never would, not even after tonight. Olivia blamed him for so many things, and most of all for their son. Hessing couldn't bring himself to think about the boy, not as anything more than an abstract. It was too painful and the thought gnawed at him that his wife was right, that he had driven his son to it, but that was too terrible to contemplate. He drained his glass in a single gulp and then poured himself another and another.

Hessing was a corrupt man and comfortable in his corruption. A favor for a favor, that was how the city worked, and Hessing had always managed to be on the right side of the equation. Mr. Nix was a different matter entirely. He had somehow established his own sphere of influence inside the Club, and not even the Duke dared to interfere. No one else could say the same, and Hessing had done his best over the years to avoid becoming personally involved with him. This time, however, there was no alternative. He didn't know what Mr. Nix would ask in return, but whatever the price, Hessing knew he would pay. He would never forgive himself otherwise. Besides, it was too late to back out now. Come what may.

*

Behind the door, the Countess found a sterile, hexagonal room. It stank of sweat and death, of formaldehyde and magic. On a workstation at the back of the room were six jars, neatly labeled, one for each of the major organs—lung, heart, stomach, liver, kidney, and intestines. Four of them were empty.

In the center, a body was sprawled out on an operating table. He was human, maybe eighteen years old, and quite dead. His chest had been expertly folded open. A dapper little man hovered above the body wearing a black butcher's apron over his shirt and tie. His sleeves were rolled up, and he was hard at work, wrist deep in the human's torso.

"Good evening, Countess," said the dapper little man mildly, without pausing in his work. "What can I do for you this evening?"

He was trying to get under her skin. It was a crude tactic, laughably transparent. The Countess was almost disappointed. She forced down the bile in her throat and summoned her most imperious voice.

"You are Mr. Nix, I presume," she said.

"I answer to that name of late. And you are the Countess Antoinette Wyman-Straus." He enunciated each word with an unseemly, knowing relish. "But we are not here to Name one another. So, I ask again, Countess, what can I do for you?"

"I require a suitable introduction for the Annual Victory Ball."

"An introduction?" Mr. Nix looked up briefly from the body.

"I know you can do it," she said. "Half the aristocracy is in your club back there getting drunk as we speak."

"It is a question of motive, not means. As I understand it, in the past three days you have managed to smuggle yourself across the border, acquire the appropriate papers and passes, and arrange this meeting." He gestured between them with a bloody finger. "None of which are simple tasks. And yet, you require my assistance with an introduction?"

The Countess felt a twinge of panic. He knew more than he should have, but her expression barely flickered.

"You need more than papers and passes to advance in this city," she said.

"That is certainly true." He moved over to the workstation and gingerly removed the last of the organs from the jar. "But you are clearly a resourceful woman. I'm sure you could find an alternative method, if you put your mind to it."

The Countess smiled. "Let's just say that I want us to reach an understanding, as soon as possible, as a courtesy. It could be useful to have someone like you on my side, or neutral, at the very least."

"Your side? And what side is that, precisely?" He sniffed the air experimentally. "You stink of the Witchling Tribes. One of the northern ones, I believe. This city, human and faërie alike, does not think well of witches."

"What about you? What do you think?"

Mr. Nix busied himself placing the heart slowly, carefully back into the body, and did not answer.

"It is true," the Countess tried again, "that the Talent runs in my veins, but it is diluted, not worthy of note, and my business is my own."

"Perhaps," Mr. Nix said. "But I am not in the habit of doing favors for strangers."

"But you will do this one for me, and perhaps one day we won't be strangers any longer."

"You are very confident." Mr. Nix straightened. For the first time, she felt the full weight of his attention. His expression remained mild, his eyes vaguely amused, but she had never felt so small, not even under her great aunt's stern gaze. It was almost as if he was devouring her, seeing through to the Purpose inside.

The Countess rallied herself. "You wouldn't have seen me otherwise," she said. She had trained and planned for this meeting. Prepared for it almost more than any other part of her plan.

"And there's something else. I know what you are." She paused. "Your Name is hidden, of course, but I can see your Shadow."

If she had been expecting a strong reaction, she would have

been disappointed. His mild expression never wavered, and his eyes kept their devouring twinkle.

"You can hide in tailored suits and fashionable clubs," she continued, "or skulk in dingy basements like a back-alley necromancer, but you have greater ambitions, and I could be helpful."

Her words hung in the air, waiting. She could feel her heart pounding. He tilted his head like a bird, as if to observe her better. Finally, he smiled, a proper, crooked smile.

"You are an arrogant little thing," he said. "But very well. I shall procure your invitation, and arrange some suitable introduction. By this time next week you shall be amongst the most fashionable of the fashionable. Will that suffice?"

"Very nicely." She wanted to sigh in relief, barely managing to keep her composure.

"And in return, you shall owe me a favor one day. After all, it could be useful to have someone with your ambitions on my side." His smile grew even more crooked. "Or neutral, at the very least. Thank you for your visit. I'd shake your hand, but…" He held up his hands, red with blood. She shrugged and removed her glove.

"I'm not squeamish," she said.

They shook hands firmly.

Part III

The Turning Point

CHAPTER TWELVE

Charles Raske waited at a table on the second floor of Spennings, an upscale dining hall on Wynford Street. He was early. Clarke and Pullman hadn't arrived yet, but that gave him time to gather himself. Spennings was the most expensive restaurant in Talis. The average appetizer cost more than his monthly wages. He hadn't been here since he was a boy, for his eldest brother's eighteenth birthday. Father had spared no expense. Not that night. Not for his heir.

It was as elegant and grand as he remembered. He needed to project strength and confidence. He and Evá had agreed that he should come alone. There were too many rumors already, but he desperately wished she had joined him. It would have been easier with her by his side. Around him sat the city's elite, the richest and most fashionable. Raske knew many of them by reputation or from the society pages, and tried not to feel too self-conscious. It seemed to him that they were all deliberately looking away from him. Even the waiters were doing their best to ignore him.

Clarke and Pullman entered together. They made an odd pair in matching pinstriped suits and starched collars. There was a sudden shuffling of chairs and cutlery as all eyes turned to them. Several dared to smile and give them a bow. Clarke shook a few hands and Pullman pronounced a few greetings, but for the most part they made their way unerringly toward their table. Raske noticed an immediate change in attitude the moment his fellow diners realized where the great men were heading. There was a sudden spate of nods in his own direction. Men suddenly remembered that they had recently seen his face in the paper. He took secret delight in ignoring them in turn. Only Clarke and Pullman mattered. He stood to greet them.

"Charles, my boy!" Clarke cried and shook his hand firmly. "Sit down. Sit down."

Pullman gave a distant nod. "Good to see you again, son," he said. They oozed condescension and corruption.

"Gentlemen," Raske said.

"How is that darling wife of yours?" Clarke asked.

"She's quite well, thank you." Raske waited for them to turn to the matter at hand, but Clarke and Pullman seemed to take pleasure in small talk. Finally, he couldn't wait any longer.

"So," he asked, "how did it go at the Mansion?"

Clarke and Pullman smirked. "The Duke and Duchess know something is happening," Clarke said.

"And that troll was sniffing around, making leading comments. You must have made an impression." Pullman gave him an approving nod.

"Interesting. I gathered that he was of the Duchess' party," Raske said. "There was some contention among the other faëries about it. Not everyone trusted him."

"Was there?" Clarke and Pullman exchanged glances and had a wordless conversation. "That is good to know."

"Excellent," said Pullman, "you're already getting to know your future constituents."

"They're only my constituents if I win," Raske said. "And if our bill passes," he added as an afterthought.

"Don't worry," Clarke said. "You've done well. We're nearly there. The hard part is almost over. All you need to do now is give a good speech and that shouldn't be a problem after your recent performance in court."

"It takes more than a speech to win an election."

"We know," Pullman said with a smile. It was not a nice smile. "We've won our fair share, after all, Clarke and me."

Raske acknowledged the point. "And what about Hessing?"

"Let us worry about Hessing," Pullman said. "And remember what you owe us. Together we'll be kingmakers."

"Dukemakers."

"I beg your pardon?"

"Talis has dukes, not kings."

"In Talis," Pullman said, "it means the same thing. We're remaking the city."

Clarke leaned forward. "Your father would be proud, my boy," he said. "So very proud."

Raske squeezed his napkin tightly under the table. This wasn't the first time Clarke had invoked his father. He forced himself to relax. Evá would be disappointed if he alienated their most important backers.

"Thank you. I'd like to think so," he lied.

Clarke nodded, satisfied. "Now, then," he asked, "how's that speech of yours coming?" Raske opened his mouth to speak, but Pullman held up a hand to stop him.

"Of course I want to hear all about it," he said. "But first, shall we have a bottle of wine?"

"I think we shall," Clarke said.

Raske watched as they devoured the wine menu with a connoisseur's passion. He wasn't sure if it was feigned or not, but he understood the message. He was very much the junior partner, but that would change. They would change it, he and Evá. She was the only one he wanted to make proud.

*

In the backroom of the Smoke & Mirrors Club, a body lurched to life suddenly and drew a single ragged breath. Then it collapsed back down onto the operating table. It was eighteen years old, or thereabouts, and mostly alive. In the corner, the satyr looked up from his newspaper. He waited, watching. Finally the body drew a second breath and then a third.

"Finally," the satyr muttered to himself. He stood, folded his paper under his arm, and knocked on the second door to the right.

"Come in," a voice called. The satyr straightened his tux, and with a final glance at the now-breathing boy behind him, entered. Inside was a spacious, warmly decorated office. The walls were lined with shelves full of all manner of volumes and occult objects.

Mr. Nix was seated in an armchair, staring into the roaring fireplace. "The boy's awake," he said to the satyr. It was not a question.

"Yes, sir."

"Excellent," he said consulting his pocket watch. "And in good time too. The boy must be strong." He rose in a single fluid motion. "Now we can begin. Fetch his father."

"He was drowning himself in drink, last I saw him."

"No matter. He'll be sober enough for this."

The satyr nodded and left without another word. Mr. Nix followed him into the operating theater with unnatural speed.

The young man was already struggling to sit up, making muffled panicked noises and thrashing about.

Mr. Nix was at the formerly dead man's side in an instant. "Easy," he said. "Easy. Little breaths. In and out. I know resurrection can be disorienting. Just sit still and wait for the room to stop spinning. That's it." Nix patted the man's arm reassuringly and eased him up into a sitting position. "If you feel nauseous, there's a bucket to your right. But it will pass. I promise."

The door opened and Baron Hessing barreled in, all previous signs of inebriation gone. He was as sober as he'd ever been. "Gregor," he cried. "You're alive!" His voice was a mixture of apprehension and a wild, desperate joy.

The newly resurrected man made a fumbling attempt at speech, but no words came, only and incoherent gurgle.

"Shhh, " Hessing said. "It's alright, son. Everything will be alright." He went to hug him, but stopped. His arms hung awkwardly, suspended in the air for a second before dropping. It was his son, alive again, but the grave clung to him with a jealous grip. Gregor's skin was pale and rotten. His limbs and flesh still bloated and deformed. Trying and failing to mask his horror, Hessing turned to Mr. Nix, accusingly. "You said you would take care of him!"

"I did," Mr. Nix replied evenly. "Despite Gregor's own best efforts, he's alive. That is what you asked for."

"But he looks…" Hessing trailed off in disgust.

"Typical." Mr. Nix sighed. "I bring your son back to life and you complain about cosmetics. The appearance can be easily fixed. Any street wish-peddler could manage that. There's a djinn on the corner of Worth and Obst who specializes in this sort of thing. I'm sure he would be only too happy to help, Commandant."

Hessing coughed uncomfortably. "I didn't mean to seem ungrateful…"

"I should hope not," Mr. Nix interrupted. "Especially since this was not an act of altruism."

"No, of course not. But I am eternally grateful."

"Quite." Mr. Nix tilted his head, studying him for a moment, seemingly satisfied. "To the matter at hand, I believe you are familiar with a Count Wyman-Straus?"

"Yes." Hessing frowned. "We went to school together."

"In that case, I am sure you'd be delighted to personally introduce his beloved widow…"

"His widow?" Hessing asked. "But Count Wyman-Straus was…well…he was…"

"…a bachelor and a buggerer through and through? Indeed. But, as I said, his *widow* requires an introduction to someone of suitable status—the Lady Anne, perhaps."

"I see." Hessing glanced from Mr. Nix down to his son. "Anything for an old friend's wife," he said at length.

"That's the spirit."

Hessing heaved a sigh of relief. "To be honest, I was expecting something a little more…dangerous."

"Well," Mr. Nix said, "that little introduction may yet prove unexpectedly dangerous, but you misunderstand. That was merely a gesture of your eternal gratitude. I have something else in mind for your payment." He gestured and Mr. Tarr emerged from the shadows in his shabby overcoat, as if he had always been there. "You also know Mr. Tarr, don't you, Commandant?"

Hessing's hand went for his gun on instinct, but Mr. Nix stopped him with a look.

"I should," Hessing answered sharply. "He's wanted for the Rook Gate Bombings! A lot of good men died because of him. Some of them were my friends."

Smirking impishly, Mr. Tarr took an ironic bow.

"Yes," Mr. Nix said calmly, "a terrible tragedy, but I would prefer it, Commandant, if instead of arresting Mr. Tarr, you were to simply look the other way, while he slips into the Victory Ball tomorrow night."

"I can't do that!"

"It seems simple enough."

"You want me to allow a known faërie agitator into the largest and most secure social event of the year. Why? I doubt it's so he can sip champagne and have his first taste of caviar."

"Not his first taste, surely. Our Mr. Tarr has a very refined palate, but no. As you say, he has other matters to attend to, matters that are not your concern."

"The hell they're not! I'm the Commandant of Police! Half of my men are probably out looking for him as we speak."

"A pertinent observation. Please remind me, Commandant, what is the highest crime listed in the City Charter, above even murder?" Mr. Nix waited with an expression of mild interest.

"Necromancy," Hessing answered reluctantly.

"Precisely, necromancy. Restoring your son to life was no

simple matter, not to mention, as you've so kindly reminded me, illegal. Death does not loosen her grasp easily. It took a great deal of skill and art. There were rituals and chants and other far less savory tasks, but then, you know all about that." He glanced down at the newspaper in the corner and folded open to a report about the Ripper, who had recently claimed his sixth victim. Hessing followed his gaze. He'd known all along who was responsible; of course he'd known.

"On the other hand," Mr. Nix continued—and suddenly, as if his strings had been cut, Gregor collapsed back onto the table. His breathing stopped. "It takes but a thought to return him to his eternal slumber. It is a much easier process."

Hessing ran to his son's side. "Bring him back!" He cried."Please! Bring him back!"

"With pleasure." Gregor jerked back to life with a gasp. "My mark is carved into each of your son's organs," Mr. Nix said softly. "My spells are etched onto his soul. He is my creature now, Commandant, and if you want him to continue drawing breath, then so are you."

Hessing sagged and held his son for the first time, tentatively at first, then closely, desperately. "I understand," he said.

"Wonderful." Mr. Nix smiled. "I knew we could reach an understanding. Thank you for your visit. You and your son are free to go with my blessings."

Hessing rose slowly to his feet and he led his son out, step by haltering step.

"Might I suggest taking the back way," Mr. Nix called after them. "Just in case." Hessing didn't reply.

As soon as they were gone, Mr. Nix turned to his little

hobgoblin accomplice. "Now that that's arranged, you know what you have to do, Mr. Tarr?"

"Yes, sir. Everything's prepared."

"And how is our associate?"

"Ravenous, sir. I haven't fed it for three days."

"Excellent."

"Anselm wanted me to make sure that you can control it."

"Her," said Mr. Nix.

"Sir?"

"Nothing. You can tell the homunculus that he need not worry. I have everything under control."

"He'll be relieved to hear it." The hobgoblin hesitated. "May I ask a question, sir?"

"Certainly."

"This Countess."

"Yes?"

"She's arranged a meeting with Anselm and the others."

"How very industrious of her."

"Yes," Mr. Tarr said. "And the People of the Water don't know what to make of her."

"No," Mr. Nix agreed, "they wouldn't." He gazed down at the hobgoblin. "But that's not what's really bothering you, is it?"

"She saw me," said Mr. Tarr. "It was only for a moment, but she saw me and she wasn't even trying."

"Ah," said Mr. Nix. "Now that is interesting." He smiled his crooked smile. "But not wholly unexpected, considering. I wouldn't worry about her, Mr. Tarr. Whatever she may believe, she's just another iron in the fire."

13

CHAPTER THIRTEEN

The Countess stood at the riverfront, peering down into the water. She could feel the eddies and currents underneath the surface, pushing and pulling. She lost herself in the ripple of the water, the calming, churning waves glistening in the moonlight. There were a few ships out on the river, passing silently by, illuminated in a lantern glow. She could reach out and touch them, see them clearly in her mind, as they came closer and closer into the embrace of the City.

Shaking Mr. Nix's hand had left her unsettled. When they touched, she had felt a power inside him as fierce as her Purpose and as vast as the City, but only for a moment and then it was gone. He had given her a glimpse, and it had rubbed her raw inside. It was quiet here. She needed that quiet, and above all else, she needed to feel clean again. She let the lapping of the water flow through her, rinsing away the filth inside that clung to her like mud.

She had chosen a secluded alley down by the dockyards, abandoned for the night. Her feet had brought her here, urged on by the City. There were many such places, where the winding streets took a sudden turn and stopped abruptly at the water's edge. The Countess knew them all now and counted every cobblestone a friend.

Lost in a reverie, she barely noticed the drunken minotaur as he staggered down the alley toward her. The City spoke of him, but only in passing. He stumbled to a halt and leaned back against the wall. His horns scratched against the bricks as he fumbled for a cigarette.

He caught sight of the Countess silhouetted against the river, and stared. "What's this?" he asked himself. His speech was slurred. "You're in the wrong place, girlie!" he shouted. "Humans shouldn't come here. It's not safe." His words were kind but there was a leering glint in his eyes.

He was upon her now, breathing down her neck. "You might get yourself hurt," he said. She didn't stir and seemed entirely oblivious to his presence.

The minotaur snarled. He wasn't used to being ignored. He reached out to grab her arm, but before he could touch her, a great force pressed down upon him with a thousand invisible hands and sent him sprawling across the alleyway. He crashed into the brick wall with a sickening thud and collapsed to the ground.

Shaking his head, suddenly sober, he climbed to his feet. "Witch!" the minotaur cried and ran away as fast as he could. His cloven feet clattered on the cobblestones. A primly dressed young woman emerged from the shadows in front of him and he started to a halt.

She regarded him with a kindly, worried expression. "Are you all right?" she asked.

He looked back at the Countess, still staring at the river, lost in her own world. "She's a witch!" he said, panicked, forgetting—for the moment—his hatred of humans.

The young woman followed his gaze. "Yes," she said. "I know."

A knife appeared in her hand. The minotaur tried to take a step back, but she was too quick. She slit his throat with a single, expert stroke, and he collapsed to the ground, choking on his own blood.

Elise watched dispassionately. Jules joined her from the shadows.

"Handkerchief?" he offered.

She took it with a grateful smile and wiped her knife clean. "You know what to do."

Jules glanced down at the minotaur and sighed. "I always get the grunt work," he muttered.

She folded the handkerchief back into his pocket. "But you do it so well," Elise said.

"Mind you, that was a bit of luck. This here's the best place to dump a body," said Jules, who'd disposed of his fair share of corpses. "The currents keep it under, and the finfolk in this part of the river are always hungry."

"I doubt that was a coincidence." Elise nodded to the Countess.

"Fair point." He paused. "How do you think she's doing?"

"Only one way to know for sure." Elise cleared her throat then stepped over the minotaur's dead body and went to join the

Countess. Behind her, Jules heaved another sigh and began to drag the body, feet first, toward the river.

The Countess came back to herself slowly. "It's you," she said in a soft, distant voice.

"Yes, my lady," said Elise. "We're here." She hesitated. "How are you?" she asked.

"I'm..." the Countess paused, searching for the right word. "Acclimating."

Elise's eyes flickered back to her brother, who looked up from his work to meet her gaze. "That's good," she said, half-questioningly.

"Yes," said the Countess. "It is. There's so much to see, so much to understand. It's beautiful."

Elise smiled at the passion in her voice, but there were other more pressing questions. "How did the meeting go?"

The Countess folded back in on herself with a frown. "I'm not sure," she replied. "We came to an arrangement."

"That was the point."

"Yes, but he saw more than I had intended, and he's not what I thought he was, not entirely."

"Dangerous?" Elise asked.

"Very." The Countess leaned in close. "He's the only one who can keep secrets from the City," she whispered in Elise's ear. "It doesn't know him."

Elise nodded. There was nothing she could say to that. They had tried to warn her, but she hadn't listened. No one truly knew Mr. Nix. They stood there in silence for a few moments, peering out over the river. It was starting to rain.

Behind them, Jules struggled with the minotaur's heavy frame. The corpse thudded on the ground, and its horns scraped against the cobblestones. Finally, he reached the water's edge. He took a deep breath, then heaved the body into the water. The minotaur sank with a splash and was gone.

"I should go," said the Countess.

"You should rest," Elise said.

"But there's still so much I need to see."

"The city will still be here in the morning," said Jules. "We just want to make sure you are too."

The Countess glanced between them. She could feel their worry and concern intermingled with something else that she couldn't quite place. Not yet. She sagged.

"Very well."

The three of them headed out into the night, toward the hotel and sleep.

*

There was a sharp knock on the kitchen door. Lemann looked up from polishing his master's shoes. The other servants had been dismissed for various reasons. Wroe and Waller had been sent on errands and Mrs. Pratchett had been given the night off to visit her daughter. She had earned it. Baron Hessing could be extremely generous from time to time. The servants weren't ignorant, however. They knew who their employer was and could guess why they were occasionally sent away for the night, but Hessing paid them handsomely for their discretion.

There was the tapping at the door again. Lemann checked the wall clock—after midnight. They were late. He rose and unlocked the back door. Two figures were standing in the rain, Hessing and a smaller man with his face hidden beneath a hat and scarf. Lemann stepped aside. They came in dripping all over the kitchen floor. Lemann took his master's coat and gloves, but Hessing insisted on unwrapping his companion personally. He removed the scarf gently.

The face beneath was pallid and bloated, but utterly recognizable. It was the eyes, discolored but as sad and expressive as ever. Hessing couldn't help but grimace at the sight, but Lemann kept his face impassive and gave a slight, welcoming nod. It was the least he could do.

"Is everything prepared?" Hessing asked.

"All the arrangements are made, sir. A room in the back wing has been prepared. None of the servants frequent the area. It's very private, sir, as you instructed. Not what young Mr. Gregor is used to, but it should suffice." He shrugged apologetically.

"Needs must," said Hessing. "Gregor will be fine." His voice brokered no argument and Lemann offered none.

"Welcome home, Mr. Gregor," Lemann said.

Gregor didn't reply. He had always been quiet in his father's shadow, but he hadn't spoken a word yet. Lemann was beginning to wonder if he could even speak anymore. Resurrection was a delicate business, and the butler didn't know which back-alley necromancer his master had employed. He didn't want to know. It was better that way for all of them.

"Now," he said, lighting a candle, "if you'll follow me."

"Quietly," said Hessing.

"Yes, sir."

They crept out of the kitchen, two old men and a former corpse. The floorboards creaked ominously beneath Hessing's feet. Stealth had never been his forte, even when he was younger. They passed through the front hall, dark and full of shadows. They could hear the rain outside pounding the pavement. Step by step they made their way across the floor. Almost there.

Then with the flicking of a match, the hall was suddenly illuminated in warm, glimmering light. Lady Olivia stood at the top of the staircase with a lamp in her hand, staring down at them. They all froze under her gaze. Lemann recovered first and managed to fade inconspicuously into the shadows with the ease of practice. He wanted no part of this. Even Hessing took a step back. No one spoke. Lady Olivia was bleary and her hair and nightgown were a mess, but her gaze was sharp, and she had eyes only for her son.

She descended slowly, unblinkingly. Gregor watched her warily as she came closer and closer. Finally they stood almost nose to nose. She held the lamp up to his face and examined his features. She didn't flinch at the sight. Her expression never wavered, but the lamp trembled in her hand.

Gregor opened his mouth to speak, closed it, and then tried again. No words emerged, only a groaning, croaking sound. Her face crumpled and she pulled him close and hugged him tightly, sobbing. Gregor remained rigid in her arms, perhaps because his limbs were not yet fully mobile, but perhaps not. Perhaps he had his own private reasons. Hessing did not smile at the reunion before him. He couldn't smile. It would have been false, and they knew him too well.

"Olivia," he said at length. She didn't respond. "Olivia."

She released her son reluctantly and wiped the tears from her eyes. Then she turned, took three steps and faced her husband. She didn't let him speak, didn't let him utter a single word. She slapped him, hard. The sound reverberated in the darkened hall.

"You think I didn't know?" she said and slapped him again. "That you could keep this from me? Any of it?" He opened his mouth to answer, but she turned away, dismissing him. "Come with me," she said, putting her arms around her son. "Your room is waiting for you. I've kept everything the way you left it."

She led Gregor up the stairs none too gently. He followed silently, dragging his feet.

"Olivia!" Hessing cried, suddenly worried. "You can't! The servants..."

"The servants will keep their mouths shut. That's what you pay them for, isn't it? Or can't you control your own people?"

Hessing sighed. "That's not what I meant. You can't just..."

"I can," she interrupted, "and I will."

Gregor kept his head down and said nothing. He had nothing to say. Even in death he had failed to escape this house. They stopped at the top of the stairs.

"This changes nothing, Theodore," said Olivia. "Nothing."

Then they were gone and Hessing was alone. His cheek stung where she had struck him. His wife hated him. That was nothing new. There was a good chance that they would be caught now, thanks to her, paraded through the courts, and tried for soliciting necromancy. But his son was alive. It had been a devil's bargain, but he was alive. All things considered, the night had gone better than expected, much better.

14

CHAPTER FOURTEEN

Raske sat at his desk scribbling and mumbling to himself. He had been at it for hours, and seemed to be growing increasingly frustrated. It was a fairly well-to-do apartment. As a city prosecutor, Raske had a sizable salary and many other opportunities, legal and otherwise, to supplement his income. The walls were filled with books—law tomes and treatises on Deeper Faërie and its denizens. It was an enviable collection, but most of them were unread, props for his latest Pro-Faërie incarnation.

The speech was not going well. It had to be perfect. Raske had too much riding on it for it to be anything less. His pen scratched against the paper sometimes in rapid bursts, other times slowly, ponderously. He crossed out a whole passage with long harsh strokes, and then started again. And again. The sounds of wheels and carts and newsboys hawking their wares drifted up from the street. Rask barely noticed. His pen scratched away. Beside him was a half-empty cup of tea, forgotten and cold. He could feel his wife hovering in the background, her presence boring in on him.

"We're going to be late," said Evá.

"The Association can wait," Raske said without looking up. He was half dressed in his best suit.

"No," she said, "it can't."

"No." He sighed. "I suppose not." He looked up almost pleadingly. "I have to get this right. The speech is tomorrow."

"And the meeting is today. Clarke and Pullman arranged everything."

"I know." He nodded. For a moment he looked like he wasn't going to say anything else. "She'll be there," he said at last.

"Yes," said Evá. "She is a founding member. You can't expect to attack the Duchess on her turf, and not expect her to show up."

"I suppose that would be too much to ask for."

Evá leaned down behind him and put her arms around him.

"Relax, Charles," she said. "You are strong, passionate, clever. Remember that. It's why I chose you. It's why Clarke and Pullman chose you." He felt her breath on his neck and her strength flowing through him. "The speech is fine, but if you really want to, you can adjust it to your heart's content." She took the pen from his hands and put it down slowly. "Later."

She kissed his cheek. "But now, we really need to go. A handful of faëries are supposed to be there. We need to put on a good showing."

"Faëries? At the Faërie Rights Association?" Raske turned and looked up at her in surprise.

"The usual handful of suspects," she answered.

He sighed. "Just give me another minute. I'm in the middle of a paragraph. I think it's flowing now."

"No," said Evá. "You said that an hour ago." She pulled him to his feet. "Get your coat and play nice. Remember to smile."

"Because I was planning on scowling," he said.

She cheekily slapped him upside the head. "I said play nice."

"Yes, dear," Raske replied, but he was smiling.

*

The clock on the mantel ticked away as they stood, hovering awkwardly in the living room. Sergeant Lund shifted back and forth, glancing around, avoiding Mrs. Obry's eyes. He'd never been completely alone with her before.

"Would you like some tea?" Mrs. Obry asked softly.

"Yes," Lund said. She headed into the kitchen. "Thank you," he called, as an afterthought.

"It's no bother," she said. "I'll just put the kettle on. I've found that I need to keep myself busy, since..."

"I understand." There was nothing else he could say to that.

She rejoined him and gestured to one of the chairs. "Please make yourself comfortable. You've had a long night. I recognize the signs."

"A long few months really," he said before he could stop himself, but she didn't seem upset at the reference. She was too practical for that. Her husband was dead. No use jumping at his shadow.

They sat across from each other. Lund crossed and uncrossed his legs nervously. He had been here before, of course, many times—the Obrys had been lavish entertainers—but it was different now. Poor old Obry, and poor Johanna.

"You said you had news," she said, interrupting his thoughts. "About the investigation."

"Yes," he said, then paused. "I shouldn't be telling you this."

"I know." She stared at him with sad, waiting eyes.

He cleared his throat awkwardly. "They've identified the bomber. It appears to be an anarchist, a hobgoblin. He has a rather large file at Headquarters."

"Appears," she said.

"What?"

"You said 'appears' and 'they.'" Mrs. Obry was an old policeman's widow and she was sharper than he'd ever been.

"Ah. Well..." Lund grimaced. "We tried, but the Commandant still refused to put us on the case."

"I see." She gave no indication of what she thought of that.

Lund leaned forward and took her hand in his. They were both shocked by the suddenness of the gesture. "But that changes nothing," he said. "I'll find the bastard and I'll make him pay." He paused. "I mean, we...that is Inspector Erkel and I..." He trailed off into awkward silence.

The corners of her mouth curled into a slight smile. "And I appreciate it," she said putting her hand on his. "Thank you."

Lund glanced around the room, looking everywhere but at their hands. He was painfully aware of their closeness. There was a shrill whistle from the kitchen.

"That'll be the kettle," she said.

*

Mr. Covét sat in the back of the hall raging impotently to himself. Heinrich loomed next to him. The troll kept his stone-hewn face impassive, but Covét knew better. Heinrich was no less angry than he was. He just hid it better, an important quality in a troll, especially one who dealt with humans on a daily basis. Covét swallowed an angry grunt. They were so fragile and petty and he had little patience left for their foolishness.

Unfortunately, the monthly meeting of the Faërie Rights Association was a mostly human affair—letter writers, pamphleteers, ladies and gentlemen of wealth and station who'd had their delicate consciences pricked. Covét and Heinrich were the only true faëries in the room, although each and every one of the others claimed faërie ancestry, at an appropriate remove, of course—the hypocrites. It was arrant nonsense. Though Covét admitted, if only to himself, that the elderly Mr. Elkin, with his slightly pointed ears and slender fingers, might not have been entirely mistaken.

Covét didn't know why he degraded himself by coming to these meetings. Heinrich had convinced him to join years ago but the troll, at least, had business interests to protect. Covét was an old revolutionary who had made a name for himself with a series of anti-human tracts, and yet here he was every month subjecting himself to the bleeding hearts and hypocrisy. It was his penance.

At the front, the Duchess and Raske, the greatest hypocrites of them all, were arguing loudly. Barbs were flying back and forth with only the barest veneer of civility. The Association had long been the Duchess' territory. She had helped found it and had nurtured its members assiduously. Judging by the expressions, however, Raske had gathered far more supporters than expected. Covét found that unfortunately telling.

"Lady Anne," Raske was saying. "You and your husband have had your chance, and you've squandered it. The faëries need more than pretty words, they need action."

"And you think you can provide action?" the Duchess asked.

"I have a proven record of doing everything I can for those less fortunate than myself."

"Yes, yes," the Duchess waved her had dismissively. "We all know about your famous little court case. You never stop talking about it. But there is a difference, Mr. Raske, between making laws and merely upholding them. Or didn't they teach you that in law school?"

"That would have been a far more potent remark, your grace," said Raske, "if you and your husband had made any laws to speak of recently, let alone enforced them."

"I think you'll find that our most recent legislation was blocked by your new friends Clarke and Pullman. If you're dissatisfied, perhaps you should take it up with them." Raske attempted to speak but the Duchess continued relentlessly. "And while you're at it, Mr. Raske, you can ask them why only months later they're suddenly the Faërie Rights Act's greatest proponents with you as their cat's paw. Though I'm sure everyone here could hazard a guess."

Raske shifted uncomfortably. He hadn't expected that. Covét snorted to himself, and above him Heinrich rumbled in agreement. For her part, the Duchess was watching Raske with growing amusement. She seemed far less worried than she had been earlier, and with a good reason. For a would-be-politician, Raske didn't seem to handle surprises very well.

In fairness, Covét was surprised himself. The meeting was not turning out how he had expected. He had never taken Raske entirely seriously, although he was beginning to reconsider. The young man was more capable than he had expected, but no less contemptible. Covét had wondered if Raske's schemes might jolt the Duchess into some form of action. There had been a time when she had offered solutions instead of platitudes, but those days were long gone. She had become complacent, and Covét did not appreciate being taken for granted. There were other options, not Raske, perhaps, but others.

And it appeared that she had been galvanized into action after all, but in the form of the Imperial popinjay, Borchard-Márai. Covét could see him sitting behind the Duchess and Raske, watching them in festooned bemusement. For a brief second, the faun had wondered if the Emperor was finally starting to take an interest. That would have been worthy news. But the fool and his moustache had been just as surprised to be there as they had been to see him. Borchard-Márai had spouted a series of trite remarks when he arrived, shook hands, and kissed fingers, but he had been wholly unprepared. Covét knew more about Imperial Faërie Policy than he did.

The others—the humans—had eaten it up, bombarding him with questions about the capital and the Emperor. Raske had lost the room before he'd even opened his mouth, just as the Duchess had clearly intended, and he was never getting it back, not even if he won every point, and argued until he was blue in the face. Covét admired her tactic, but she had sidestepped the issues. There was no substance here, no real difference between her and Raske. They were as bad as each other, and as a whole the Association was more interested in hobnobbing with royalty.

"Politics," Covét muttered. "Human politics."

Heinrich nodded. He could read the undercurrents just as well as the faun, clearer even. He was better informed of the factors in play. Faërie rights were being subsumed into human politics, just another piece on the board to be maneuvered. It had hurt Covét's pride to be a "cause" for fashionable ladies, but this was worse, far worse. In the humans' petty maneuverings he could see the shadow of far greater dangers. They were afraid, all of them, and they were burying their heads in the sand. When they finally looked up, they would blame the faëries. Covét was sure of it. Something would have to be done before that happened, and soon. He couldn't sit on the sidelines any longer.

15

CHAPTER FIFTEEN

It was late. Everything was quiet save for the scratching of her pen. Lady Anne was writing letters in her sitting room, with a fresh cup of tea by her side. The city noises were faint and distant. She had a mountain of correspondence: contacts and friends across the Twelve Cities that needed nurturing. She flexed her wrist and took another sip. No rest for the weary or the wicked. Lord Edward strode in, looking harried.

"Good evening, Edward," she said after a moment, when it was clear he wasn't going to speak.

"You took the envoy to the Association without telling me," he said.

She put down her teacup with a clink. "This feels familiar," she said. "Weren't we discussing secrecy just the other day? Forgive me. My memory isn't what it used to be."

Lord Edward blinked. His face tightened for a moment, but then he sighed and nodded. "I deserved that," he said and sat down slowly. "In truth, I wasn't expecting you to wait this long. But why would you bring him to the Association? To make a point?"

She narrowed her eyes. "You know me better than that." Her voice was icy calm. "Do you truly think I would jeopardize all our work on a whim?"

Lord Edward waved his hand in apology. "I didn't mean that," he said. "Not like that. I'm sorry." He sighed again.

"I know," she said. She had seen the circles under his eyes and the tension in his shoulders. The pressure was mounting, and he was starting to miss a step. This wasn't the first time he'd forgotten to tell her something. She patted his arm softly.

"I know the Association," Lady Anne said. "The ladies and gentlemen with their deep purses and bruised consciences, and the faëries with their bitter memories and fading hopes. I've spent a great deal of time cultivating them on your behalf."

"And I'm grateful," said Lord Edward.

She smiled slightly, but continued. "I know their foibles. They're all so parochial, even Raske," she paused. "No. Especially Raske. Poking around, trying to carve out support, unable to see past his ambition."

Lord Edward looked up. "You were the one who told me not to be too hard on him."

She shrugged. "I still believe it would be easier to make use of him, and his wife."

"His wife?" asked Lord Edward.

"From what I could gather, she's the brains of the operation. What brains they have, at least."

"Interesting."

"Typical," Lady Anne corrected. They shared a smile. "I thought," she continued, "to give them all a glimpse of the larger picture, remind them why we are still their best champion, and I wanted to get a sense of him."

"Hmm," Lord Edward murmured. "That might work. So what did His Excellency, Borchard-Márai have to say for himself?"

"He used many words to say little. The Emperor is trying to keep well above the Faërie Movement."

"The safest place to be," agreed Lord Edward.

"He unbalanced Raske, as well."

Lord Edward reached over and took a sip of his wife's tea. "Not a bad day's work, then. At least one of us is making progress."

"I wouldn't say that," she said.

"Oh?"

"The mood was different this time. Not the ladies and gentlemen, they can always be relied upon for their predictability, but the faëries. They were angrier, less patient."

"Less patient." Lord Edward repeated and leaned back with an angry sigh. "We can't move any faster," he said. "Any drastic measures would have consequences for all of us. Step by step. They know that."

"I'm not sure they do."

Lord Edward exploded to his feet. "Well, that's what you're there for! To remind them!"

"I've been telling them the same thing for years."

"It's been true for years."

"Yes," she agreed softly. "But they've stopped believing me."

Lord Edward moved to the window and stared down into the street. "Don't they remember?" he asked. "Perhaps they're all too young. When my father made his first gesture for Faërie Rights, they turned on him. I still remember the mob howling at our gates, the human mob. It wasn't even equal rights he offered, not even close, and they nearly deposed him."

"I know," she said, again softly.

"He had them lined up and shot. Should have put their heads on pikes." He never raised his voice, but it was sharp and bitter.

"That was over sixty years ago," she said.

"Yes." He turned. "But do you truly think anything has changed?"

"No." She met his gaze unerringly.

"Do they?"

"No," she repeated, "but they don't care anymore."

"Then we've lost control of the Movement."

"Perhaps not yet, but soon."

He nodded. "It was only a matter of time, I suppose. Very well. I shall have to take precautions."

"Such as?"

"I'm summoning Brigadier Kronberger and the Ducal Guard. I'll leave them outside the city for the moment, but I want him close at hand."

"The Guard," she said, and frowned. "With the envoy still in the city?"

"Let him see what he sees. I don't have time for Imperial politics at the moment. One problem at a time."

She stood and put her hand on his shoulder. "The mob didn't get your father. It won't get you."

"No," he agreed. "Not while I have soldiers."

She shook her head. "This is a recipe for disaster," she said.

"I know," he agreed. "But the storm will pass. I have the

soldiers, I have the police, and I have you. We just have to hold on a little longer."

*

The Thirsty Goblin was dark and crowded, filled with grim and hungry faces. Mr. Covét seemed out of place with his dusty frockcoat. These were not the artists and intellectuals who frequented its Café Goblot incarnation during the day. This was a different crowd—rougher, deadlier. There was a preponderance of suspicious glances and a few welcoming nods. He had friends here as well.

Covét made his way to the back room, where four figures—a hobgoblin, a headless man, a homunculus, and a man with the nose of a vulture—sat in the darkest corner, heads bent in hushed conversation. Mr. Tarr was the first to notice him, but the hobgoblin said nothing. Covét was almost upon them when there was a fluttering of wings in the shadows, and the tall birdlike figure turned his beak suddenly.

"You," said Droz sharply. "What are you doing here?" The others twisted in their seats and regarded Mr. Covét solemnly, though Brunet had no eyes to see.

"I've just been to a meeting with the Ladies and Gentlemen of the Faërie Rights Association," said Mr. Covét.

"And?" Droz sneered.

"There was an Imperial Envoy."

"Did you and your troll friend offer to shine his boots?" Droz asked. He would have said more, but Anselm put a restraining hand on his shoulder.

"I'm sure that was...enlightening," said the homunculus. For his part, Mr. Tarr leaned back with an amused twinkle. He knew what was coming.

"I know you're up to something," Mr. Covét said. "It's been obvious for months."

"And?" Anselm asked, not bothering to deny it.

"And," said Mr. Covét, "I want in."

Mr. Tarr smiled smugly, but said nothing.

"Help us?" Droz snarled. "You? You're tainted by them, making your living off the humans and their ilk. I wouldn't be surprised if you were here to spy for them."

"How dare you!" Covét was furious. He had many flaws and his share of enemies, but no one had ever accused him of human sympathies before, especially not some ignorant birdman barely out of his nest.

"Enough," said Anselm. "Mr. Covét's loyalties are not in question." He looked up at the faun. "I've read your pamphlets. Very inflammatory. Very vigorous. We'll need faëries like you. But that's a question for another day."

"The question for today," said Brunet, speaking for the first time, his voice echoing outward from his neck, "is can you fight?"

"Yes," Mr. Covét said without hesitation, swallowing his bitterness—of course he knew how to fight. "I was a soldier once."

"Very well," Anselm said. "Pull up a chair."

As Covét sat, Mr. Tarr slapped him on the back. "Now the fun begins," he said.

Covét didn't reply. He still believed that they were all doomed to failure; but at least this time, he would die with his own kind.

CHAPTER SIXTEEN

Auberon Square was crowded. They had been gathering beneath the shadow of the First Duke of Talis for a few hours. The crowd was mostly human, but a few faëries had braved the trip. The city's mood had not gotten any friendlier. They were mostly middle class and well-to-do moderates—faëries and monstrous humans—willing to be convinced. There were true fairies in the throng fluttering their wings to get a better look, and other creatures with hands where ears should be and strange limbs. They jostled with the humans, but both sides held their peace. After all, that's why they were there—to improve Faërie-Human Relations.

At the back of the crowd, the Countess watched the proceedings with interest. The City had led her here, nudged her, and she had let her feet follow. It wanted to show her something.

Ever since she'd arrived in the Talis, the Countess had seen signs of someone courting the faëries ahead of her, making her job more difficult. It had been an unexpected complication. Now she understood. Raske was clearly the one Covét had been referring to, the one whose unwanted overtures had poisoned the well. She would need to deal with him—and quickly, judging by the size of the crowd.

*

Raske was standing at the foot of the pedestal in a well-ironed suit. It was a good-sized crowd, but there were less faëries than he'd hoped. By the look of them, Clarke and Pullman agreed. They joined him beneath the pedestal and shook hands.

"Thank you for coming, gentlemen," Raske said. They looked out at the assembled gathering.

"A fairly good turnout from the monstrous humans," Pullman offered.

Clarke frowned."Refugees and immigrants," he said.

"I believe they prefer just to be called 'humans' these days," said Evá, pushing through the crowd. She gave her husband's arm a reassuring squeeze. "The Charitable Ladies have arrived." She nodded to the procession of women in purple hats, who were shouldering their way with eminent politeness toward the front.

"What would we do without them?" asked Pullman.

"Careful," said Clarke. "They're one of our largest contributors. Though I do wish you had convinced more faëries to come, Charles."

"We've got the *humans* and the Purple Hat Brigade, what more do we need?" Pullman said grandly. Evá frowned at him.

"It's still early," she offered.

"Not early enough. Not in this weather. It looks like it might rain at any moment."

"That makes the size of the crowd all the more impressive," Evá said.

"Perhaps," said Clarke. "But that only means it could have been even larger in the right weather." He muttered darkly to himself about weather magic.

Raske shook his head. "I doubt the Duke would have gone to the trouble of arranging for a rainstorm," he said. "Not when there are far more efficient methods of deterring turnout." He tilted his head toward the Ducal Palace bristling with armed guards. Clarke nodded. It was a fair point.

Raske found that he couldn't take his eyes away from the Ducal Mansion. Evá had suggested the Square as the setting for the speech, as a way to show that they weren't afraid of the Duke, that they were willing to take the fight to him. "It is time," she had said, "to reclaim the promenade as a place of the people, human and otherwise."

That had been the theory at least, and it had seemed like a bold move at the time with visions of vast crowds dancing in their heads. But now with the statue looming above him, and the Ducal Mansion to the right, Raske felt suddenly, terribly small.

*

Lord Edward unstoppered the decanter and poured three glasses. Lady Anne and Borchard-Márai were at the window gazing down at the rally. The Duke had invited the envoy reluctantly, but Lady Anne was right and he knew it. This was a necessary piece of political theater—a show of unity. He joined them at the window and handed them their glasses.

"I'm not sure why you're allowing him to go forward with this display, Lord Edward," said Borchard-Márai.

"Are you saying that the Emperor would have interfered?" he asked.

"Perhaps." Borchard-Márai took a sip and sighed contentedly. "Stability must be maintained at all costs. That nobody down there is undermining you, and worse, he's rubbing your nose in it."

"Oh, I agree," said Lord Edward. "But this is all perfectly legal under the Charter. Mr. Raske or one of his supporters has been very thorough, very careful. He is a lawyer, after all. Legally I can't deny his right to speak."

"And even if you could," Lady Anne added, "in the current climate that would only stir up trouble and potentially drive more people to him."

"Yes," said Borchard-Márai. "Speaking of the current climate, the Emperor has some concerns."

"With the climate?" Lord Edward asked.

The Duke and Duchess exchanged worried glances. Finally, they were getting to the heart of the matter, the real reason for the envoy's presence, or as much of it as Borchard-Márai was authorized to say.

"With this faërie nonsense. It's destabilizing, and worse, it's spreading. There have been incidents."

"Incidents?"

"Last week in Argen a fight broke out between policemen and a band of faëries—ogres and the like—and just yesterday a monstrous human from Deeper Faërie attempted to assassinate the Grand Duke."

"I'm not responsible for other cities," said Lord Edward.

"No, but the Emperor is."

"And?"

"And he wanted me to tell you that while he is sympathetic to the difficulties and appreciates the subtleties and restraint of your policy…"

"Spare me the platitudes."

"Very well, your grace," Borchard-Márai matched the Duke's glare. "Respectfully, His Serene & Imperial Majesty commands you to get your house in order. Immediately."

"Respectfully?" Lord Edward's lips twitched angrily. Lady Anne sent him a quelling glance. He nodded and took a deep breath. "The situation is well in hand," he said after a moment.

"Well in hand?" Borchard-Márai raised an eyebrow. "Your grace, you have a serial killer on the rampage, and an anarchist hobgoblin bombing the city…"

"That hasn't been confirmed."

"The inspectors seemed fairly confident earlier."

"How do you know that?"

"I have my sources."

"You've been spying on me," said Lord Edward.

"You're going to lecture the Emperor on spying? You have the largest intelligence network in the Crescent."

"Second largest," Lord Edward replied. "I could never compete with Imperial resources. Nor, of course, would I ever dream of doing so."

"Of course." Borchard-Márai frowned. He had been out maneuvered slightly. "The point is that you are losing control. We need stability in the region now. Or we may have to provide it ourselves."

The Duke and Duchess shared another glance full of meaning.

That was a blatant threat. No Imperial Envoy would have made such a statement without authorization, without orders from the highest level. The Imperial court hadn't been this active in city politics for decades. Something had changed and the Lord Edward had no idea what it was. That was the most disturbing part. Borchard-Márai had not been exaggerating the size of the Duke's spy network. He should have known.

"Imperial interference," said Lord Edward, "wouldn't solve anything at this juncture, and it most certainly would not provide stability."

"Why now?" Lady Anne interrupted.

"Excuse me?"

"The faërie situation has been precarious for decades throughout the Twelve Cities, not just here in Talis. Why is the Emperor suddenly so worried?"

Borchard-Márai drained his glass and sighed. "There are rumors," he said.

"Rumors about us?" Lord Edward asked.

"No," Borchard-Márai said. "Rumors about the Witches." The Duke and Duchess stared at him in shock.

"I need another drink," said Lady Anne. Lord Edward could only nod.

*

In the distance, the bells struck the hour. Raske sighed. He couldn't wait any longer. No one else was coming. If only Anselm and his comrades had agreed to mobilize on his behalf. They would have been able to fill the Square, rain or shine. But it was still more than enough to give the Duke something to think about.

Evá gave him a quick, reassuring hug. "It's time," she said.

He nodded. And took a deep breath. "I know."

"Good. Now, don't forget to enunciate."

"Yes, dear."

"And remember, forget the crowd. Clarke, Pullman, and the Association are the ones who matter. They're the ones with the purse strings. The rest is window dressing."

"No pressure, then," he said. Evá gave him a long, searching look.

"You'll do fine," she said. "I believe in you." And then with a final peck on the cheek she disappeared down into the crowd.

Raske inhaled and exhaled. His breath turned to mist in the air. There was nothing else for it. The speaking permit had cost almost all his savings, that and the bribes. This was his last, best opportunity. He straightened his tie. Raske was a good orator, his old professors had always said so, and the newspapers concurred. "Think happy thoughts," he muttered to himself and stepped out onto the dais.

The crowd erupted into enthusiastic applause, although some of them, no doubt, were simply glad it was finally starting. A few curious spectators on the promenade looked on in interest. Raske gave a half wave and waited for the noise to die down. Then he took a deep lungful of air and began.

"We are gathered here today," Raske said, his voice unexpectedly loud in the sudden silence, "in what was once a place of tyranny—tyranny of the Witches, tyranny of magic. We are standing, all of us, in the shadow of a great man, Lord Talis the Liberator, a man of vision, and bravery, a man who was not afraid to fight against tyranny and make this a place of freedom!"

There was a small smattering of applause, mostly from the humans. The others shifted restlessly. They had not come to hear another paean to the glory of the Lords of Talis. Evá flitted through the crowd, distributing flyers. A few people took them. One four-headed man took one copy for each head. But more often than not, they turned her away. She kept a demure smile in place and moved on.

"But," Raske continued, "it has been two hundred years since that blow was struck for freedom, and this place is in danger of once again becoming a place of tyranny, not from willful malice but from slow decay and apathy. For too long the promise of liberty has been left half-answered. For too long the Liberator's heirs have allowed their illustrious ancestor's promise to go unfulfilled. It was not only the Liberator and his human allies who drove the Witches out, but faëries too, and what we now call *monsters*. It is time that we honor that sacrifice. It is time that all men, human or otherwise, were allowed their full rights as citizens!"

The applause was warmer than before. This was what they had come to hear. Raske seemed to grow slightly, basking in their cheers. From the corner of his eye, he caught Clarke and Pullman exchanging pleased glances. He had them. Everything was going according to plan.

*

Raske was not what the Countess had expected. At first glance, he had seemed damp and grasping, but he was winning over the crowd. She could sense their enthusiasm vibrating in the air. Her great aunt had been right. There was a deep reservoir of discontent ready to be exploited, but Raske had tapped into it first. That was dangerous. There was nothing inside him but ambition, no substance, nothing she could turn to her purpose.

There was no other option. She would simply have to thwart that ambition.

The Countess gathered herself. Stealth was her greatest ally. Unleashing her power with all these people watching was risky. A single pair of eyes could ruin everything. Even more dangerously, the Invocation of the City was incomplete. There was no telling how the mystical energies cooking inside her would react, but her Purpose demanded action and she obeyed.

She released her power into the world. It expanded eagerly, formlessly, but the Countess pulled it back. This would require absolute precision to avoid detection. She was keenly aware of the magic-sniffing dogs lurking by the Ducal Mansion, and on the edge of her awareness she could sense the magicians in their college across the river. Their understanding was narrow but deep.

She employed a combination of mind artes and aeromancy, to use the human terms. It felt grubby and sordid to cage her magic in such small, clumsy boxes, to chain herself to texts and formulas like some common sorceress, but it was necessary. She could not sing a storm into being and lose herself in the melody of the world. She might as well have simply shouted her identity from the rooftops. Nor was there time for a ritual incantation, even if she could have managed it in the crowd without being foolishly obvious.

Glancing around, she began to softly mutter a few, lilting words under her breath, and trace a number of eldritch shapes in the air. There would be a price for this. Without a ritual or song, she would need to provide the power to shape the world herself. The Elements were a particular and exacting mistress. Mere flesh and blood was never enough for them.

She carved a long, cherished summer's evening from the depths of her memory—one of the few times she and her mother had spent free from their all-consuming Purpose. It was a piece of herself that had warmed her on her long, lonely road. She cast it out and purged it from herself, gone forever, leaving emptiness in its wake. The winds and weather could be fickle but they accepted the sacrifice greedily, accepted her.

The Countess felt herself expand upwards. She was apart, gazing down at the crowd, seeing their thoughts and dreams glowing below. She watered the discontent she found in the minds around her, and carefully planted new seeds. It was simple if you knew how. Then she turned her attention to the sky and expanded even further. She was in the air now, in the clouds. She filled them to bursting, until at last she descended in a hundred thousand raindrops. She was the storm. The storm was her. And she raged, louder and louder.

*

Borchard-Márai rubbed his mustache idly. "It's not a bad little speech," he said. "The rhetoric was a little trite, but he's a fairly competent orator."
Lord Edward glared at him. "Forget Raske," he said. "Tell me about the rumors."
Borchard-Márai was far too practiced in the art of diplomacy to allow anything more than the shadow of a smirk cross his lips. Besides, there was nothing amusing about the rumors. "The Witchling Tribes are on the move," he said. "There are reports of Witches coming down from the mountains."
"For what purpose?" asked Lady Anne.
"We don't know. We're not even sure the reports are valid, but we can't take the risk." He fixed them with a serious glance. "More

importantly, there are whispers about a Leonora—the Witchling Heir to the Throne of Talis."

"That's not possible," Lord Edward said. "That line is dead."

"It's only a rumor," said Borchard-Márai. "But perhaps your illustrious ancestor was not as thorough as history suggests."

The Duke and Duchess glanced at each other, but said nothing.

"And it's not just the Witches," Borchard-Márai continued. "More and more faëries are migrating into the Cities every month. They're running from something."

"We've noticed," said Lord Edward.

"Everyone's noticed. The Emperor is trying to pivot to meet the threat, whatever it may be, but there are some…disagreements about how best to proceed."

"Count de Grimvard," Lady Anne supplied. The Chancellor was always planning something.

"Yes," said Borchard-Márai. "The Emperor would prefer a less antagonistic approach, but de Grimvard is gathering supporters. The moderates are losing ground."

"And where do you stand, your excellency?" she asked.

"With the Emperor, of course. We need to stand together, especially if the Witches are returning."

"Together." Lord Edward said with a sigh. "There doesn't seem to be a great deal of unity in the capital." He sneered down at the crowd. "Or here, for that matter. Look at them down there—the self-righteous and the desperate."

Borchard-Márai nodded. "Hence the Emperor's concerns. He can handle de Grimvard and the rest, but only if you and the other Dukes can handle your own problems."

Lord Edward shook his head. "That shouldn't be too difficult. Despite the harsh rhetoric, Raske isn't offering anything new, no solutions that we haven't already suggested, no ideas my wife hasn't already voiced. His agenda is empty."

"As you say."

The three of them turned back to the window. The storm was intensifying outside. The downpour had become nearly torrential—a cascade of water and bitter wind. The crowd was beginning to disperse in ones and twos, and in bunches. Raske was raising his voice in a desperate attempt to call them back, but he was no match for the elements.

Lord Edward's lips twitched into the beginnings of a smile. "Raske will find a new issue soon. This one isn't turning out as he'd hoped."

"The weather's taken care of that," said Borchard-Márai. "No one's going to stay much longer, not even the reporters. Unless he's got another card up his sleeve, your Mr. Raske is finished."

"It would appear so."

"Think about what I've told you," Borchard-Márai said."And for all our sakes, try not to prove de Grimvard right."

He put his empty glass down on the table. "But now I shall take my leave. You have a great deal to think about. Your Grace." He bowed. "Lady Anne." Then he turned and walked away, leaving them alone.

Lady Anne joined her husband at the window and put a hand on his shoulder. They peered down at the thin, straggling ruins of Raske's big rally. "He's right. It was a good speech," she said.

Lord Edward frowned. "That man down there believes only in his own ambition and was willing to twist and overturn my family's legacy to achieve it."

"Yes," she agreed, "but you've always had a talent for channeling other's ambitions, Edward. Use him."

"Perhaps I will," he said. "But we have other problems now."

"Yes. The Witches. Had you heard anything about that?"

"No," said Lord Edward.

"Then you had better verify the rumors and quickly. Your family has unfinished business with the Witches."

"I know."

"And still no mention of the succession," Lady Anne said. "Do you think we were wrong?"

"No," he said. "If they're worried about the Witches returning, then the succession is an even bigger problem."

"You sent for Kronberger?" she asked.

"Yes," he said. "Though I'm not sure he'll be enough."

"Worst comes to worst," she offered, "we still have your little secret weapon."

"Let us hope it doesn't come to that," said the Duke. "For all our sakes."

*

The crowd scattered around her, but the Countess remained somehow apart from them. They ignored her and passed by without seeing, but she saw them and their rain-soaked faces. She saw everything. Raske and his wife were arguing with four or five men in great coats. It appeared that his political aspirations were not proceeding according to plan. All it took was one little storm and a sprinkling of discontent in their minds. The Countess smiled to herself, but there were other, far more dangerous enemies waiting for her. She could feel her Purpose itching beneath her skin, screaming louder even than the voice of the City. It wasn't satisfied. It was never satisfied.

She looked up at the Ducal Mansion and found them immediately. There they were, the Duke and the Duchess looking down from a small window on the right. They were barely silhouettes, but she knew it was them; at last, it was them. She saw her enemies clearly, but they did not see her. Then they were gone.

She turned. It had been a productive evening, and the night promised to bring its own developments. Behind her stood Mr. Tarr and Mr. Brunet, exactly where the City told her they would be.

"Gentlemen," she said with a nod. The City whispered to her of Mr. Brunet's lost head, and the hobgoblin's mischievous heart.

"Countess," said Mr. Tarr. "I understand you wanted to talk."

She smiled.

CHAPTER SEVENTEEN

The parade ground was crowded. The 7th Ducal Regiment was on evening maneuvers. They had been at it all day—drilling, drilling, and more drilling. They had gone through most of the field manual twice already—firings and maneuvers, forming battalions, advancing, retreating, and street firing. Twenty rounds in all. Over and over again. The Brigadier was clearly worried about something, but Lt. Berg and the other officers were as ignorant as the rest. The Guard was the last bastion of civilization in a hostile world. Vigilance was necessary and the increased training regime usually presaged a fight, but there had been no major incursions recently.

Not that there was a shortage of potential dangers. Ft. Ammassari was near the Borderlands, where the protection of the Twelve Cities faded and the wilder Lands of Faërie began.

Refugees streamed in constantly, more and more each day. The goblin kingdoms to the east had grown bold since the last war, and were forever sending raiding parties. And then there were the snowcapped mountains to the west, where the Five Witchling Tribes had fled after the revolution.

Lt. Berg forced himself to focus on the task at hand. It was no use worrying about the future. The present was troublesome enough. The formation was slipping and his men were to blame. Private Skane was falling behind. He opened his mouth to rebuke him, but the sergeant beat him to it. Rudbeck was a grizzled old soldier. He had learned his trade on the battlefield and had proved a welcome boon for Berg, whose own experience came largely from the training field and the manual.

Suddenly, the exercises were called to a halt, saving Berg any further embarrassment. A colonel came running from the command center.

"All officers report to the mess hall," he shouted. "Immediately!"

Everyone knew what that meant. Before he joined the others, Berg turned to Rudbeck, who nodded encouragingly.

"I'll tell you what I can," Berg promised.

*

No one seemed to know what was happening. The officers were all muttering among themselves. Lt. Berg hung back. He was relatively new to the regiment, and unlike the others he had worked his way up from the ranks. He seldom felt comfortable here.

Brigadier Kronberger entered to a fluttering of salutes and the room instantly fell silent. Kronberger, with his polished uniform and pointed mustache, was the picture of a proper soldier. A war hero, most forgot that his origins were as humble as Berg's.

"At ease," he barked. "We have been ordered to proceed to Silver Point. Make preparations for an overnight march." There was a rustling at that, but the officers held their tongues.

"Once at Silver Point, we must be ready for deployment to Talis at a moment's notice." This time not everyone could contain their reaction. A murmur rose. Kronberger held up a hand. "I don't know what's happening any more than you do," he said. "But if the Duke deems it necessary, we will march on the city."

"Yes, sir," they chorused.

"Dismissed."

As the assembled officers filed out, Kronberger called for Berg to remain.

"Walk with me, Lieutenant," he said.

"Yes, sir." They headed out to the parade ground, where Berg noticed a few jealous glances from his fellow officers.

"You're a good soldier, Lieutenant, capable. All you need is a little seasoning."

"Thank you, sir."

"This could be your chance to make a name for yourself," Kronberger said. "Serve well and there may be a promotion in it for you, perhaps even a medal."

"Yes, sir." Berg tried not to let his excitement show. He failed miserably.

Kronberger smiled, but his amusement faded quickly. "See to your men," he ordered. "We have a lot of work ahead of us."

*

Heinrich sat in front of the fire with his spectacles perched on his nose. Piles of papers were stacked around him. He always found pouring over his accounts to be methodically soothing, and he was in desperate need of soothing. His nerves were jangled. Chaos was the enemy of good business and he could feel it spreading, infecting the city and everyone in it. Heinrich had spent years trying to leverage his contacts and maintain stability at all costs, the Duke and Duchess on the one hand and Anselm and the Dissidents on the other.

He realized now that he had grown too complacent, too sure of his influence. The Duke and Duchess shared his desire for stability, but not his methods. They had plans of their own and, as the Imperial Envoy had reminded him, other influences acting on them. Worse, he had misjudged Anselm. The homunculus turned out to be as radical as the rest, more so even. He took Heinrich's money but he no longer listened to his council. He never truly had, and now he would drag their people with him into madness.

His disapproving maid entered. "There is someone here to see you," she said. "He came the back way and knew the proper signs."

Heinrich nodded. "Bring him in," he said. He had been expecting Anselm to send someone, but he started in surprise when he saw the old faun come through the door. Covét looked almost as surprised to be there as he was to see him.

"I wasn't expecting him to send you," Heinrich said. "I always thought you were too smart for that."

Covét grimaced. "You were at the same meeting I was," he said.

Heinrich nodded to himself. He should have known. Watching the Duchess and Raske bicker over the faëries as if they were their own personal fiefdom while the Imperial Envoy held court had shaken Heinrich's confidence, but Covét was a romantic turned cynical, and all the more prickly for it.

"You saw what I saw," Covét continued, "and it bothered you just as much."

"Yes," Heinrich said. "But that doesn't mean Anselm's plan is the answer. He's risking everything on one throw of the dice."

"We've tried it slow and steady," Covét said. "We've been trying for years."

"We've made some progress."

"No, you've made some progress," Covét said, gesturing at the house around them. "But only as much as they've let you."

"That may be so." Heinrich brushed the thought aside and narrowed his eyes at the old faun. "But we've also tried Anselm's way before. You know that better than I do."

Covét glanced down and said nothing.

"I've heard you talk about those days in this very room," Heinrich said. "The chaos and the madness. You called Anselm deluded and anyone who followed him a fool. Were you wrong?"

"Circumstances have changed," Covét said.

"Were you wrong?" Heinrich bit out each word. They echoed in the small office.

"No," said Covét. "I wasn't wrong. Anselm's plan is madness. His revolution is as doomed as the last."

"Then why?"

Covét sat down next to him by the fire, and fixed his tired, weary gaze on him. "Because it doesn't matter," he said. "Because the humans are trying to co-opt us, and when that fails, they will purge us. And I will never be co-opted, and I will not be purged without a fight."

Heinrich stared at him, aghast. "You can't really believe that."

"There are more faëries pouring into the city every day. More than ever before. Do you know why?"

"No." Heinrich hesitated. The muse's words echoed in his mind, but he kept them to himself. "Do you?"

"No," Covét said. "And neither do the humans. They're afraid, and soon they're going to do something about it, before the faëries outnumber the humans. We have to do something first."

"You've been thinking about this for a long time."

"Yes."

Heinrich wasn't convinced. "The Duke wouldn't do that."

"Perhaps not," Covét allowed. "You know him better than any of us, but could you say the same for whoever replaces him? Or Parliament? Or the Emperor?"

Heinrich had no reply.

"I've said my piece." Covét nodded and rose. "The choice is yours, but remember that this is happening with or without you. And when it does, would you rather be with us, or on your own?"

Then the faun was gone, leaving Heinrich to his lonely thoughts.

*

Raske sat at the dining room table, his head down, and a half-empty bottle of whiskey in front of him. Evá hovered behind him, unable to keep still. She fiddled with the pictures and straightened items on the mantelpiece.

"It wasn't a bad speech, Charles," she said. He didn't respond, didn't even stir. "It's not over. There will be other days, other causes. You can come back from this. We can come back." She put her hand on his shoulder. He grimaced slightly. It might have been an attempt at a smile, it might not. Evá was relieved. It wasn't much, but it was something at least, an acknowledgement, the first in over an hour. All was not lost.

"There were a few thousand out there," she said. "Nothing to sneeze at."

"No," Raske agreed glumly, "that would be the weather."

She took his head in her hands. "None of that. It was a fairly good turnout, all things considered, and the papers can spin that into a success."

"But they won't," he said. "Clarke and Pullman have abandoned me."

There was a knock at the door. Evá frowned. A visitor at this hour? Clarke or Pullman, perhaps, come to strategize, but she doubted it. Charles was right; they had already abandoned him, not that she could blame them. His political prospects were finished for the time being. She'd have made the same calculation in their shoes. It still stung, though, and there *had* been something strange about the weather.

Evá went to the door and opened it slowly. A messenger stood in the hallway in rain-soaked finery. He presented a letter without comment, wrapped in string and adorned with the official City Seal. Evá took it with a frown, and went to collect a couple of coins for a tip. The messenger wrinkled his nose at the thought and left in a huff. She shrugged and turned her attention the letter.

"It's from the Duke," she said.

Charles took it from her numbly and broke the Ducal Seal. Inside was an expensive sheet of parchment with gold-embossed lettering. He read to himself silently for a moment.

"We are 'cordially' invited to the Victory Ball," he said, disbelief coloring his voice.

"Interesting," Evá said, intrigued. Perhaps they had made an impression after all. Meanwhile, Charles's disbelief rapidly turned to fury.

"Cordially invited?" He spat."Cordially!" He threw his glass against the wall. It shattered.

Evá ignored his tantrum, didn't even flinch at the sound. She was deep in her own thoughts. "Why, I wonder," she said.

"Why? To gloat," Raske said. "To laugh in our faces and parade our defeat in front of all of high society."

"Perhaps."

"Perhaps?" Raske stared at his wife. "Do you really think he isn't gloating right now?"

"No." She shrugged. "But the Duke seldom does anything for only one purpose. Gloating is just a part of it. He could have slammed the door on us forever, but instead he left a crack open."

"A crack?" Raske was incredulous.

"Think about it," she said. "Think! The Duke has won a thousand political battles and where are his enemies now? He doesn't parade them. He buries them, sometimes literally. So why are we different? Why are we humiliated instead of buried?"

Raske watched her in dawning comprehension. "The faëries," he said. "It's because of the faëries. We came at him through his wife's little fiefdom. He needs to make an example of us."

"He already has. I'm sorry, but we failed, Charles, miserably. Although I doubt anyone could have done much better, even with Clarke and Pullman's full support. The Duke doesn't need to make an example of us. No. This is an opportunity and a test."

"A test?"

"He wants to know if we can swallow our pride and be useful."

"Useful." Raske didn't like the taste of the word. "Who the hell does he think he is?"

"The Duke of Talis," she replied simply, "and your only way back in from the cold."

"No." He shook his head. "I will not debase myself."

"Yes," Evá said, "you will. For tomorrow. For us. For me."

They were standing almost nose to nose. He stared down at her for a long moment. "Very well," he said. "But I don't like it."

"You don't have to like it." She smiled and kissed him gently. "You just have to be patient. I'll find us a way. You can't win every battle, but it's the war that counts, and we're not beaten yet. Are we?"

"No."

"No," she repeated. "Not by a long shot."

CHAPTER EIGHTEEN

Hessing found his wife in the hall outside Gregor's room, an uneaten dinner tray in her hands. She was not as fragile as he had feared, but there was still something brittle about her. He fiddled with his cufflinks.

"How is he?" Hessing asked. She almost didn't answer.

"I had Mrs. Pratchett prepare his favorite," she said. "But he won't eat."

"That's not surprising," said Hessing. "He isn't exactly alive anymore."

"I noticed," Lady Olivia snapped. "I just didn't think it would be like this..."

Hessing interrupted her. "What did you tell Mrs. Pratchett?"

"Oh, don't worry about it," she said sharply. "Thanks to you, I have a reputation for madness in this household."

"That wasn't my doing, Olivia."

She glared and moved to pass him, but he blocked her way.

"We need to talk," he said.

"I have nothing to say to you," she said—but then she saw something in his expression. "Very well," she said.

"Not here." He led her, whether by accident or design, to the master bedroom, the room they'd once shared. They stood in awkward silence.

"Well?" she demanded at last.

"You knew."

"I suspected," she said. "I know you, after all."

"Then why the tantrums? Why didn't you say something?"

"Tantrums?" She put the tray down with a crash. "I see. Because you were a fountain of honesty and communication."

"I couldn't say anything," he said. "Not until I had a solution."

"Oh, I know. That's always been your way. You never mention a problem until you know you can solve it, but our son was not a problem to be solved."

"I'm sorry."

"Of course you're sorry." She scowled. "That's what all this is—you being sorry—but none of it changes what you did before, to him or to me."

"To you?"

"Please," she said. "Don't lie to me. You've had your pet doctors drugging me for months. Very convenient, I'm sure."

"There was nothing convenient about it," Hessing said. "There's nothing convenient about any of this." He looked down. "There's a price."

"Naturally," she said. "I'm not an idiot. No one performs necromancy out of the goodness of their heart."

He gazed at her solemnly, but she was unyielding. "You did this," she said, "and you will pay the price, whatever it is."

"You don't know what you're saying."

"No," she said, studying his face for a moment. "I know exactly what I'm saying. Goodbye, Theodore. We're done here. I'm going to check in on our son now, and no, you can't follow me." She left without a backward glance. She hadn't used Gregor's name once. Not since he'd come home.

"Goodbye," Hessing said. There was nothing more to say.

*

Lund climbed the stairs laden with groceries. They were unexpectedly heavy. Mrs. Obry's apartment was at the top of the fifth floor walkup. He hadn't fully considered that when he offered to help carry her bags. His legs and arms ached in protest. He wasn't as young as he used to be. Mrs. Obry followed behind him and passed him on the landing to open the door. They entered her apartment and she ushered him into the kitchen.

"You're very kind," she said.

"Happy to help," he said, hiding a grimace. If she noticed, she stayed silent. "Did you need help with anything else, Mrs. Obry?"

"No," she said. "Thank you, Sergeant."

"I have a name besides Sergeant," he said softly. They stared at each other for a long moment. Lund felt as if they were on the brink of some invisible milestone. Finally she half smiled, half shrugged.

"Thank you...Frederick," she said. "And you can call me Johanna."

The two of them had known each other for nearly twenty-five years, and in all that time had never once called each other by their first names. It felt strangely awkward.

"How are you?" he asked unable to take the lingering silence any longer. "Really?"

She glanced down. "Not too bad, considering. Some days are better than others," she said.

"I thought I might..." Lund hesitated. "Look in on you," he said. "See how you're doing from time to time."

"I'd like that," she said after a long moment.

Lund smiled tentatively. "Good."

*

Heinrich stared across the street at the crumbling apartment building for a moment, and then double-checked the scribbled note in his hand. He was at the right address. He folded the note back into his pocket and headed out into the thoroughfare. Carts and carriages swerved out of the way. He received a number of heated glares and muffled curses, but they died down quickly when they saw him. It was a human neighborhood. He was probably the only faërie for blocks around; but he wasn't just any faërie, he was a troll. None of them could even hurt him and they all knew it. He continued uncaringly into the building without a backward glance. He was used to the bitter fear in their eyes.

An old man was sitting in the lobby reading his newspaper, with a cat on his lap. He glanced up at the troll lazily.

"You'll be wanting the second floor," he said. "Room 2C."

"How do you know?"

"Everyone wants Room 2C," said the old man. Then he grinned a toothless grin. "And she's waiting for you."

Heinrich shivered, but he supposed such things were to be expected from the Oracle.

He climbed up slowly. The stairs creaked ominously beneath his weight. The Oracle was a notorious recluse. He had called in countless favors to get the address, but now that he was here, he was nervous. Heinrich had never employed mystical guidance before. He avoided magic generally, as unreliable and bad for business, but something was happening in the city. The muse's warning still echoed in his mind, and if he was going to profit from the situation, or, at the very least, survive, then he needed to understand. The Oracle was his last hope to find another way.

He reached Room 2C and took a deep breath. The door opened before he could knock. An elderly woman peered up at him with a vacant, flighty expression. Her face was a tangle of wrinkles and laugh lines.

"You must be Heinrich," she said. "Come in. Come in."

Nonplused, he bent down and followed her into the apartment. It was shabby but homely. A number of newspaper clippings were pasted to the walls.

"Sit down," she said, waving her hands wildly. "Make yourself at home."

"Thank you, ma'am." He sank onto the couch, cautiously. It groaned in protest but held, barely. She sat across from him in a flurry of limbs.

"I'd offer you a cuppa," she said. "But I only have two teacups left, and you'd probably break them."

"Did you 'see' that?"

"Hmmm? Oh no, nothing like that." She glanced down pointedly at his giant stone-like hands. "Just a feeling."

"They say..." he paused uncertainly.

"Yes, dear?" she prompted.

"They say you can lie."

"So they do," she said, suddenly shrewd.

"And can you?"

"Yes." She answered promptly. There was nothing flighty about her now.

"I thought Oracles couldn't lie. That you were the mouthpiece of the Fates or something."

"Oracles can't lie," she agreed. "Just me."

"How?"

"With great difficulty." She studied him serenely. "But that's not why you're here."

"No," he said. "Something happened the other night at the Duke's. There was a...force, a presence. The faëries all felt it and Grand Master Undur practically collapsed."

"But that's not what's worrying you."

Heinrich looked away. "The muse said something. She must have felt it more keenly than the others."

The Oracle held up her hand. "I know what she said, or I can guess."

"I need to know what it means."

"You want to know what it means. There's a difference." She leaned forward. "Knowledge is not cheap," she said. "What would you offer me in return?"

"I am a very rich man," said the troll, "but I don't think you want money."

"Very good." She nodded, satisfied. "Most men try to buy my services. I thought you might be smarter than that."

"What would you have of me?" Heinrich asked.

"Well," she said brightly. "I could use a new tea set."

He cracked a smile. "Done."

"Excellent." She sighed. "Understand that what you do with this information is entirely up to you. I am not legally, mystically, or morally responsible."

"I understand."

"Very well." She studied him. "The City is awake."

"What does that mean?"

"Power," she replied. "Power the likes of which we have never seen. Not for centuries."

Heinrich paused taking that in. "What should I do?" he asked.

"I can't tell you that," said the Oracle, "but I can tell you that the city will burn if you fight, and it will burn if you don't. The peace you hope for is lost, and it's never coming back."

Heinrich closed his eyes and slumped back on the couch. He could feel his world slipping away. All his hard work had been for nothing, and in the end his decision had been made for him. He opened his eyes and found the Oracle studying him with sad, knowing eyes.

"I'm sorry," she said. "I wish there was another way."

"Me too," he said. "Me too."

*

The Countess was led blindfolded first through a number of winding alleys, and then down into the underground chambers and catacombs beneath the city. The ground inclined steeply and she stumbled a few times. The noise of the city above, the clatter of hooves and carts had been first muffled, then distant, and now it was gone, lost behind them in silence. They were too deep.

Her companions said nothing. The little hobgoblin in front of her whistled from time to time, but it echoed strangely in the close quarters, and the headless man behind stayed silent. Their path bent and curved. Sometimes she could have held out her arms and never touched a wall. Other times, it was impossible to stand upright, though doubtless the hobgoblin had no such difficulties.

She banged her head once or twice to the sound of his barking laughter.

The Countess could feel the weight of clay and brick above, and smell the stench of the sewers beneath her feet. Her dress was ruined, but Elise and Jules had warned her to procure a pair of sturdy boots, so she was prepared for that, at least. The walls were rotten brick and crumbling mortar. Fungi grew in the cracks. She could feel them beneath her fingers when she reached out to catch her balance. The air was heavy and moist, and unexpectedly warm. She occasionally struggled to breathe, but said nothing. They were waiting for her to falter, watching for weakness. She was certain of it. Just as she was certain they had taken more twists and turns than were strictly necessary even for secrecy's sake.

This was the city beneath the city, buried and decayed—a labyrinth of tunnels and passages, of chambers and dead ends. Rats scurried in the walls, and she thought she felt an eel swim past her feet. There were other things too, creeping nameless things that made their home in the dark, but she was not afraid. Not here.

Despite the blindfold and the myriad of twists and turns, the Countess knew exactly where she was. The answer came up from the rotting bricks and sludge, and down on the heavy air. The City was speaking to her, and she was learning more and more how to listen. The real difficulty would be in keeping her awareness hidden and her Witchling connections secret. Mr. Nix had seen through her easily, seen more, perhaps, than she knew, and that was troublesome. But there was only one Mr. Nix, and he was something else entirely.

They turned a corner and clambered, splashing, up a few steps and passed through a door. The air was freer suddenly, and filled with the sickly sweet smell of sorcery. The claustrophobia of the tunnels was gone and the Countess could hear the sound of voices. She recognized a few faërie dialects.

"We've arrived," Mr. Tarr said needlessly and removed her blindfold with a flourish.

The chamber was vast and cavernous, illuminated by hundreds of lanterns, dangling from the cave ceiling. Boxes stockpiled with weapons and cursed artifacts were crammed into every available alcove. Faëries—goblins and minotaurs, trolls and fauns, sprites, ghouls, and other nameless creatures—toiled in this subterranean world. They all had lean, hungry looks, and anger in their eyes. Not all their anger was directed at the Countess. Some of them were glaring at the hobgoblin. There was nothing friendly about it. Mr. Tarr seemed entirely unperturbed, though he bit back a whistle. Caldrons bubbled in one corner, and a whole section had been commandeered into a makeshift laboratory equal to that of the Imperial University in Amendroz. The Countess was impressed. This was a level of sophistication and enterprise far beyond what she had been told to expect. That would make some things easier, and others far more difficult.

Anselm and Droz, the homunculus and his birdlike lieutenant, were waiting for her. Anselm shook her hand, but Droz disdained such pleasantries. They offered her a seat on a dusty crate, with a mocking curtsy in a parody of manners. She thanked them for their generosity without a hint of irony. She knew how to dissemble, perhaps better than them.

From the corner of her eye she noticed a small box, hingeless and black. "Danger," the City whispered to her, but she could tell that on her own. She recognized the make of the box, felt the spells radiating out from it, and heard faint echoes of a song of deep slumber. There was something else. She could feel it reaching out—a great presence, ancient and vast. She had never felt the like.

"You wanted to meet us," said Anselm.

"Yes." She forced her attention away from the box. "I did."

"Why?"

"I wanted to offer you my assistance."

"Then join the Faërie Rights Association." Droz snorted.

"The Association is a joke," she said promptly. "A meaningless sop—well-meaning naiveté at best, and self-serving hypocrisy at worst. Anyone with eyes can see that," she said. "Or without." She nodded at Brunet.

Droz grunted. He couldn't disagree and that annoyed him most of all. Mr. Tarr leaned back against a wall and watched the proceedings with a growing smile. The Countess was proving more dangerous by the second. It was delightful, or would have been if not for a few nagging doubts.

"And you want to do more?" Anselm asked.

"I can do more."

"That's not an answer," said Droz sharply.

"I'm here," she replied. "I came alone. I wouldn't have done so otherwise."

"You could be a spy."

"I could be," she said calmly, "but I'm not."

"We have only your word on that."

"That's all you'll ever have unless you test me." She studied them. Droz was indignant and hostile, Mr. Tarr amused and barely containing his laughter. Brunet was unreadable without a face, though his body language suggested caution, and Anselm was watching, waiting, weighing her words, content to let the others question her.

"Test you?" asked Brunet. "You have given us nothing besides confidence in your own abilities. What exactly are you offering?"

"My services and an ear in the highest corridors of power."

"How could you have an ear in the corridors of power? You haven't even been in the city for a week."

"No," said the Countess, "I haven't, but I'm already sitting here before you. Give me another week and imagine where I'll be sitting then." No one said anything for a moment.

"We don't know you," said Anselm. "No one does. We don't even know where you come from. How can we trust you?"

"Because no one knows," she replied instantly. "That is my strength, but it's also your leverage. I'm placing myself wholly at your mercy—my life, my secret. You could destroy me at any time." It was a lie, or at least an exaggeration, but it was true enough as far as it went. She let that truth resonate through the air.

Droz was unconvinced, but Brunet made a rumbling grunt that echoed from his chest.

"I suppose we could at that," said Anselm. "But if we are to work together, if I'm to trust you even a little, there is one thing I need to know."

"Who I really am." She had been expecting that, and had a number of lies prepared.

"No," said Anselm, startling her. "I understand secrets and the need to keep them. There are many reasons to hide one's identity, not all of them dangerous. But I need to know what you want."

"Revenge," the Countess answered without a moment's hesitation. That was her Purpose. It flowed through her veins.

Anselm nodded, unsurprised.

"On who? The Duke?" Droz asked sharply. They all waited with baited breath, dimly aware that her answer could change everything. That this was a turning point for the Dissidents, for the Countess, for the city itself, but they waited in vain.

She would neither confirm nor deny it.

Part IV

The Victory Ball

19

CHAPTER NINETEEN

Inside the Armory, the 199th Annual Victory Ball was in full swing at last. This was the crowning glory of Lord Edward's family, a celebration and a memorialization. His ancestor had started a rebellion from within these very walls, and his heirs had nurtured that story into a legend; effectively, if not altogether subtly, welding themselves onto the city's mythos. In many ways it was the central pillar of their reign. None of the other Cities fetishized their Dukes to this degree. Not even the revolutionary Young Magicians, who had sparked the movement and eventually produced an Emperor, had been as mythologized as the First Lord of Talis.

Lord Edward was the custodian of that legend and he was in his element at the Ball. The Duke and Duchess were perfectly at home here, expertly weaving their way through the crowd, smiling and laughing, shaking hands, and slipping amongst the masked revelers and dignitaries. The great, the good, and the obscenely wealthy orbited around them in all their finery. Some were gentlemen decked out in coats and tails, with sashes draped over their shoulders. Others presented themselves in full martial glory, all epaulettes and polished medals.

The women glided with practiced skill, a whirligig of satins and colors, studded with pearls and gems gleaming even brighter than the soldiers' medals. In the minstrel's gallery a small orchestra moved smoothly from waltz to foxtrot to minuet and around again. Society reporters mingled with the crowd, taking photographs and scribbling notes. All of them were human. This was the Duke and Duchess' world, and they were lord and mistress of all they surveyed.

*

Outside the rain was starting to fall harder, and a cool wind was blowing. A cordon of police lined the perimeter, where a growing number of faëries gathered. Covét was among them, looking out of place in his faded professor's garb, but there was no mistaking the rage in his eyes. The crowd was bigger than he had expected.

They came in many shapes and hues; some gnarled and wizen, others tall and radiant. With hooves and scales and wings and horns they came—the minotaurs and goblin men, the elves and pixies, sprites and fauns, and other nameless things. They had long, sad faces and angry eyes. In their hands they carried cardboard signs and homemade banners. And in the cold and the rain they began to murmur and chant. Some called for equal rights. Others snarled anti-human slurs.

Most of them had no idea what was coming. Even Covét had

only the barest notion, but it was enough. He found Heinrich in the crowd. The troll was hard to miss even among this assembly.

"You came," Covét said.

"Yes," said Heinrich. "I came." His voice was tired and solemn.

"I didn't think you would."

The troll gave a creaking shrug. "In the end," he said, "there was no choice."

Covét studied him curiously, but Heinrich would say no more on the matter.

"Well, I'm glad," said Covét. "It's good to have at least one friend here with me."

He watched as the policemen on the line cast each other tense, nervous glances, and gripped their weapons tighter. There was violence in the air and they could sense it. Covét glanced up at Heinrich.

"I never thought we'd end up here," he said. "On the front lines, after all."

"Nor me," said the troll.

A black carriage pulled up outside the Armory, just too late to be called fashionable. Raske emerged wearing a dress coat, perhaps a size too large. At his side was Evá, demure as ever in her elegant little dress. At the sight of them, the faërie murmurs grew louder, angrier. None as angry as Covét.

Raske stared at the protesters, his face a combination of seething humiliation and despair. Evá followed his gaze.

"Forget them, Charlie," she said. "They are the past. Tonight we mingle. Tonight we survive. The Duke invited us."

"Yes, I know," he sighed. "I'll be a good little bootlicker."

"No," she said sharply. "Tonight you are Mr. Charles Raske, Esq., a city prosecutor and a gentlemen of high expectations, and you will act like it." She reached up and tilted his head down to hers. "For me."

He took a deep breath. "What would I do without you, Evá?" he asked.

"Starve," she replied matter-of-factly.

Arm in arm they turned inside and headed in toward the music and the lights. Behind them, the faërie chanting grew steadily louder.

*

The Countess admired herself in the mirror. It truly was an exquisite dress, and Elise had proved to have unexpected styling talents. Skills she'd picked up as a lady's maid on one of her previous assignments. The Countess had never felt so refined and sophisticated. She was accustomed to tattered hand-me-downs, the relics of old glories. This was her first Ball, her first party of any kind, and she swallowed down her nerves. She needed to make a good impression, to seem as though she belonged. She had been constantly drilled on etiquette and proper lady-like behavior, while her Purpose forever reminded her that she was better than them. Tonight would be the first test, but the frills and finery were merely distractions. There were other, far greater, worries to concern her.

The City was humming inside her, warning of a danger she couldn't quite understand. Memories, thoughts, sensations flickered through her. They threatened to overcome her, and they still might. Coiled at the core of her, the Purpose murmured in anticipation. Something was coming.

"You're going to be late, my lady," Elise said. She was hovering in the background, admiring her handiwork.

"Fashionably so," the Countess replied.

"If you say so, my lady." The Countess spared Elise a sideways glance. Her face was blank, but her eyes twinkled slightly. She was becoming bolder, more familiar. The Countess treasured that. Her great aunt would have considered it presumption, but she saw it as a sign of loyalty.

"Shall we?" The Countess headed out into the main room where Jules was waiting. He stared at her, stuttering for a moment.

"Well?" she asked.

"G-green," he managed. Elise nudged him sharply in the ribs.

"Forgive my brother, " she said, but the Countess waved it away.

"There is nothing to forgive." Her face turned solemn. "Be careful tonight," she said. "Both of you. Something's going to happen. I don't know what, but I would hate to see either of you hurt."

The siblings exchanged a wordless conversation. "We know the risks, my lady," Jules said. His face was still red, but there was determination in his eyes. "And we know how to stay unseen."

"But thank you for your concern," Elise said. "You should be careful too, my lady."

The Countess smiled at them and the gratitude in their eyes. No one had ever showed them any concern, certainly not her great aunt. She had their loyalty before, but now she had their devotion. Her Purpose murmured its approval, but she didn't care. She was already fond of Elise, and Jules' obvious infatuation was flattering. She had never had friends before. It would be a shame to lose them. A few doubts whispered in the back of her mind, but she pushed them aside. She had a Ball to attend.

*

Sergeant Lund huddled against the wall. He was cold and wet.

The rain was dripping from his helmet and down his neck. He shivered and pulled his coat tighter. Lund had been assigned to guard one of the back entrances into the Armory by Hessing himself. It was a lonely, miserable job, and promised to be a lonely, miserable night. At least he was away from the noise and the throng, but he would rather have been inside with Inspector Erkel. Guarding the gentry while they wined and dined and congratulated themselves was not his idea of a good time, but at least it would have been warm and dry.

He was partially protected from the elements. A great gargoyle loomed above him, though thankfully it was dormant. Lund's fingers shook slightly as he struggled to roll up a cigarette. In the distance he could hear a dull roar. The faëries were chanting, spoiling for a fight. Maybe it was time they got one. Poor old Obry. He hadn't deserved to die like that, and the bomber was still roaming free, taunting them with his damned whistling. They hadn't caught the Ripper yet, either, but Lund didn't care about that any more than Erkel did. He finished rolling his cigarette and took a long, warming drag. He coughed.

"Good evening." The voice startled him from his reverie, and he snapped to attention when he saw who it was.

"Sir," he sputtered. "Sorry, sir, I..."

Hessing waved his apology away. "Never mind, Sergeant. I understand perfectly." The Commandant was imposing in his full regalia—freshly pressed uniform and cape. "Long night."

"Yes, sir," Lund agreed.

"Can't be helped." Hessing reached into his pocket and pulled out a cigar. "Would you mind if I joined you?"

"Not at all sir," Lund replied, as if he had any choice in the matter. Hessing flashed him a friendly grin and lit his cigar with a flourish. They stood there a moment in expectant silence.

"Reminds me of back in the day, when I guarded the Old Duke, but I suppose that was before your time," Hessing said. Lund remained silent. "You were with me in '86, weren't you? When we arrested the rebels?" Hessing smiled sadly. "The good old days."

"Yes sir," Lund said mildly. He remembered the 'good old days' very differently, but he had been amply rewarded in the years since.

"Not as young as we used to be, Sergeant," Hessing continued. He paused and glanced down at his companion. "Why don't you go take a walk, stretch your legs a bit." His gaze was suddenly sharp and demanding. "Say five minutes or so."

"Five minutes," said Lund. "Thank you, sir." He saluted. He'd known this was coming since Hessing arrived in person. His posting made perfect sense now. It wasn't the first time they'd done this dance. He was curious, but kept it to himself. Hessing had his fingers in too many pies, and Lund had made it this far by never questioning him.

Hessing took a long drag, and waited until Lund had disappeared into the night. Faithful, dependable Sergeant Lund. He needed more like him. Finally he signaled into the darkness. Nothing. He turned and started. Mr. Tarr was standing right behind him. The hobgoblin was staring up at him with a far too innocent smile; in his hands was the ominous black box.

"What's in there?" Hessing asked.

"Don't worry, Commandant, sir, I promise it's not a bomb." Mr. Tarr grinned. "Not exactly."

"Now see here, that's not very reassuring," Hessing rose to his full imposing height. "I'm going out on a limb here for you and your master…"

Mr. Tarr was unimpressed. "I have no master," he said. "You, on the other hand, have two. Choose. Now. And if you're looking for reassurance, just think of your son." He paused. "Now then, shall we proceed?"

Hessing glared down at him, but his anger was hollow and they both knew it. He sighed and pulled out his set of keys. "Quickly," he said, unlocking the door. "And I never want to see you again."

"Never is a very long time," said Mr. Tarr, then slipped inside with a mocking whistle. Hessing slammed the door behind him and turned the key.

Lund returned a few moments later.

"Well, Sergeant," Hessing said. "I suppose I should head inside myself. Join the party."

"Yes, sir," Lund replied. His mind was a jumble. He hadn't gone far, and on his way back he had caught sight of the small figure talking to Hessing, but it couldn't be. The hobgoblin. The shabby coat. The whistling. All the witness statements had agreed. Hessing had to know that.

"Goodnight, Sergeant."

"Goodnight, sir." Lund saluted, but inside he was reeling. The hobgoblin had killed one of their own, one of Hessing's favorites. The man Lund knew would never let that stand. The Commandant repaid loyalty with loyalty—that's why Lund had stayed with him so long. It didn't make any sense. Erkel would understand. He was the clever one. Lund clung to that thought. There was an explanation. There had to be.

Across the street, a figure slipped away in the darkness, a camera under one arm, protected from the rain. He had seen what he needed to see, but his errand was far from over. His master wanted the pictures developed and delivered tonight. Only then would his debt be repaid.

CHAPTER TWENTY

Borchard-Márai was impressed. The Imperial Envoy considered himself a keen student of political theater and the Victory Ball was one of the finest examples he had ever seen. The Duke and Duchess were a formidable partnership, both of them virtuosos at playing the crowd. There was a reason that Lord Edward had long been considered the strongest of the Dukes, even in the face of the recent difficulties. It was one thing to read the files and hear the stories, but witnessing them in person was another matter entirely. They hadn't lost their touch, for better or for worse. Borchard-Márai would report as much to the Emperor. It should help soothe his mind, although there were other more long-term concerns that would still need to be addressed.

The Duke broke away from a number of local nobles and approached him.

"An impressive performance, your grace," said Borchard-Márai.

"Thank you, your excellency." The Duke smiled politely. "But the speech is still hours away. That is when the real performance begins."

"I shall look forward to it." The envoy bowed his head. "I see Mr. Raske has joined us this evening."

Charles and Evá Raske were standing apart, looking stiff and grim, obviously ostracized from the festivities. A number of young officials with sharp faces were circling them like jackals.

"Yes." The Duke's smile was entirely genuine this time. "I invited The Honorable Charles Raske. It seemed the least I could do."

"I see." Borchard-Márai raised an eyebrow.

"Yes," said the Duke. "But I believe I shall leave him to his own devices just a little while longer. Now, if you would excuse me, your excellency."

"Of course," Borchard-Márai said, frowning. The Duke was up to something; he would have to discover what it was before he returned to the capital.

*

It was nearly midnight when Hessing appeared at the Duchess' side with a young woman in a green dress. Lady Anne turned from Grand Master Undur in relief.

"Theodore. It's been too long," she said with only half-feigned enthusiasm. Of all the grabbing, grasping, bloated egos there, Hessing was the closest to a true friend. He had the double advantage of being both useful and loyal. "I'm sorry that Olivia couldn't make it."

"She would have come, but in the circumstances," he said gruffly. "I hope you understand."

"Perfectly," she said.

"You've been very kind." He cleared his throat. "But I wondered if I might present Lady Antoinette, Countess of Wyman-Straus."

The woman at his side curtseyed gracefully. "Delighted to meet you, your grace."

"Her husband and I went to school together," Hessing continued, "many moons ago."

"And where is Count Wyman-Straus?" the Duchess asked, turning to the Countess.

"He passed away last winter, your grace."

"I apologize," Lady Anne said with a suitably contrite expression. "I did not mean to rake over fresh wounds."

"It's quite alright," the Countess said with a smile. "You couldn't have known."

Her smile faltered slightly as she noticed a familiar figure watching her from the sidelines, still dapper and immaculate in white tie and tails. Mr. Nix gave her a slight nod. He had performed his part exactly. The introduction had been made. She owed him a favor now. That was a problem for another time, however. She returned his nod, but he had already disappeared into the throng.

*

Mr. Nix found Evá Raske lingering on the sidelines, waiting for him. He followed her gaze. Raske was surrounded by a circle of young men—ministers and undersecretaries—all festooned with the sashes and ribbons of rank. Raske was growing increasingly red and flustered, but there was a bitter anger in his eyes. The men erupted suddenly in a burst of laughter.

"She's your 'muse', is she?" chortled one of the festooned ministers.

"How romantic." Another sniggered.

"Perhaps she's why he's been such a miserable failure."

The two observers exchanged glances. "He seems to be experiencing difficulties," Mr. Nix commented.

"Character building," Evá answered evenly. "When the time comes, he'll hold his nerve. Faërie Rights just wasn't the meal ticket he'd hoped for."

Suddenly, the crowd circling Raske parted, and the Duke emerged. The Duke and Raske stared at each other for a long moment, and the onlookers held their breath.

"Bow," Evá muttered to herself. "Smile and bow."

Finally, Raske gave a stiff bow and Evá let out a sigh of relief. Mr. Nix gave her an amused glance. "Right on schedule," he said.

"It was a good speech," said the Duke. "You acquitted yourself well, quite well."

Raske blinked at that and swallowed back an angry response. "Thank you, your grace," he managed.

"Good." The Duke nodded. He had watched the young man reign in his emotions, with approval and private amusement. "Very good. I believe you'll go far, Mr. Raske, and I know that I would much rather have you working for me than against me."

Watching, Evá blinked in surprise. "You were right," she whispered.

"Did you doubt me?" asked Mr. Nix.

"No. Of course not. I just didn't truly expect him to move so quickly."

"He's under siege and he has always understood your husband.

He'll make good use of him. I know Lord Edward quite well." Mr. Nix smiled.

"Apparently so."

"Now, I hope your dear husband will have more of a stomach for criminal law than he did for faërie politics. You received the file, I assume?"

"Under the door, as expected."

"Everything was in order?"

"Photographs, transcripts, financial documents," Evá listed. "Everything an ambitious young lawyer might need for the case of his career, even sooner than anticipated."

"Excellent," said Mr. Nix. "And here is one final piece of evidence." He slipped her a photograph subtly. She quickly hid it in her dress.

"I hope the timing will not be a problem," he continued. "As his 'muse', you came to me highly recommended. I was told you could handle men like him."

"I can," she replied without hesitation. He studied her, looking for any hint of doubt. There was none.

"Good," said Mr. Nix. "Now handle him."

*

As the witching hour approached, the music slowed to a halt. The Duke strode up onto the rostrum to give his annual Victory Ball speech, as he and his ancestors before him had done every year of their reign.

"Ladies and gentlemen," he said into the sudden silence. "Thank you all for coming to the 199th Annual Victory Ball!" There was polite applause and a handful of drunken cheers. "We are gathered here to celebrate one hundred and ninety-nine years of peace and liberty; one hundred and ninety-nine years of prosperity; one hundred and ninety-nine years since Lord Frederick the Liberator cast down the Tyranny of Witches forever!" The crowd roared its approval. The Duke smiled, basking in the applause, but slowly, sporadically, the cheers faded, and heads began to turn. Then the whispering started, confused and nervous.

The crowd parted uncertainly and a figure emerged. He was a little hobgoblin man carrying a small metal box in his hands. The whispers died down and everyone watched in stunned disbelief. The hobgoblin grinned at the crowd, daring them to stop him.

He made his ponderous way to the very center of the room and set the box down, gently. For a long moment, nobody moved. Nobody dared to breathe, and then, as if of its own accord, the box sprung open with a creak. Mr. Tarr stood utterly still, glancing around at the watching, expectant crowd. He paused, as if for dramatic effect, and then he spoke three words into the silence.

"Faërie freedom now!" he cried.

And all hell broke loose.

CHAPTER TWENTY-ONE

A tentacle emerged from the box, impossibly large, black and terribly strong. It waved about cautiously, stretching and testing the air. Another tentacle followed, and then another and another. For a moment the assembled crowd remained unmoving, as if spellbound. They stared up at the thrashing, searching tentacles with disbelieving faces—the Duke, the Duchess, Hessing, Raske; even the Countess could not quite believe her eyes at first.

She had known there was something inside the box, something ancient and dangerous, but had thought she would have time to study it and prepare. There had been no inkling, no premonition of an attack. For the first time since she had come into her power, the Countess had been completely and utterly surprised. It was not a pleasant feeling.

The City had spoken to her of many secrets and hidden threats, some barely decipherable, others dead and buried along with their keepers. The City had little conception of time. But there had been no mention of this, nothing, not a hint or a whisper. She did not believe It would have willfully kept anything from her, which meant the City had somehow been kept silent, or ignorant. She was not sure which was more disturbing.

Someone in the crowd let out a shriek and the strange pall was broken. The yelling began and the great, the good, and the obscenely wealthy began to run. There was chaos—people jammed together, tripping over gowns, jostling, pushing, screaming—as they fought their way toward the door, any door. All that mattered was getting out, getting away. The tentacles reared back at the sudden commotion. Perhaps they heard the noise, or perhaps instead they sensed the fear wafting on the air. They quivered in excitement.

Then, suddenly, a twisted, misshapen monster exploded from the box in a writhing, ravenous mass of tentacles and teeth. It rose to its full height, higher and higher, until it crashed through the arched ceiling into the night air, sending chunks of marble and concrete hurtling down onto the people below.

It was a Creature from the Depths, a Monster of the Ancient World, revealed at last in all its terrible beauty. There were tentacles missing and others were torn and mangled, the scars of titanic battles fought long ago in the lonely places beneath the waves. It had been called from its home by the old songs, herded by mermen, caged and left hungry. The undines had spelled it down to fitful sleep, but it was awake now—and raging.

*

Outside, Covét and Heinrich stared up in shock. The Creature was looming out of the Armory, reaching up into the night sky.

The mob fell silent. The chants and slurs died down. The minotaurs and goblin men, the elves and pixies, sprites and fauns, the policemen and bystanders were all held in rapt attention. It was a dreadful sight, and beautiful. No one who saw could help being moved, and frightened. Covét had spent a lifetime scribbling and agitating, hating the humans for taking the wonder from the world, and here at last was a true wonder, deep within the city walls. They were kin, him and the Creature, separated by an unbridgeable gulf, but kin nonetheless. Covét had never felt so small or so proud.

Then they heard the screams. People came pouring out onto the street. Humans in their uniforms and sashes, shouting, crying, pushing, and afraid. So afraid.

"Anselm told us that we couldn't miss the signal," Heinrich rumbled.

"Well," Covét nodded up at the troll, "he wasn't lying."

Above them the Creature gave a mangled roar and there was the sound of distant gunshots. Covét took a deep breath. This was it. Now or never. He could feel the hate boiling inside him, decades of pent up rage, and something else. For the first time in many years, he felt the treacherous hint of hope.

"Faërie freedom now!" he cried and the old faun charged at the nearest policeman headfirst, Heinrich right behind him.

*

The Duke stood alone on the dais in the ruins of his speech, staring up uncomprehendingly at the growing colossus. His mind rebelled at the sight. This could not be happening, not here, not now. He had never heard or read of anything like this. No one had, not for millennia, not since before even the Time of the Witches.

"Your grace!" A few plainclothes detectives had managed to

summon the presence of mind to try and spirit the Duke away. "We have to get you to safety!"

They grabbed him and half ran, half dragged him, shielding him with their bodies. He followed them willingly at first, but the falling debris shook him from his stupor.

"My wife," he said franticly. "We need to find my wife!"

The detectives exchanged nervous glances. "Don't worry, sir," said one.

"Her own security will have her well in hand," said the other. The Duke was far from reassured. It didn't look to him as if anyone had the situation well in hand.

"Anne!" he screamed into the noise and confusion. "Anne!"

He glanced around wildly, catching sight of Borchard-Márai's Imperial white uniform, and Hessing looking as bereft as the Duke felt, but he couldn't find his wife. She had been standing just below the dais when he'd started the speech, but she was gone now, lost in the crowd.

He tried to turn back, but the detectives wouldn't let him and they had been joined by a handful of soldiers, members of the Ducal Guard.

"Our priority is your survival, your grace," a soldier said, and they marched him out of the hall, still calling desperately for his wife.

*

Hessing had somehow survived the immediate chaos. His thoughts were whirring dangerously, and there was a terrible pit in his stomach. Mr. Tarr was gone, leaving the Creature to wreak destruction in his wake. Hessing searched the room wildly. Mr. Nix had remained, leaning against a pillar, seemingly as unruffled as ever. Sensing Hessing's gaze, he turned and regarded him with a provocatively mild expression, but his eyes were filled with vicious laughter. He had planned this, all of this. Hessing was sure of it. He wanted to kill the smug little man, wanted to tear him apart with his bare hands, but he couldn't. The thought of Gregor was always on his mind. Besides, Hessing had other concerns at the moment—namely survival.

He had faced monsters and faëries before and lived to tell the tale, but this Creature was something else entirely. They needed to contain it somehow, trap it, and kill it. A few policemen and guards had taken up positions amidst the rubble, and had opened fire on the creature. Inspector Erkel was among them, shouting orders, stiffening their resolve. Hessing knew he could be relied upon to hold the line. Erkel gave Hessing a brisk nod from across the room. Hessing returned it and then continued his survey. He saw Borchard-Márai cowering in the rubble, burrowing beneath a fallen soldier trying to hide. Hessing ran over to him and crouched down beside him. He plucked the rifle from the soldier. He aimed and fired. It was hard to miss at this range. He fired again. The crisis gave him something else to focus on besides his guilt.

The Creature was raked by gunfire. Bullets tore into it, spilling black, inky blood, but that only seemed to enrage the beast. It responded with teeth and tentacles, striking blindly, knocking down columns, gnawing, searching, killing. A tentacle found one unlucky soldier and sent him flying headlong into the far wall with a sickening crunch. Hessing joined Erkel, pinned down behind a pillar. They exchanged identical glances, the same thought clear on their faces. There was nothing they could do. They needed more men, more firepower, perhaps even magic if the Duke allowed.

"Fall back!" Hessing shouted. He reached down and pulled

Borchard-Márai to his feet. "We need to fall back!" Then he turned and ran. Erkel and the others followed him slowly, stumbling through the rubble, trying desperately to avoid the Creature.

*

Not everyone was able to escape. Lady Anne was still trapped within, the Countess by her side. Their dresses were caked with grime, and they were covered with cuts and bruises, but they were alive. For now.

The Creature roared, knocking over a column with a stray tentacle. As it came crashing down, Lady Anne was directly in its path. The Countess hesitated but there was no time for calculation. She muttered a spell softly under her breath. It was a simple spell, small, barely worth noticing, nothing compared to the storm she had summoned the night before, but after days of restraint it was a blissful relief. Her power surged through her veins and leapt from her body eagerly with invisible fingers to clutch the falling pillar.

It shattered under the Countess's will and she reached down to pull Lady Anne out of the way. She had tried to be gentle, but objects were so breakable and the Creature's very presence bred decay and rot. She looked around anxiously. Her plan required secrecy. Her Purpose demanded it. Lady Anne was lying stunned and bleeding. She didn't seem to have noticed anything, and the room was empty except for the dead and the dying. The Countess was safe, except for the Creature, of course.

It gave another primal roar and she turned to face it, gathering her power. There was no other choice.

A spare tentacle struck at her lazily, but she batted it away. The tentacle reared back, puzzled, then attacked again. There was a resounding clang as it struck an invisible shield. She had summoned it quickly about herself, weaved it from thought and enchantment.

Suddenly the Creature was upon her in a torrent of tentacles and teeth. Her hastily composed shield shattered like glass under the sudden onslaught. The Countess stumbled back, then rose to her full height. She was a witch and this was her city. She held it inside her now and she would protect it, whatever the cost—and there would be a cost.

In that moment, though she had not grown an inch, she seemed as tall as any giantess and her power burnt cold around her. She stood revealed at last in all her might. Witches were human once, perhaps, or nearly human, but living in the Faërie Lands, practicing magic for untold generations, had changed them into something else, something colder, wilder.

The Countess felt the Creature truly notice her for the first time. It turned the crushing weight of its attention upon her, and for a moment she strove with it, armed with certainty and purpose. But the Creature was too strong, too vast, a relic of creation's more chaotic and frightening visage. She crumbled in on herself and was sent sprawling. The tentacles followed greedily, prepared to devour her whole, but they fell back suddenly.

Mr. Nix was standing perfectly still over her, an island of tranquility amidst the destruction, perfectly untouched. He looked down at her curiously. She could feel him in her mind.

"I said you were an arrogant little thing," he said. "But I didn't think you'd be foolish enough to contend with the Creature." Mr. Nix gave her a knowing smile. "Especially not with an incomplete Merging in your head."

"I don't know what you're talking about," she said.

"I saw geography and memory in your eyes," he said. "And I know an invocation when I feel one."

"What else did you see?"

"Don't worry," Mr. Nix said. "Nothing I hadn't seen already." The Countess was not reassured.

Then Mr. Nix turned to face the hulking, tentacled monstrosity. He reached out his hand and a few tentacles were drawn to him. They approached him not in rage, but inquisitively. They nipped at his fingers, almost playfully.

"Hello, old friend," said Mr. Nix. "It's been a long time." He murmured softly and caressed the tentacles gently, petting them. "There, there, it'll all be over soon. I'll take you home, to the Old Sea," he said."You'd like that, wouldn't you?"

The Creature gave a mournful call, the likes of which had never before been heard on dry land. The whole world shuddered at the weight of its sorrow and longing. Its loneliness clawed through the Countess, washing away all thought, all emotion, all purpose. She realized with a start that she was crying, but tears could not express the depth of feeling. The Creature was so alone, so terribly alone.

"I know," Mr. Nix said. "But the Others are waiting for you. You won't have to be alone again." He continued stroking the tentacles tenderly, almost consolingly. "I promise."

And then he spoke a Word and the Word was a Name. It was a Name that the human mouth had not been meant to utter; yet it rolled from his tongue easily. The sound of it echoed through the ruins of the ballroom, filling it with a presence as vast as the Creature itself. It was as if the air had gone out from the room. The Countess could feel the potency of the Name throbbing through her ribcage, heard the echo of years beyond count, and felt the shadow of mortality like a sliver in her heart. She hid her eyes and covered her ears. Even the glorious, burning Purpose inside her seemed to retreat and bury itself in the farthest corners of her self. It was too much.

Then that writhing, ravenous mass, that Creature from the Depths, that Monster of the Ancient World let loose a heartbreaking wail of such abandonment, and then collapsed, as if its strings had been cut, down toward the street. The force of its falling broke through the outer wall in a shower of masonry and glass and the street cracked beneath it. Hundreds of humans and faëries were crushed to death, unable to escape in time. The Creature lay dead in the ruins of the Armory. A last few tentacles twitched and then were still.

Inside, Mr. Nix stared down at the creature. For a brief moment his face lost its customary composure, replaced with an expression of infinite yet fleeting sadness. "I'm sorry," he said. "Forgive me."

And for the moment all was silent. All was peaceful.

Part V

The Riots

CHAPTER TWENTY-TWO

The whole front of the Armory was shattered. The outer wall had crumbled beneath the Creature's weight. The world had become a confused hell of crushed stones and death. Sergeant Lund pulled himself to his feet. It was still raining. He ached. His bones had been jarred and his head was spinning. It should have been a lonely, quiet night, but first Hessing and the hobgoblin, and now this. It didn't take much to connect the dots, and Lund did not like the picture it was making. He tried to blink the world back into focus. But this was not the time for those thoughts. He wasn't the only one stirring.

The faëries were starting to climb back up as well. He didn't know how it had started, but the cordon had been breached. After months, even years of pent-up tensions, fighting had finally broken out, and after a brief lull it was starting up again without mercy—humans and faëries biting, clawing, stabbing, and shooting each other. Lund hadn't been in a brawl like this in decades. He hadn't missed it.

A spindly-armed faërie with sunken eyes and long, sharp nails flew at Lund out of the dust, hissing and slashing. Lund tumbled out of the way. His revolver was spent, and he'd lost his baton earlier in the night. He tried to throw a punch, but his opponent was fast, too fast. It ducked and sliced and then there was pain. Lund's uniform was torn and bloody.

The faërie wasted no time pressing its advantage. It was on top of Lund in an instant; its long fingers around his throat, and nails burying into his flesh. Lund struggled, but to no avail. The grip was too tight. He fumbled blindly with his right hand and found a fallen shard of masonry.

He grabbed it, desperately, and struck the faërie, hard. Its grip barely loosened. Lund was choking, starting to feel weak. He struck again—once, twice. Finally, it let go and fell back. Lund followed, no longer slow and achy but enraged. He raised the stone high with both hands and brought it down on the faërie's skull, over and over again. He didn't stop. He couldn't stop. Not until the skull was bashed in, and the faërie's face unrecognizable.

He rose unsteadily to his feet, covered in blood, some of it his own, and glanced around. The others weren't faring so well. Most of the police force that he could see was dead or dying. He wouldn't be far behind.

Lund turned and gave an audible sigh of relief. The man before him was a mess. His uniform was tattered and covered in dust and blood. His face was bruised and bleeding and there was a piece of shrapnel in his arm, but it was Erkel and he was alive. Lund had feared the worst. He controlled himself with difficulty.

"Sir," he said.

"Lund," Erkel nodded. "It's good to see you."

"You're alive. I thought that Creature had…"

"Yes, I'm alive. Barely." Erkel grimaced. "And the night isn't over yet."

"There's something I have to tell you," said Lund. "Something you need to know."

"Not now," said Erkel. "The Commandant has ordered everyone to fall back and regroup at Headquarters."

"Hessing!"

"Yes, he's made it too, so far at least."

Lund shook his head. "You have to listen."

"No time." Erkel said. "We have to get out of here first."

It was hard to argue with that. Lund peered into the gloom. He could see a troll leaving a trail of destruction that belayed its gentlemanly attire, and what appeared to be an elderly faun in a berserker rage was following in his wake.

Lund nodded. Suspicions could wait.

*

They ran and kept on running. Blindly, desperately. The image of the Creature still loomed in their minds, all teeth and tentacles. Raske held Evá's hand tightly, so tightly that he threatened to break it, but she didn't complain. She was clutching him just as tightly. It had been a madhouse of scrambling and screaming. People had climbed over each other, trampled one another to death in an attempt to get out. Raske still wasn't sure how they'd escaped. He had been certain that this was the end, but suddenly a path had opened up through the crowd. Someone had smashed a window, and Raske followed, dragging Evá behind. It wasn't until they were outside that he realized who it was, the last people he wanted to see—Clarke and Pullman.

The old men had a finely developed survival instinct, though Raske himself was no better. They had turned to see who had followed them out, and Pullman smirked slightly at Raske in dark amusement. Clarke had smiled his most dangerously friendly smile, but whatever he had intended to say was lost. More people were streaming out but the Creature had not halted its attack. The four of them ran, staying together more out of circumstance than inclination. If he was honest, Raske wouldn't have minded feeding Clarke and Pullman to the Creature himself.

He quickly realized, however, that escaping from the Armory wasn't enough. The whole city had been engulfed in chaos. The faëries, the ones he and the others had tried so hard to court, were attacking. His dreams were in ruins, but the only thing that mattered now was keeping him and Evá alive.

"Wait a moment," Clarke said. The portly man was panting heavily. "I just need a moment to catch my breath." Pullman came to a halt beside his colleague. He looked little better. They were both too old for running.

Raske hesitated. He knew what Evá wanted him to do—leave the old men to their fate. Her eyes were pleading with him, urging him onwards. He was tempted, but found that he couldn't. They would die if he left them. He could see them beaten and humiliated, but not dead. That was more than he could do. He wasn't that vicious.

"All right," he said. "But we can't linger for too long." Pullman nodded his thanks. Raske couldn't look at his wife. He knew he would see only disappointment, the same disappointment he felt. He wished he was strong enough for this.

The four of them waited in awkward silence, huddled behind a barrel. There was nothing for them to say, and no time to say it.

An ogre suddenly charged out of one of the side streets followed by a ragged band of fauns, satyrs, and imp men. It gave a roar when it saw them. Raske rose quickly, the others close behind. The small mob moved to surround them and Raske wavered.

Clarke didn't hesitate, however. The sudden danger had revived him. He grabbed Raske and shoved him into the ogre. In the confusion, he and Pullman were gone. Raske scrambled to his feet and pulled Evá behind him, cursing Clarke.

The ogre charged.

*

Lord Edward hadn't felt this panicked in years, not since the revolt against his father when the rioters had penetrated into the Mansion itself. The detectives had half-dragged him from the Ball into an armored carriage surrounded by Ducal Guards. Then they had fought their way out through the crowd with their sabers drawn and pistols bared. They had left more than a few dead faëries behind them in the street, those foolish enough to try and take their anger out on the Duke.

As the carriage climbed the hill up toward Auberon Square, he turned back and peered out the window. He could see fires in the city illuminating the night sky in a burnt orange, and even in the Old Quarter the carriage thundered past looters and isolated fighting. This was worse than he'd ever imagined. He'd felt the rumblings, of course, spent many sleepless nights plotting and scheming as he felt the city slowly slip from his grasp. But someone had unleashed a Creature of the Ancient World against his city, against him. Even when the Young Magicians and the

Witches had threatened to tear reality apart under the weight of their magical war, they had never dared unleash such a thing in the Cities. No one could have been meant to survive that, him least of all. Someone had changed the rules.

Finally, he reached the Ducal Mansion. The gates shut behind them quickly. Soldiers were running about the grounds, taking up positions, and setting up artillery and rifle pits. The Duke was hustled inside, up the great marble staircase and into the East Wing. A long hall had been commandeered years ago, transformed into the most important instrument of the Duke's rule—the telegraph room.

The noise and clatter was practically deafening. There were four long tables, almost the length of the room, covered with telegraph machines and typewriters. Someone had found an old map of the city and hung it on the wall. Officers, government ministers, clerks and even Grand Master Undur were all clustered around it. Everyone stood when the Duke entered, but he waved them back to work. This was no time for formalities.

"Any word on my wife?" he asked.

"No, your grace," one of the officers answered.

"Then get word," he said.

"Yes, your grace." The officer saluted and sprang into action, issuing orders left and right, but Lord Edward's mind had already moved on. This was the most dangerous moment of his reign.

"Now," he said, "what do we know?"

One of the operators, Mr. Oliver, a dusty civil servant with sharp eyes, bowed. "We have received unconfirmed reports that the Creature that attacked the Ball is dead."

"Dead?" Lord Edward was surprised. "How?" He turned to

Grand Master Undur. His ceremonial robes and sashes were tattered but he was unharmed. He shrugged almost apologetically.

"It wasn't us, your grace," he said. "My magicians and I know better than to engage in open magical combat without your permission."

"Even when that Thing is trying to kill you?"

"Especially then," said Undur. "That was a Leviathan, or something like it. It can make magic..." He paused. "Unpredictable."

Lord Edward nodded. He understood the theory. Every child of the Cities knew the dire consequences of thoughtless magic, but he couldn't help but notice that the Grand Master and his entourage had somehow reached the Mansion before him.

"So what did kill It?"

"Unknown, your grace." Mr. Oliver turned back to the map on the wall. "There have also been reports of rioting in the Faërie Quarter, and a number of isolated incidents throughout the city." He pointed to a number of places on the map. "There are more coming in by the minute."

"Thank you, Mr. Oliver."

"Your grace."

Lord Edward turned back toward the clattering mass of telegraphs and operators. He was searching for someone and found him in the back at the far table. The operator was a young, weedy-looking man with darting eyes and quick fingers, but he was discrete. He started slightly when he felt the Duke looming behind him.

"I need you to send a coded message upriver to Silver Point."

"Of course, your grace." His fingers were immediately at the ready. He knew all the codes and ciphers by rote.

"To Brigadier Kronberger. Stop," Lord Edward whispered. "Rioting in the streets. Stop. You are ordered to proceed immediately. Stop."

Clack, clack, clack went the operator's hands. "Message sent, your grace," he said after a moment.

"Good." The Duke patted him on the shoulder, and then headed back to the others.

"Send someone to Police Headquarters," he ordered. "Find out where Hessing is, or if he's even still alive. And the envoy." He'd forgotten about him. "The Emperor won't be pleased if his cousin is killed on our watch."

"Your grace?" Grand Master Undur approached him flanked by two of his adepts. "Let us help," he said. "We could not risk magic against the Creature, but faëries are a different matter. They have sneered at our College for generations. Let us show them what human magic can do."

Lord Edward studied him for a moment. He saw bitterness in the old magician and eagerness, but also calculation. "No," he said. "Not yet. Your point earlier was well taken. Magic is a risk."

The Grand Master grimaced. Undur knew his flight from the Ball would be remembered, and he knew he needed to counterbalance any hint of cowardice before it was too late. "Your grace," he tried again. "The Quarter is where their power is strongest. They have crones there and spirits and elementals. Even your Guard will need assistance."

"Perhaps," Lord Edward allowed. "But there has been no magical combat inside our city walls for almost two hundred years. We will try more terrestrial methods first."

"I understand, your grace." Undur and his men withdrew in a

huff. Lord Edward let them go. Magicians were a temperamental lot, and he didn't have time to soothe their egos.

The situation was even more of a mess than he had believed. An attack on the Ball followed immediately by rioting across the city. That couldn't be a coincidence. There was coordination here. This had been planned in detail. His mind was whirring through the possibilities, but he kept circling back to his wife. He had left her. She would be fine, he told himself over and over, with as much sincerity as he could muster. He almost believed himself.

*

The Dissidents came roaring out of the secret places of the city from the sewers and forgotten doors, up ladders and tunnels into the waiting night. They had prepared their weapons and curses, made their plans and nursed their long grievances underground. There were hundreds of them, thousands, criminals and radicals hand-picked for their devotion and savagery. They carried their guns and torches aloft and a select few bore the fruits of their subterranean labors—bombs and explosives mixed with magic, along with cursed objects and charms to spread disease and fear to their enemies. Now at last their time had come.

Anselm was at their head. He had no guns or knives in his hands. He carried no bomb or hex. Those around him, they were his weapon. They were his curses. He had nurtured them, fed their hatreds, shaped their plans. At every street he passed, more came. They left their shops and hovels. They left their houses and beds. They grabbed whatever weapons they could find—a shovel or a kitchen knife—or just themselves with their claws and horns and teeth. They had made no plans but they too had grievances aplenty, and in this mob they saw their chance.

Droz, Brunet and others fanned out into side streets calling loudly for all to join them and fight. It seemed to Anselm that the Faërie Quarter had been emptied down to the last imp and child, and they all marched with him.

They had not always looked kindly on him—a false faërie forged by human science and magic. They had spat at him and shunned him. But tonight, they were his completely—his freedom fighters, his soldiers, his comrades.

"Onward, my brothers!" he shouted. "Arise and fight! This is our night of vengeance!"

CHAPTER TWENTY-THREE

Hessing was bone tired, and covered in dust and grime. A ragtag band of guards and police had gathered around him. Borchard-Márai was crouched on the ground, rocking back and forth. Hessing shook his head. Keeping the man alive was a waste of time, but there would be hell to pay if an Imperial Envoy was killed in the city, even more so if the Commandant of Police directly let it happen. There would always be questions, insinuations, and Hessing had more than enough problems already.

The area around the Armory had turned into a warzone. All was chaos and blood. The faëries had regrouped far too quickly, and they outnumbered Hessing's men ten to one. He could see them, circling, snarling, clawing—some gnarled and wizen, others tall and radiant, all of them angry, all of them fierce. Behind them, Hessing could see fires in the city. The fighting was spreading.

He ran his hand through his hair, tiredly, and it came away bloody. He'd been hit somewhere and he hadn't even noticed. There was no time for that now. He needed to think, to act. This had all been planned. Someone had rallied the faëries when he and the Duke weren't looking, too busy chasing anarchists and worrying about politicians. They should have known better. He should have known better. Then there was Mr. Nix, playing his own little games, dragging Hessing into it—and he was in it now, in it up to his neck. Mr. Nix had trapped him, made him an accomplice, for his own amusement, perhaps. No one could ever quite tell why Mr. Nix did what he did.

Hessing had known the box was dangerous, incriminating even. He'd gone in with his eyes open, had entrapped too many people himself in the same manner not to know he was being set up. But despite the repeated assurances, he'd assumed it was a bomb, a mystical bomb, perhaps, but a bomb nevertheless. It was Mr. Tarr, after all. The little hobgoblin loved fire. If he had died in the explosion, Hessing would have considered that fair recompense—a life for a life, his for his son's—and a fitting punishment for his betrayal. Best of all, no one would ever know. But there had been no explosion. The Creature was dead; Hessing and the Duke were still alive, and the city was falling apart around them.

Two figures emerged out of the dust. Hessing and the others brought their weapons to bear—but they were human. It was Erkel and Lund, both looking worse for wear. Hessing nodded at them. Old comrades were hard to come by these days, and he'd need all the help he could get. The faëries seemed to be massing for another attack. They needed to escape and quickly.

"Good," he said, "you're here. We need to get back to Headquarters. The night is young. We can still salvage the situation." The others nodded tiredly, but a few of their backs straightened slightly, as if it had never occurred to them that all might not be lost. It wasn't much, but it might be enough.

"The Duke will be summoning reinforcements," he continued. "We just need to survive and hold as much ground as we can."

He glanced down at the gibbering envoy. Headquarters was half a burning city away. Borchard-Márai would never make it. Hessing ran an eye over his remaining men. Erkel and Lund were the most dependable. He'd hoped to send them both to protect his family and smuggle them to safety, if necessary. He knew he could trust them to keep his secret, as he had trusted them many times before, but he needed to get Borchard-Márai to the Duke. Lord Edward would need to be able to reassure the Emperor that his cousin was alive, or they might all hang no matter what happened.

"Erkel," he said.

"Yes, sir?"

"Take one of the guards and get the envoy to the Mansion alive, at all costs."

"But, sir." Erkel frowned down at the envoy.

"I know," said Hessing, "but there's no time to argue. His survival is paramount."

"Yes, sir." Erkel exchanged glances with Lund, who looked as if he wanted to say something, desperately, but kept his mouth shut. Erkel pointed to one of the guards at random.

"You're with me," he said. The guardsman was young, barely

eighteen, but he had a rifle and knew how to use it. Erkel pulled Borchard-Márai to his feet gingerly, nursing his wounded arm.

"Let's move," he said. The three of them headed off toward Auberon Square, half dragging the envoy with them.

Hessing didn't bother watching them go. Even wounded, he had never known Erkel to fail. But the inspector's allegiance had always been more mercenary. Lund, on the other hand, was a simpler man. His loyalty ran deeper. Hessing would need that loyalty.

"Sergeant Lund," he said.

"Yes, sir." There was a wariness in the man's eyes that he'd never seen before.

"I need you to do something for me. I need you to go to my family and keep them safe. Lemann is there, but he's only one man."

"Of course, sir," said Lund, but inside he was frowning. Everyone knew that Gregor was dead, but Hessing had referred to his family in the plural. Force of habit, perhaps, but it was not like Hessing to make a slip of the tongue. Though that wasn't the only thing out of character lately.

Hessing put a hand on his shoulder. "I know I can trust you with this," he said. "Whatever happens. Whatever you see."

Lund blinked and searched the Commandant's eyes. Did he know that Lund had seen him and the hobgoblin? No. There was no suspicion there, just pleading. Hessing was begging in his own way. Lund had never seen him do that before.

"Take this," Hessing said pressing an old coin into Lund's hand. "Give it to Lemann, witch-side up. He'll know I sent you."

"Of course, sir," said Lund. "I'll keep them safe." He could say nothing else, and maybe he could figure out just what was going on, provided they all survived long enough. He threw in a salute for good measure and slipped out into the city, pausing only to relieve a dead soldier of his weapon.

Hessing nodded to the remaining men. "Come on," he said. "We have a long fight ahead of us."

*

Rain poured down through the open ceiling into the ruins of the ballroom. The Creature had brought down most of the building with it. Stones and brickwork, pillars and posts lay strewn across the hall, burying the living and the dead. In the downpour, the Creature had quickly turned from a great terror into a putrid, slimy corpse. It was deathly, terribly quiet save for the sound of rain and an odd scratching sound. The cries and screams of the dying had faded down into a few scattered whimpers, and then nothing.

Suddenly the silence was shattered. There was a clatter, as a pile of rubble shifted and partially collapsed. A hand reached out into the air, then another followed by a head. It was the Countess. She half stumbled, half crawled out into the open air and took a deep, gasping breath. There was another hand emerging from the wreckage. She reached down and grabbed it, pulling the Duchess from out of the rubble. They collapsed into a heap and leaned against each other for a long moment taking short, shallow breaths. They had been digging their way out for what seemed like hours.

The rain on their faces was a blissful relief. The Duchess cupped her hands together and drank, while the Countess rubbed the sweat and grime from her forehead. Her arms ached. Everything ached. She felt dizzy and tired, but the open air helped, even as the Creature's putrid stench filled the air. It didn't bother

her much, though she saw the Duchess hold back a retch. She could feel the City rejoicing in her survival, eager to share and be joined. Her own power rose up in answer. She could feel it gurgling up inside her, itching to be used. It could take away the pain, the tiredness. She could be strong again. When she closed her eyes, the runes and incantations swam before her in the darkness, nudging her, waiting, wanting to be cast. She concentrated, clearing her mind and pulling her awareness inward. Her thoughts, which had become fuzzy and unfocused, gained a renewed clarity and sharpness. She would need all her wits about her, but she would have to be very careful now. Her fight with the Creature had weakened her.

Beside her, the Duchess stirred sluggishly. It was harder for her. She was only human.

"We can't stay here," said the Duchess. Her voice was tired, but there was a burning focus in her eyes, a certainty despite her exhaustion and frailty.

The Countess glanced at her and nodded. That much was obvious. "No, my lady."

"You saved my life," said the Duchess. "Call me Anne."

The Countess smiled slightly in acknowledgement.

"If my husband..." Lady Anne took a deep breath and steadied herself. "If my husband is still alive, they will have taken him to the Mansion. Either way, that's probably the most secure building in the city."

"If we can make it," said the Countess.

"If we can make it," Lady Anne repeated. "But we have to try."

"Agreed," said the Countess.

"We can do it," Lady Anne said in her most reassuring voice. Neither of them quite believed it.

Irons in the Fire

The Countess stood slowly and reached down to help Lady Anne to her feet. "I'll follow you," she said. "You know the city. I don't."

In the back of her mind, she could feel the City's laughter, but she kept her face grim and scared. They crawled and stumbled out of the ballroom through a crack in the wall, holding each other up.

The streets were on fire. Bands of faëries were ravaging past the ruins, flying, stomping, and shouting as they went. Any human unlucky enough to cross their path was set upon with teeth, and claws, and horns. A small group of policemen and guards were retreating down an alley, firing wildly as they went. The Countess recognized Hessing's rotund figure among them, shouting orders even as he aimed and fired. He was far more active than she would have imagined. The Duchess was watching them as well, cursing.

"Too late," she muttered. "We'll never catch up with them."

"We could make a run for it," the Countess offered, but she was shaking her head as she said it.

"No," said the Duchess. "It's too dangerous. We'll have to make our own way."

The Countess nodded. Her mind was racing. She had believed herself largely untouchable. None of the faëries and monsters in Talis should have been able to harm her, even without the City whispering in her ear, but that was before the Creature. The others had all been afraid of its tentacles and teeth, but she had felt the depths of its age and power. She had been forced to reveal her true nature and it had taken the greater part of her strength to survive.

She had already made one slip tonight—another might ruin her cover forever, especially if the Duchess saw. Mr. Nix was another matter. He had seen her perform a spell. He must have had his suspicions before that, even said as much, but a true adept could learn much from seeing another's powers in action. She shuddered to think what he had seen in her. The violence was escalating, and that was worrying. It wasn't supposed to happen yet. Her Sisters were not ready and neither was she. That was a problem for the future, though. Tonight, she needed to keep Lady Anne alive. This was a much better chance to earn the Duke and Duchess' trust than she could have hoped for.

She would just need to be careful, very careful, if she was to survive intact. She just hoped Elise and Jules were alright.

CHAPTER TWENTY-FOUR

Elise stared down at the city. The Countess had been right, something was coming, not that Elise had ever doubted her. Fires were burning below, and faëries were marching in the street. They were organized. She glanced over at her brother but he was intent on the destruction. After the Countess had left for the Ball, they had retreated to their lodging house. It was small and out of the way. They thought that would keep them away from whatever was coming. They had underestimated the danger, badly. Elise was not used to making that sort of mistake.

"They're dragging people into the street," Jules said. Elise nodded. She could see them—breaking down doors, throwing homemade bombs, pulling others out into the road, beating and biting them. It was madness, but she had no sympathy for any of them. They had brought this upon themselves many years ago. This was justice, though it had come early.

"They're heading this way," Jules said. "They'll be upon us soon."

"We may have to fight our way out," she said.

"I'm not sure we can."

She opened her mouth to berate him, but stopped when she saw his expression. He wasn't afraid. He was calculating the odds and found them wanting. She reconsidered. They were well trained, but there were only two of them and the faëries were multiplying.

"We have to get out of here," she said.

Jules agreed. "We should stick to the roofs," he said. "Keep above the fray."

"If we have to," Elise said with a sigh, but she knew it was a good plan. There was no point dying for nothing, even if slaughtering as many of those heathens in the street as possible would have been immensely satisfying.

She caught Jules shaking his head at her. He shared her allegiances but not her fanaticism. "We'll have our chance," was all he said.

"I know." She turned to leave, but he didn't follow immediately. "If we don't go now," she said, "we'll have to do this my way, after all."

He blinked. "I just hope she's alright out there," he said.

Elise gave a small smile and put her hand on his shoulder. "You know what she is," Elise said. "You know who she is."

"Yes," he said.

"Then stop worrying about her and come on."

He nodded, once, twice, then marched toward the door. Elise

smiled at his back. His little infatuation was amusing, so long as it didn't interfere with the larger plan. She liked the Countess as well, and she cared less and less for their orders.

Elise took a deep breath and followed him. They had a perilous night ahead of them.

*

Mr. Tarr was dancing giddily through the streets. This was even better than he had imagined. Mr. Nix had promised him anarchy to his heart's content, as much chaos as he could ever want, and he had delivered—first that beautiful, wondrously chaotic Creature from the Depths, and now the rioting. Humans killing faëries; faëries killing humans. People running hither and thither like so many headless chickens. It was exhilarating.

He stole a woman's hat and placed it delicately on the head of a dog-faced man, just to see what would happen. The look on their faces was hysterical. He pulled down a cyclops' trousers just as it was about to smash a poor drunk's skull. No one saw him. Perhaps they caught a glimpse of his shabby old coat from the corner of their eye, as he left confusion in his wake. But they all heard his whistling and his joyful, malicious laughter.

No one really knew what they were doing or what was happening, not the Duke, not Anselm, certainly not Mr. Tarr. That was the beauty of it. All was flames and confusion, fire and death, and he was right in the middle of it, the happiest little hobgoblin of chaos. He thought he had understood anarchy, but Mr. Nix had showed him pandemonium at a whole new level. He would have to get the man something later to show his appreciation; a fruit basket, perhaps, with a surprise inside.

He whistled and danced and stabbed a man randomly, just for

fun, then whistled and danced some more. This was the best night of his life, and there were still several hours until dawn.

*

Raske collapsed against the alley wall, breathing heavily. A harpy had nearly clawed his face off, only moments before. Clarke and Pullman had just left him, abandoned him and his wife to die. He wished he could say that he was surprised, but he wasn't, not even remotely.

Evá joined him a moment later. Her breathing was steadier. They were almost home. Somehow she managed to look demure even while running for her life with her hair down and her gown torn and tattered.

"No wonder Anselm and the others didn't join me," Raske said. "Not when they had this planned the whole time." He spat.

She shrugged noncommittally. It didn't matter anymore. The situation had changed. She glanced around to make sure they were really alone. Clarke and Pullman's presence had prevented her from bringing this up earlier. They would have asked inconvenient questions and tried to make plans of their own, but there would be no reconciliation now. Raske could accept political abandonment, but he would not forgive their cowardice tonight. It was better this way.

"You need to see this," she said producing a file from her person. "A contact of mine slipped it to me at the Ball."

Raske stared at her incredulously. "Now?" he said. "You're showing this to me now? We're in the middle of a bloody riot."

"I know," she said. "Trust me, Charles. That's why it has to be now."

He took it reluctantly and flipped through the contents quickly. He still thought she had gone mad. The Creature was enough to alarm anyone, and his preternaturally composed wife had always struck him as being wound a little too tight. Perhaps she'd finally snapped and gone into shock.

Then he stopped, the words on the page finally sinking into his tired mind. He went back over the file slowly. The riots and the danger were forgotten. The lantern light was faint, and it was barely enough to read by, but the photographs spoke for themselves.

"I'll be damned," Raske said. "I never would have believed it. Not him." He glanced up. "You trust your source?"

"Absolutely," she said. He nodded. He had implicit faith in her judgment.

"This changes everything," he said. "I have to get this to the Duke. He said he wanted me to work for him. This is my chance." He barked a laugh. "With this, I could..."

"Do anything you wanted," she finished.

"Yes," he breathed. Whole vistas were opening before him. Faërie Rights would be nothing compared to this. He would be Charles Raske, the Man Who Brought Down Hessing.

"And if you get it to him now," Evá said. "Prove your loyalty in the midst of the riot, then the Duke would owe you everything."

He nodded. The old fire was back in his eyes. His ambition had been rekindled, redirected. He could be relentless when he had a purpose. He wasn't always successful, but he never let up. That was his great strength, why he had been chosen—by Clarke and Pullman, by Evá, and, though he didn't yet know it, by Mr. Nix.

Evá watched the emotions play across his face and smiled to herself. Like she had told Mr. Nix earlier that evening, she knew exactly how to handle men like Raske.

*

Covét ducked beneath the policeman's strike and stabbed upward into the man's ribs. He had found a rifle and bayonet among the dead. It had long since run out of ammunition, but the bayonet was still sharp. He hadn't felt this alive, this pure in years. After decades of pent-up rage, taking the human's money, listening to their insults, this felt righteous. It felt right.

There was frenzied simplicity to the fight, though Heinrich had to save his life once or twice when he overreached. They were winning. He wasn't sure how it happened, but they were. Another man charged out of a storefront wielding a kitchen knife. Covét blocked the first blow, but the second sent him sprawling into the ground. He glanced around wildly. Heinrich was dealing with two men, one in a grocer's apron, another wielding a shovel. He would be no help at the moment.

Covét rolled out of the way and kicked blindly. His hoof smashed into the man's knee and he sank to his knees with a cry. The faun stood and prepared to make the killing blow, but the man threw himself at him and waved the knife wildly, cutting the faun's leg. Covét stumbled back, bleeding. They circled each other, both limping.

The man was almost as old as he was, and had a matching look of anger in his eyes. Covét jabbed the bayonet forward clumsily. The man parried, just as awkwardly. They were not fighters by training, but by circumstance. Covét thrust and stabbed with the bayonet, but the man dodged and blocked.

Finally a thrust broke through and slashed his cheek. The man stepped back and prodded the cut, almost in disbelief, as if he couldn't understand how a faun, especially an old one, could have hurt him. Then his eyes clouded with rage, and he attacked madly. There was no skill to it, no rhyme or reason. Covét fell back, hard pressed under the assault, until his back was against the wall. The man charged, a victorious gleam in his eye.

Covét closed his eyes, sure he was going to die, and cursing himself for his folly. He had let his emotions get the better of him and was paying for it now. He should have stayed in his apartment writing pamphlets where he belonged.

There was a strangled cry and a gurgling sound. He opened his eyes cautiously. The nameless man had skewered himself on Covét's bayonet. He stared in disbelief. The man's body lurched forward pinning him to the wall, but that didn't matter. He was alive. Covét couldn't believe his luck.

He grunted, slowly extricating himself from beneath the body. He took the man's knife and put it in his coat. Another weapon would be useful. Heinrich was waiting for him. He had found that he had an unexpected talent for destruction. He was a troll, after all, but even he was starting to look a little haggard.

Human mobs were starting to form, rampaging through the streets killing any stray faëries they could find. Not everyone cared about the politics or Human-Faërie relations. Some were just looting—smashing store windows and robbing the dead and the dying. The excitement was starting to fade. For all his revolutionary ideas, Covét preferred order. He was starting to wonder if there would be a city left by morning.

As they headed out, Covét saw an odd, mismatched pair staying low, slipping from alley to alley and trying to stay hidden. The first was a policeman—older, tall and lanky. He was half-carrying, half-dragging his companion along. The other man was younger and more rotund. His imperial white uniform was stained with dirt and blood, and he seemed stunned, almost insensible. In the lantern light Covét caught a glimpse of their faces and started.

He knew the policeman, vaguely—one of Hessing's old gang—but he'd met the other man just a few days ago. It was the Imperial Envoy. Fate had given him this chance. With Borchard-Márai in their hands the Dissidents would have a powerful weapon.

He surged after them, but then hesitated. Even in the midst of the fighting, Covét was a thinker. Anselm had always struck him as fairly reasonable, but he couldn't say the same of the others. The thought of an envoy in Droz's talons made him shudder. They were playing with fire tonight. It would not do to enrage the Emperor needlessly. He stopped and barked a laugh. Heinrich glanced down at him as if he'd gone mad, and perhaps he had. He was still thinking in the old ways. Nothing would be the same after tonight.

But he had waited too long. The policeman and the envoy were already gone. Lost in the chaos.

"Did you see them?" Covét whispered sharply.

"Who?" Heinrich asked.

"The policeman!"

"I have seen many policemen," the troll rumbled with vicious pride.

"He was with another man, wearing white."

Heinrich shook his head.

"We need to find him," Covét said. "It was Borchard-Márai."

Heinrich blinked and looked around with new interest. He understood the possibilities immediately, but there was no sign of them now. "How?" he asked.

Covét cursed. He had let a perfect opportunity slip through his fingers. He vowed that he would not make the same mistake again.

*

The Countess wiped her forehead, but only succeeded in

smudging the dirt and sweat. Her hair had come undone and her grand dress was in ruins, but she was wholly unharmed. There wasn't a single scratch on her. The same could not be said for her companion. The Duchess was covered in cuts and bruises, but she had avoided serious injury thus far. It had not been easy. Two human women alone in the riots had seemed to be easy targets for every passing faërie. Lady Anne had done her part, leading them through the familiar streets, but it was the Countess who had kept them alive, kept them hidden.

She could feel the City welling up inside her. It shouted warnings in her mind, told her when to run, when to duck, when to wait. All the while it whispered underneath, in a constant bubbling stream, the history of every building or piece of debris, or body. There were so many. Her Purpose knew them as her enemies. The City knew them as a part of itself. She simply knew them, and wished she didn't.

Now. The command roared through her and she ran across the street gesturing Lady Anne to follow. The made it just in time and ducked down an alley. A small mob marched past at their head a horned beast with a human head impaled on both his horns. Lady Anne swallowed back a cry. Beside her, the Countess struggled not to scream. Not at the horrors around them, but at the sudden, terrible pain inside. The ritual had reached its apex.

It was a torrent. It was a storm. She was drowning. She was burning. She was the City and the City was her—every street, every sidewalk, every building and square. She was them all. They were her limbs and organs. They were her flesh. She was in every broken window and gutted building. The fires burned inside her. A thousand feet and hooves tread upon her skin. She felt the people as well, all of them, human and faërie. She knew every atom of their being, every moment of their lives, every random act of chance across generations that had led them here. They were as much a part of the City as the roads and architecture. They flowed into her and she flowed into them. She was splintered, scattered, a part of her being imprinted on every atom, every moment, every cobblestone. She was etched into all of them, and it hurt.

She was lost, adrift in the pain, and the knowledge, and the being. She was as vast as the City, and the City was as small as her. She felt its deep, abiding love—free of judgment or prejudice, yet tangled and sprawling run through with irony and contradiction. The City had teeth and claws, and guns and knives, and magic, so much magic. She could feel it reaching out, tenderly embracing the rotting remains of the Creature. It tasted of the sea, of all the deep, dark places where the City could never go. It was too ancient and too strong to be wholly devoured, but it too was now a part of the City. The Creature's death was woven into its history.

As she became more accustomed to her communion with the City, she became conscious that her awareness was not absolute. There were empty places that she could not see, places hidden beneath the shadow of Mr. Nix, and of the man himself she could find no sign at all.

The Duke, however, loomed large, his worry and determination bleeding out into the streets. She could feel his love for Lady Anne pulsing like a beacon through the veins of the City. Their love was a thin thread that had kept Talis tied together for many years. She could see its depths and calluses. It was beautiful.

She saw Elise and Jules, as well, fighting for their lives across the roofs of the city. She felt their determination burning bright inside them, knew their loyalty and their most private selves, and with a terrible lurch, she saw their secret orders. Her great aunt had commanded them to kill her, if she failed, as if they could. It left a bitter taste in her mouth. She would remember this, when the time came.

A new pain roared through her without warning. Her great and glorious Purpose was burning through her veins, pulling her back down into her own flesh and blood. It was clawing its way through her, claiming her. She was caught between the two vast certainties coiling inside her mind. There was hardly any room for her self. She was being subsumed.

She whispered her name to herself, her true and secret Name. The name that had bequeathed her Purpose and opened the path to the City's heart. The Name that was her. She whispered it over and over until it reverberated throughout her body. She was not Purpose alone, and she was not the City. She was less than either and more.

The Countess came back to herself, dizzy and gasping. She had fallen against the wall. Lady Anne was hovering over her, frantically searching for a wound.

"Are you hurt?" she asked.

The Countess sat up slowly. "I'm fine," she said.

"You collapsed."

"Don't worry about me." She shook away Lady Anne's ministrations. "We need to keep moving. It's not safe."

Lady Anne didn't look convinced, but she couldn't argue. They were exposed in the alley, and the longer they stayed in one place, the worse the risk. The Countess allowed Lady Anne to help her stand. In truth, she was still a little dizzy. The City and her Purpose were both still roaring inside her.

Someone was watching them. She turned and found him instantly perched on a rooftop across the street. It was the ubiquitous Mr. Tarr. The City told her of his movements. He had been everywhere tonight and had many places still to go. In that moment she knew all of him—his life's story, his motives, the long history of his coat, the lyrics of his favorite song—everything that was not touched by Mr. Nix.

For a moment, their eyes met. She glanced at Lady Anne, then winked at him surreptitiously. Let him and his master make of that what they would. She had strength of her own now.

Mr. Tarr watched the two women disappear into the city. In between following Covét and saving his life, Mr. Tarr had been keeping an eye out for the Countess, partly out of curiosity, and partly because Mr. Nix had suggested it. She had seen him, again. Looked right at him, pierced his best concealment charms without even trying, and she had winked. It was the wink more than anything that made him laugh. Whoever she really was, whatever side she was on, the Countess was going to be his kind of fun.

25

CHAPTER TWENTY-FIVE

The ship rocked back and forth. Lt. Berg could hear the rain pounding on the deck above and could feel the engines rumbling. He grimaced and tried to control his stomach. Seasickness had troubled him since boyhood. That's why he'd joined the Ducal Guard. It was an honorable profession with room for advancement even for a poor fisherman's son, but most importantly of all it was on land and far away from the fishing village where he had grown up. He spent most of his time training on the Duke's Estate. But the fates were clearly laughing at him, because now here he was crammed in a cargo hold with fifty other soldiers heading down river.

The orders had come through only an hour before from the Duke himself. Brigadier Kronberger had taken the officers aside. Apparently riots had broken out in the city. The faëries were in open revolt and an attempt of some sort had been made on the Duke's life, though they were all ordered to keep that a secret. They couldn't afford rumors at a time like this.

Berg had never been to Talis. He'd lived all his life on the outskirts and hadn't met many faëries in that time. Most of them had immigrated to the Cities. A few goblins occasionally came down from the mountains, and in his village they had traded fairly often with the mermen of the river. He knew that a number of true fairies had set up a Brugh-in-Exile in a hill only a few miles from where he grew up, but he had already joined the Guards by the time they arrived.

Berg had no particular feelings about Faërie Rights. It didn't much matter to him whether they got the vote or not, but orders were orders. And no one tried to kill the Duke. The old man was well loved outside the city. Life had been good under his rule. He kept the trade flowing and mostly left everyone to their own devices. Berg owed the man personally, as well. He had come far in the Duke's service with the promise of further advancement. Brigadier Kronberger had taken him under his wing, and intimated that one day Berg might succeed him. This would be his first opportunity to distinguish himself.

There was a distant roll of thunder and the ship rocked slightly. Berg clutched his stomach. He just wished the riverboat would move faster. He glared at the other soldiers, daring them to comment, but Sergeant Rudbeck looked as bad as he felt, and poor Private Skane was practically shaking. Berg retched in the corner.

It would be better once the fighting started. He hoped.

*

Lemann had barricaded the doors at the first sign of trouble.

This was not his first riot, although this one seemed worse than usual. Hessing had many enemies who might use the unrest as cover to settle old scores. The butler couldn't be too careful. All the lights in the house had been doused. The windows were bolted. Most of the servants were huddled in their quarters, waiting out the night, but the footman and coachmen had both been armed from the hunting cabinet. Lemann had ordered them to patrol the ground floor, careful to keep them away from Lady Olivia and Master Gregor's room. As things stood, tonight would be more than dangerous enough without adding that particular uncertainty into the mix.

Lemann would protect them personally. He had an old shotgun and a short sword and knew how to wield them both. Hessing had hired him for his discretion, but kept him for his efficiency and hidden capacity for danger. He knocked softly on Master Gregor's door.

"Enter," came a whisper.

He creaked the door open and checked on his charges. He found them together in a heavy silence. The Baroness was seated on the bed, shivering, looking everywhere but at her son. Lemann still was not entirely sure what he thought about the resurrection. It would be good to have Master Gregor back, if he was truly back, but Lemann had heard stories. There were always complications, and there were some problems magic could never solve, but it was not his business to have an opinion.

The Baroness finally turned toward him and gave Lemann a nod. Master Gregor followed her gaze sluggishly, as if in a daze. His twitching and jerking movements were painful to watch. Lemann was almost afraid that Gregor would come apart at the seams, but the enchantments held, and there was a spark of something in his eyes, recognition perhaps, that offered a glimmer of hope. Lemann nodded to them both and put a finger to his lips. They weren't out of danger yet, and there were long, watchful hours ahead.

Waller, the coachman, was waiting for him in the hall. He gave Gregor's room a curious glance, but shrugged. Everyone knew of the Baroness' overwhelming grief. He had more important things to think about. Where she chose to wait out a siege was her own business.

"Problem?" Lemann asked. Waller wouldn't have come upstairs if it wasn't urgent.

"Wroe sent me," replied Waller. "There's a man downstairs."

"And you let him in?" Lemann was incredulous. There was no point in locking the house down if Wroe and Waller were just going to invite people in the moment his back was turned.

"He's a policeman, pretty banged up. Says the Baron sent him."

Lemann frowned. "Take me to him," he said.

*

The policeman was waiting in the kitchen. Wroe's hands were shaking but he managed to keep his gun pointed at him. The policeman appeared to be more amused than threatened, but mostly, he looked tired. He was covered in dirt and blood, but underneath he seemed mostly unharmed. He was only a little younger than Lemann and it took the butler a moment to recognize him. One of the old guard.

"Sergeant...Lund, isn't it?" he asked.

"Good," said Lund. "You remember me. That will make this easier."

Lemann narrowed his eyes. That could mean anything.

"The Commandant is alive," Lund continued. "He sent me to

help keep his family safe." He reached into his pocket gingerly, careful not to startle either Wroe or Waller. They seemed far too jumpy for men with their fingers on the trigger.

"And told me to give you this." He pulled out an old coin, predating the Glorious Revolution, and turned it over. "Witch-side up." There was a silhouette of the Old Witch-Queen proudly displayed on one side.

Lemann relaxed. Lund was telling the truth. Hessing had sent him, but there was something puzzling him.

"Keep his 'family' safe? Are you sure those were his exact words?" he asked.

"Yes," Lund answered without hesitation. "I thought that was odd too."

"Then you had better follow me, Sergeant Lund," said Lemann, but there was something he had to take care of first. "Wroe, Waller," he said, "good work. Keep patrolling. Dawn is still hours away."

"Yes, Mr. Lemann," they said. He nodded, satisfied, and led Lund up the stairs.

The policeman didn't speak and moved surprisingly quietly. Lemann studied him curiously. The Baron obviously trusted him and Hessing was a good judge of character. In his line of work, he had to be.

Sergeant Lund was of an age. He had clearly served under Hessing for a long time, owed him everything, but it was more than that. Hessing had sent the sergeant here to protect them, and in doing so was sharing his most dangerous secret, a secret that Lemann himself had barely accepted. There had to be more to Hessing's trust than simply his faith in the man's mercenary tendencies. There had to be more to Lund than the others.

They reached Master Gregor's room. "Wait here," said Lemann. Lund nodded without question. Lemann entered and had a brief hushed conversation. Lund couldn't make out the words, but there was a familiar urgency and fear in their voices.

Finally, Lemann emerged. "Come in," he said. He only hoped Lund was the man Hessing thought he was.

"Sergeant Lund, milady."

The Baroness was standing when Lund entered. "Lady Olivia," he said, and bowed awkwardly. This was not his area.

"I remember you," she said studying him. "You're one of Erkel's men. We've met before—five years ago at the Policemen's Ball, I believe. My husband spoke highly of you."

"Thank you, your ladyship," he said. She was saying the right words, and he was flattered that she had remembered him, but her face was tight and nervous. She was hiding something. Finally, she seemed to have found whatever she was looking for and stood aside. Lund saw who was sitting on the bed, and his world changed.

He had never officially met the Commandant's son, but he had seen him many times at Headquarters or the Policeman's Ball, and watched the boy grow up from afar. There was no mistaking those features, even when they were pallid and bloated, stitched together by a necromancer's needle. The young man had his mother's nose and his father's eyes. Suddenly everything made sense.

Lund didn't have all the pieces, not yet, but he understood enough. Gregor was alive. Hessing had made a deal to save his son. Nothing else mattered. Lund thought of Hessing and the hobgoblin talking in the rain. He thought of Obry dying in a hail of fire, and his widow sitting at her kitchen table, so strong.

She was a good woman, and she deserved better. She deserved vengeance, and he wanted to be the one to give it to her. He had felt so betrayed, but now the anger was gone and only the uncertainty remained. Lund closed his eyes and sighed. In the end, he had no choice.

"The Commandant sent me to keep you safe," he said, opening his eyes. "Both of you."

The Baroness gave a sigh of relief, and behind her Gregor's lips twitched into what could almost have been a smile.

*

Mrs. Obry woke with a start. Something was wrong. She reached over in the bed and found only cold emptiness beside her. The last of sleep faded from her mind. John was dead. He'd been killed months ago. She rose uneasily and wrapped herself in a shawl. It was a chilly night and she wanted to curl up back in bed, but something had woken her. She had been a policeman's wife long enough to trust her instincts.

She went to the window and pulled the curtains back. There was destruction, fire, and a small mob marching through the streets below. It had finally happened. The tension had snapped. She considered running, but there was nowhere to go. If John was still alive, he would have insisted on going out and leaving her alone. He couldn't help himself.

She was more alone now than she had ever been, but she was still quite capable of taking care of herself. Mrs. Obry turned away from the window and checked that the door was bolted shut. Satisfied, she dragged the kitchen table slowly, creakingly, over and pressed it hard against the door. Her limbs ached, but she wasn't done. Retrieving a carving knife from the kitchen, she retreated to the bedroom, locked the door and pushed the dresser in front of it.

John had kept a rifle in the closet. She pulled it down and checked that it was loaded. That done, she sat down facing the door with the rifle in her hands and the kitchen knife on the bed beside her. There she waited. She could wait all night if necessary.

She hoped Sergeant Lund—Frederick—was all right. He had been very kind these past few months, keeping her informed of the investigation. Worrying about him felt oddly comforting. She was used to worrying on nights like this. It was familiar, but she couldn't help but wish that it was John she was worrying about instead.

Outside she could hear the sounds of the riot coming closer. She gripped her gun tighter. Let them come. She would take as many of them with her as she could. For John.

*

Police Headquarters was in chaos. People were running about here and there, and they were starting to cluster into factions. Inspector Cambor and his task force had attempted to take control, but he had been violently shouted down. Inspector Vorn and the others weren't willing to take orders from him. The inspectors were all the same rank, and they all had their adherents. No one knew who was in charge. Only a handful of them had been around for the last major uprising, and they had only been patrolmen at the time. None of them knew what to do.

Hessing barreled into the maelstrom, bleeding but determined. All eyes were on him instantly. He took in everything at a glance—the confusion, the fear, and the insurrection threatening to boil over. He charged through the ranks to the front of the chamber. They parted in front of him.

"Lock down the building," Hessing barked as he went. "Prepare for a siege." A number of men rushed to obey.

"There's no time for fancy speeches," he said turning. "So I won't give one." His voice echoed in the sudden silence. "We have a long night ahead of us. But I know you are up to the task, each and every one of you." He met their eyes steadily, saw their backs straighten. Good. He would need that belief. "Now," he said, "who told you that you could stop working? Get to it!" There was a sigh of relief and a rustling, as everyone was filled with renewed purpose.

The senior officers gathered around him. "Start sending patrols out," he ordered. "We need to get the city under control, and more importantly, we need to know what is happening." A few inspectors broke off running, grabbing men left and right.

Hessing didn't watch them go—his mind had already moved on to the next problem. "Inspector Vorn, get some men on horseback. Ride down the mobs—human or faërie, it doesn't matter. I want them off my streets."

"Yes, sir." Vorn left, glaring at Cambor.

"Has anyone contacted the Duke?" asked Hessing.

"No, sir," said Cambor. "The telegraph lines have been cut."

Hessing sighed. "Get someone on that immediately, preferably you."

"Yes, sir."

"And would someone get me a coffee." Hessing rubbed his eyes. The situation was deteriorating, but all was not lost. There was always a moment of chaos, when both sides were spent. Whoever acted decisively in that moment would win the day. He just needed to get his men into position to take advantage, and he hoped the Duke was doing the same. He could deal with everything else later.

*

The Duke ran out of the telegraph room as fast as he could, guards trailing behind him. Inspector Erkel and Borchard-Márai were in the antechamber, slumped in their chairs. Wounded, battered, catatonic, they looked half dead. The Duke took a deep breath and controlled himself. Every time stragglers arrived at the Mansion his hopes flared, but so far in vain.

"Gentlemen," he said. "It's good to see you."

"Your grace." Erkel could barely stand, but he managed a half bow from his seat. Borchard-Márai didn't say a word. He had collapsed and was staring blankly at the far wall. The Duke raised an eyebrow questioningly.

"He's been like this since the attack on the Ball," said Erkel.

"Someone get these men a drink," said the Duke. One of the servants hurried out. "Any idea what happened?" he asked.

"No, your grace." The inspector replied. "All I know is that the Commandant was planning to regroup at Headquarters."

"He's alive? Good."

"He was when I left him."

"And my wife?"

Erkel managed a wincing shrug. "I didn't see her, your grace."

The servant returned with a tray and two glasses of whiskey. Erkel thanked him and took small sips. Borchard-Márai barely noticed him, but seemed to inhale the drink.

"Permission to rejoin the Commandant?" asked Erkel when he was done.

The Duke took in the man's injuries. He was beat up, nursing his arm gingerly, and bleeding on the carpet. "No," the Duke said.

"Not yet. I may need you here. For now, get yourself patched up. You'll be no use to me dead."

Erkel started to protest, but the Duke waved his objections away. "That's an order, Inspector."

"Yes, your grace."

"Take Inspector Erkel to the doctor," said the Duke.

As he was led away, Erkel leaned in close. "I'm not sure the envoy is as catatonic as he seems," he whispered to the Duke.

Lord Edward nodded his thanks and scrutinized the envoy thoughtfully. Borchard-Márai seemed to be coming back to himself, slowly. The drink had helped. He stirred.

"The...Emperor," he mumbled. "I have to...have to inform the Emperor."

"Don't worry, your excellency. It will all be taken care of."

Borchard-Márai fixed him with a bleary stare and sat up straighter. "Lord Edward," he said. "I'm sorry that I seem to have let you down."

"You've done nothing of the sort."

"The Emperor," the envoy tried again. "He'll send troops. He can help."

"And that would be much appreciated, but I've summoned my Ducal Guard, and for tonight, at least, that will have to suffice."

Borchard-Márai tried to rise, but the Duke put a quelling hand on his shoulder. "It's quite alright, your excellency. There's no need to task yourself. It's been a trying evening." He glanced at the guards. "Kindly show the envoy to his rooms. Get him something to eat and drink." He turned back to Borchard-Márai. "I shall send you my personal physician."

"You're too kind," Borchard-Márai muttered.

"Not at all." He turned to leave but stopped one of the guards.

"Don't let him leave his room," he said. "Or send any messages. Understood?"

"Yes, your grace."

"Good." The Duke headed back into the telegraph room. The envoy would be a problem for the morning. It was best to deal with the situation one crisis at a time.

Gunshots erupted outside, far too close for comfort.

"Your grace!" Mr. Oliver called urgently. The Duke joined him, peering cautiously out the window.

A handful of rioters had reached Auberon Square. The Guard opened fire from their entrenched positions. An ogre stumbled and fell; a sphinx dodged and pounced, nearly reaching the outer gate before it fell. The Duke watched as the remaining faëries broke and fled. It had been a feeble attempt. Only the sphinx had come close, but the fighting had reached the Mansion. Others would not be far behind. Lord Edward remembered hearing them as a boy pounding on the doors, smashing windows. That would not happen again. Not while he was still Duke. This needed to be contained.

"Find the magicians," he said. "They won't have gone far."

"Are you sure that's wise, your grace?" Mr. Oliver cringed. He had spoken without thinking. "Forgive me. I spoke out of turn."

"No," replied the Duke. "I'm not sure at all." He gave Mr. Oliver a faint smile. "And there's nothing to forgive. You've always been a good and loyal servant."

"Thank you, your grace."

The Duke watched him go. Mr. Oliver was right. Matching magic with magic could have dangerous consequences. There are some areas in the Crescent still impassable centuries after the Young Magicians and the Witches had done battle. There were places in Talis where magic had torn holes in reality, and the best that the magicians had ever managed was to sew up the scars. But the faëries, or whoever was leading them, had unleashed a Monster in his city. That was unforgivable. It was time he met them on their own terms, whatever the risks. And magic was not his last resort. He still had what his wife called their secret weapon.

He sighed. There was still no word on Anne.

CHAPTER TWENTY-SIX

The Smoke and Mirrors Club was crowded. The nymphs and waiters, those who had made it at least, huddled at the tables. Even Éponine La Roux and her mother fluttered in a corner with the other dancers. They had all brought their families, if they had them. They knew of no safer place. There was no music now, no customers. They all sat in terrified silence listening to the screams and shots outside. There were many doors to the Smoke and Mirrors Club, and the mob had reached them all.

The satyr in a tux moved among them from table to table with a kind word and a reassuring hand on the shoulder. "Don't worry," he said. "The enchantments will hold. He will not turn you away. I promise."

Most nodded and thanked him, but they were not so certain. Few of them knew their employer well. He was distant and often preoccupied with his own plots and schemes. It was unwise to ask too many questions, but he paid well, and good work was hard to find for their kind. For his part, the satyr did know his employer well, as well as anyone could, and he was no more certain then they were. Mr. Nix was a difficult man to predict and he did not appreciate it when things were done without his permission. There would be a price to pay from each of them.

"I promise, Éponine," he repeated. "You'll be safe here."

"In the future," came a voice from behind them. "Try not to make promises that aren't yours to keep." They all turned as one. Mr. Nix had arrived without anyone noticing.

"Sir," said the satyr. "I didn't mean…"

"I know what you meant," Mr. Nix said. He glanced around the room, his face expressionless.

"They have nowhere else to go," the satyr said. "Please."

Mr. Nix studied him for a moment, and then nodded. "You can set up some beds in the back. It would be better if there were no immediate evidence of their presence."

"Why? No one can enter without your permission."

"Yes," said Mr. Nix. "But that does not mean it would be advisable to be open about it. Everyone knows that I am neutral and I prefer to keep it that way, given the current circumstances."

"True," said the satyr. "That could be unfortunate."

"Just so." Mr. Nix turned back to his waiting employees. "Of course you can stay," he told them. "Stay and be safe."

"Thank you," Éponine said and the others followed suit. Mr. Nix merely smiled.

"I'm willing to pay the price for them," the satyr whispered in his ear. "No matter what."

Mr. Nix's smile did not slip. " I know," he said. "Pour me a drink."

*

Inspector Cambor arrived on Broad Street with his men right behind him. The street was deserted, but a forest of telegraph poles stretched out before them, running the length of the city. They had been stripped of their wires, and the broken lines lay on the sidewalks and in the road, intermittently sparking. Broad Street ran more or less straight from Police Headquarters into the Old Quarter and the Ducal Mansion. Repairing this line would be the most direct method of reestablishing contact.

Cambor's men were policemen. They had never been trained for telegraph repair, but he had chosen those with the quickest minds and nimblest hands. They had already restored almost a quarter mile of wire, moving pole by pole, and they had begun to develop a system, cumbersome, perhaps, but effective. The smallest and most fleet of foot were already clambering up the next pole, with a roll of wire and tools on their backs. Cambor remained on the ground with the others, watching the street nervously. They'd had no difficulties as of yet, but signs of the faëries' path of destruction were all around them. They were getting closer to the front, but had no way of knowing just how close.

For, perched on the nearest telegraph pole, Droz and the other Winged Faëries watched them as they climbed upward, and waited for the right moment to strike. A harpy shifted its wings restlessly, eagerly.

"Hold," Droz whispered. "Hold."

The humans climbed closer and closer. Nearly there. Droz glanced around. His brethren were ready. So many of them. The pixies, harpies, thunderbirds, gargoyles, wyverns, and countless others without name all waited for the word. It was their time at last. It was his time.

"Now!" Droz cried and the first wave launched itself, swooping down and attacking in a flurry of wings and claws.

The men climbing on the poles shouted, and tried desperately to fight back, but they were clinging on for dear life, unable to maneuver. The faëries dove and lunged, and looped around again. The pixies swarmed in vast numbers, devilishly fast, with sharp teeth. The harpies were slower, but their arms were longer, their grasp tighter. The humans didn't stand a chance. Some of them fell, screaming. Others died still clutching the pole.

The shouts alerted Cambor below. He immediately grasped the situation and turned upwards, shooting. Most of his men were armed only with truncheons and cudgels, but those with pistols and old-model muskets opened fire sporadically. Looking down, Droz nodded and released the second wave of the attack, leaving the tops of the telegraph poles bare. Then he reared up himself and stretched his wings out of the shadows, fully visible at last in all their dark, feathery glory. His nose, once merely birdlike, was now a beak—sharp and pointed. His true form stood revealed—a birdman, a spirit of the air. He was himself at last, and descended upon the humans with ferocious intensity. He dodged bullets gracefully, feeling the air whir and burn around him as they passed.

He aimed for Cambor and struck the Inspector at full speed. The force sent Cambor sprawling into the gutter. Droz was on top of him in an instant, pinning him down with his wings. His fingers had become claws and dug into the Inspector's chest. Droz sank his beak into Cambor's shoulder, through the flesh until he met bone. Cambor screamed and reached blindly, fumbling for his pistol. Droz was merciless, pecking into him again and again. Finally, Cambor found his weapon and pawed for it. Grasping the handle, he turned the pistol up awkwardly and pulled the trigger.

A gunshot rang out at point blank range. Droz flinched back in an explosion of feathers. Cambor wasted no time. He rolled to his feet, bleeding and in pain, and ran, firing over his shoulder. The other policemen, those who had survived the onslaught, followed after him. Pixies and harpies hounded after them and drove them from the street. Although wounded, Droz gave a taunting screech of victory, echoed by a hundred birdlike voices. The field was theirs at last.

*

Mr. Nix sat at the bar with a peculiar expression on his face. The satyr had never seen it before. He thought it might be sadness. The others had already filed into the backrooms, leaving the club empty and forlorn. Outside, the sounds of fighting had moved on, leaving an eerie stillness.

"If I may ask, sir," said the satyr as he handed him his drink, "what's wrong?"

Mr. Nix blinked and seemed to come back to himself. "Wrong? Nothing really." He paused. "It's just that I knew her in the old days."

"Her?"

Mr. Nix said nothing. The satyr nodded. He understood. "Did you know it would be her?"

"No," said Mr. Nix. "Not until after."

"It was necessary," the satyr reminded him.

"It's always necessary." Mr. Nix smiled a bitter half-smile. Then he pushed his glass back toward the satyr. It scrapped across the bar echoing in the club. "Drink," said Mr. Nix.

The satyr took a half step back. "You know I don't," he said. "I can't."

"Yes," said Mr. Nix. "And yet you work for me here every day—a life of temptation, every day a struggle. I understand that. More than you know." He gave the glass a final nudge. "Drink," he repeated. "It is my price for them."

The satyr's hands shook as he gulped down the glass, slowly at first, then greedily. Mr. Nix watched him avidly, seemed to drink in his companion's need. "Another," he said.

"Sir, I can't..."

"Another." Mr. Nix's voice brokered no argument. Resigned, the satyr poured himself a second drink. He wanted it, of course. He always wanted, but he never drank. That was his power, his strength, ever since Mr. Nix had given him a second chance. He had promised to pay the price, whatever it was, but he hadn't expected this. He raised the glass to his lips. There was no choice in the end.

"Wait," said Mr. Nix. "It is enough that you were willing." The satyr lowered the glass more reluctantly than he would have liked.

"I've started," he said. "Once I've started you know I can't stop."

"You will," said Mr. Nix.

"How?"

"I will stop you." It wasn't an apology, but it was enough. "Now you should go check on the others, make them comfortable."

"Yes, sir," said the satyr. He turned to leave, then paused. He had to know. "Sir?" he asked. "What could my price have possibly had to do with anything?"

Mr. Nix studied him for a moment. "Nothing whatsoever."

"Is that a lie?"

"Everything is a lie," said Mr. Nix. "One way or another."

As the satyr headed to the back room, he thought he heard his master say, "thank you," but it was probably just his imagination.

*

Anselm was waiting on the corner of Vale Street when Covét and Heinrich arrived. The homunculus was impervious to the rain and seemed tireless. Brunet was not far behind, coming from the opposite direction. They met each other amidst the burning city, grinning broadly. Droz landed among them in a flutter of feathers, black as shadows. His wings were visible now, large and outstretched. His sharp beak was speckled with blood, and his wing was bleeding.

"The telegraph lines have been cut throughout the city," he reported. "The Winged Faëries and I have seen to it." A roar of approval greeted his words.

Faëries were trailing in from all directions, some singly, others in groups. They were of every shape and size imaginable and they were all smiling; those, at least, with the requisite anatomy. Even Brunet, headless as he was, radiated excitement. He was practically vibrating. A gargoyle pounded its chest gleefully. Even Covét was beaming, as broadly as he was able. There was a giddy sense of victory in the air, a strange euphoria, vicious and infectious.

Anselm had lost control of the rioters early in the night. Decades of resentment could be channeled, but not controlled. Many faëries had taken to dragging people into the streets, raiding their homes, beating, burning, clawing, biting in a glut of indiscriminate violence. The original plan had called for greater precision, but that didn't matter now. They were winning. The

Duke had scurried back to his Mansion, and the police were falling back.

"Running like frightened rabbits." Brunet's voice was full of dark glee at their retreat. He counted every dead policeman as revenge for his lost head, although Inspector Vorn himself had remained elusive thus far. He only hoped another faërie did not tear apart his quarry first.

Covét looked around as if in a daze. "I never really believed until now," he said, holding his hand out to Anselm. "But we've done it."

Looking at the faces of his fellow faëries awash with victory, Covét could see the future clearly for the first time, not as a distant dream, but as something tangible. He could almost reach out and touch it. It was more even than he had imagined. It was exhilarating.

"Not yet," said Anselm, but he shook Covét's hand. "Now it's time to finish what we started." Anselm turned to the assembled hordes. "We march on the Duke!" he cried. "Just as his own ancestors once marched on the Witches!"

"Down with the Duke!" the crowd roared. "Freedom!" they cried. "Liberty!" There was no mention of equality, not anymore. They surged forward, marching toward Auberon Square with Anselm and Covét at the head.

"Freedom! Liberty!" the crowd chanted. "Revenge!"

*

Mr. Tarr had left Covét to his own devices. The old faun could look after himself for a change. There was too much fun to be had blazing a path of chaos and flames across the city. Mr. Tarr wanted to see everything, do everything. The memories of tonight would nourish him for months, even years to come. Anarchy at its purest. He turned this way and that, picking alleys and roads at random, allowing his feet to take him where they would. Sometimes he ran, or skipped, or flew, however the mood struck him. He made his way by chance and happenstance, until he found himself down by the docks.

The warehouses were deserted. Even the lights in the taverns were out. The workers were either cowering in their homes or out in the streets, looting and pillaging. The mobs had come and gone, moving deeper into the city, leaving only destruction in their wake. Windows had been smashed. Boxes and barrels had been overturned, their contents spewed onto the streets, and across the river. Mr. Tarr could see a number of factories on fire, illuminating the night sky. It was glorious.

From the corner of his eye, Mr. Tarr saw movement on the wharfs. Dozens of ships were disembarking on the quay. There were hundreds of soldiers, perhaps more, each with rifles on their shoulders and the Ducal emblem proudly engraved on their helmets. Mr. Tarr slipped closer, more careful now. The Guard was known to employ magicians, and the Countess' inexplicable ability to pierce his charms was already a cause for concern. But something was wrong. The soldiers were not moving in clean, orderly ranks, but quickly and warily. There was movement in the river. Mr. Tarr peered closer. It was hard to be certain in the dark, but he thought he saw shapes rippling beneath the surface—the People of the Water. They had come.

When the attack came, it was fierce and swift. The mermen and merrows emerged in sudden fury, their spear points sharp, their aim deadly. Their spears and javelins rained down on the soldiers, killing and maiming dozens. An officer—a Brigadier, if Mr. Tarr was reading the insignia correctly—with a handlebar mustache and a fur coat hurtled down the gangplank, narrowly dodging a spear. The finfolk were pressing their attack. They had not felt this pure in many years. But these were not thugs and policemen, or pampered parade-ground troops, but soldiers, veterans of a thousand goblin skirmishes. Already they were forming into ranks and returning fire.

Brigadier Kronberger surveyed the burning city for a moment, and tilted his head, listening to the rumble of gunfire, of screams and shouts and nymph war songs. The finfolk were fierce but undisciplined. It would be a sharp fight, but short. Then they could move on to the real battle. He nodded to himself, his expression grim.

"You have your orders," he said to his assembled officers. They nodded. "Good. Then secure the bridgehead. We can't afford to leave these animals at our back."

"Yes sir." They saluted. The soldiers began to spread out, ready for battle, firing and tossing grenades into the water.

"Lt. Berg!" the Brigadier cried. Berg emerged from the ranks, still a little green, but he seemed to have perked up at the fight. He saluted. Kronberger didn't bother to return the courtesy. There was no time. "Take your men into the city," he ordered. "I want to know what's going on in there. We're blind, Lieutenant. Be my eyes." Berg glanced at the waterfront almost wistfully. "Don't worry, boy," the Brigadier said. "There'll be more fights before the night is out."

"Yes, sir." Berg saluted and hurried to obey.

In the distance, Mr. Tarr watched them go, intrigued. This could be an opportunity. He wanted desperately to tweak the Brigadier's mustache, and perhaps turn the young lieutenant next to him inside out, just to see what would happen. But the arrival of the Guard meant the situation had changed. The Duke was starting to regain control. Pity. Still, the fun wasn't over yet. He could still cause a little more mischief before morning. He let out a tiny whistle and skipped back toward the city. Brigadier Kronberger's eyes flickered to where he had been only a moment before, but missed him, barely, his attention drawn back to the battle. Perhaps, Mr. Tarr mused, this would be interesting after all.

Part VI

The First Battle of Talis

CHAPTER TWENTY-SEVEN

Lieutenant Berg and his men scouted ahead of the column. They crept silently from street to street with their eyes alert. They were veterans, all of them, and they knew better than to ignore any possible avenue of attack. Sergeant Rudbeck kept one eye on the sky for any harpies or wyverns, and Private Skane was watching the ground with particular intensity. He had once encountered a particularly nasty burrowing creature in the foothills.

Brigadier Kronberger had lost contact with the Duke almost immediately after the first summons and had received no further information on the state of the city. It was immediately apparent to Berg that the Duke had been right to summon them. The city was eerily still, but the air was filled with the distant murmur of fighting, and the streets were littered with bodies and debris. Of the faëries themselves, however, there was no sign. Not until they turned down an alley toward Broad Street.

Berg could hear the sound of trampling feet and hooves, and feel the ground tremble beneath him. Even the windows seemed to vibrate. Berg signaled the others and stole down the alley, Rudbeck and Skane close behind.

Partially hidden in the shadows, they peered onto the avenue. There were faëries—hundreds, thousands of them. They passed the alley in a continuous wave, until Berg lost count. So many shapes and sizes, more than Berg had ever seen, or even imagined. A lifetime on the Border had not prepared him for the cornucopia of horns and scales, of wings and talons, of fair shapes and monstrous forms. Some bore torches. Others glowed with an inner fire. All were grim and determined, intent on violence.

Berg and Rudbeck exchanged worried glances and retreated back toward the side street. They had seen all they could. They huddled in the corner, Skane keeping watch, while Rudbeck lit a match. In the faint light they studied a map of the city. Berg had tried to commit it to memory, but there was no clear order, no system. Talis was a haphazard outgrowth of roads and avenues. Even lifelong residents occasionally got lost. The faëries were proceeding down Broad Way toward the Old Quarter. There could be no doubt as to their intentions.

"We have to get back to the Brigadier," Lieutenant Berg said. "Immediately."

*

The Ducal Guard marched up from the Docks in perfect order, rank by rank, regiment by regiment. They had emerged from the waterfront victorious, if wounded. Brigadier Kronberger was riding at the vanguard of the advancing troops. He was a proper martinet, even in the midst of battle. Rain poured down his helmet and dribbled down his cheeks, but he paid no heed to the elements. He had braved fiercer storms. As Berg and his men approached, Kronberger called a halt. He and his officers dismounted and joined Berg.

"Report, Lieutenant," he said.

"Yes, sir." Berg saluted. "The faëries are marching on Auberon Square," he said pointing to the map. "Thousands of them. They must have nearly emptied the Quarter."

Kronberger nodded to himself and resisted the urge to stroke his mustache. "We'll head them off," he said. "Here." He tapped the map at the Rook Gate. "We can move in parallel. We might be able to beat them there if we double-time."

"The Gate was destroyed," Lieutenant Berg reminded him.

"Doesn't matter." Kronberger shook his head. "It's a choke point, even in ruins. They still have to pass through. If we get there first we can break them." He turned to his other officers. "Move out," he said. "Double time."

"Yes, sir." They departed in a burst of orders.

"We must protect the Duke," said Kronberger. "No matter the cost."

*

Anselm, Covét, Heinrich and Brunet were marching, all four abreast. Above them swarmed Droz and his winged cohorts, and behind them came a horde of chanting, triumphal faëries. More were joining every minute. They streamed in from throughout the city, intent on pulling the Duke down from behind his high walls, and tearing him limb from limb. They were drunk on euphoria and bloodlust.

Some of them had already begun practicing, exercising their

rage on whatever lay before them. They fanned out, breaking windows, busting down doors, dragging people from their houses out into the street, where they were set upon from all directions, beaten and dismembered. A few bands of humans tried to stop them, but their anger and fear was no match for the faëries and their long-simmering fury. No one could stand against them.

They were almost at the ruins of the Rook Gate, where it had all begun. It had been over a month, but Parliament and the Duke had made little progress in repairing the damage. Suddenly, there was the sound of hooves, and mounted policemen wielding pistols and sabers emerged from the alleys and cross streets. Someone seemed to be regaining a semblance of control.

The swiftness of the assault sent the mob scrambling back. The policemen were counting on that element of surprise. They were still heavily outnumbered and untrained for anything on this scale. Broad Street was thrown into confusion.

The faëries wavered, but held. Of all the instruments of the Duke's regime, they hated the policemen and jackboots the most. Covét and Heinrich rallied the faëries and they began to fight back with renewed fury. The policemen's charge had ultimately been foolish. It was effective at running down stragglers, but was ill suited to a crowded street fight. The riders soon found themselves isolated and surrounded, fending off attacks from all sides.

Vorn was in command, shouting orders desperately amidst the clamor and noise. He had a piercing officer's voice, recognizable almost a block away, where Brunet was rallying a wendigo and ogre for a counterattack. The headless man turned instantly. He had no eyes or ears, but he could see and hear well enough. It was Vorn—the man who had cleaved his head from his shoulders—at last.

Brunet barreled toward his enemy. Faëries and policemen dove out of the way. A six-foot tall headless man in a berserker rage was an imposing sight for anyone, even a troll or ogre. He tossed a goblin out of the way, and then he was upon Vorn, throwing him from his horse and sending him sprawling to the ground with a sickening crash. Vorn was an inept tactician and a mediocre investigator, but he was one of the best fighters on the force. He was on his feet in an instant, trading blows.

He had lost his weapons, but he was lean and fast. He had already killed Brunet once before. But the headless man was stronger now. The powers that had reanimated him had also lent him greater strength. He gave as good as he got, better even, and they tore into each other. Neither was quite able to get the upper hand. Brunet was strong but in his eagerness and anger he was making too many mistakes, while Vorn was starting to slow down, trying desperately to think of a way to kill someone who was already dead.

A volley of gunfire erupted suddenly and faëries fell screaming around them. Brunet and Vorn looked up from their fight. Ahead, soldiers were taking up position in orderly ranks blocking the street. Their bayonets gleamed. Their faces were calm. Vorn and the other policemen immediately broke for the soldier's line. He and his fellows had no problem running from a fight they couldn't win. The Guard let them pass, then quickly closed ranks.

Frustrated, Brunet found Anselm, Covét and Heinrich preparing to attack. The police had barely fazed them and they had come too far to stop now, Ducal Guard or no. He gave them a bow of assent. They would win or die together.

They charged. The faëries thundered behind them, screaming, screeching, roaring.

The Guard let them come, quietly, patiently. The front rank kneeled.

"Wait for it," Lieutenant Berg said. "Wait for it." In the second rank, Private Skane's nose itched. He could see the faëries charging, monsters and creatures. He took careful aim. They were close now, so very close.

"Volley fire present," Lieutenant Berg shouted. "Fire!"

And the world exploded in noise and death.

CHAPTER TWENTY-EIGHT

Hessing was pacing back and forth in his office with terrible jerking movements, slamming each footstep hard into the floor. Every about-turn threatened to send something flying off the shelves. He was full of coiled rage, ready to strike. He wanted to be on the streets, bashing heads, taking action, anything to dull the gnawing worry. Instead he was chained to his desk at Headquarters, giving orders, projecting strength and control. It was a lie. There was no control tonight, no order, only indiscriminant chaos, and he was to blame. His mind wound around and around that thought. It was all his fault.

Hessing wrenched open his desk and pulled out a glass and half-empty bottle of whiskey. He forced himself to pour it out, and not drink it from the bottle. There needed to be some civilization tonight. He could control himself, if nothing else.

Hessing knocked back the glass and poured himself another drink.

There was a tap on the door. Cambor entered without waiting. He was bruised and bloody and there were scratch marks on his face and neck. He sagged against the desk. They were all getting too old for this.

"The telegraph?" Hessing asked, pulling out another glass and pouring the remaining whiskey into it.

Cambor shook his head. "They have pixies and harpies atop the poles, picking us off one by one." He accepted the drink gratefully. "We're policemen," he said, "not soldiers. My men are good in a fight, but this is something else."

"Damn it!" Hessing slammed the desk, sending the empty bottle shattering to the ground. "We don't even know if the Duke made it out of the Ball alive, if there's anyone in charge."

Cambor leaned forward. "Wasn't there supposed to be a Psychics Communications System?" he asked. "With adepts trained in long-range communication?"

"Yes," said Hessing. "The magicians' favorite project."

"Then where is it when we need it?"

"Budget cuts. Parliament voted against it. The training was too expensive. Telegraph was cheaper."

"Lovely."

A constable raced into the office, out of breath and bleeding. Hessing and Cambor exchanged grim looks.

"Take your time, constable," said Hessing. "But not too much time."

"Thank you, sir," the constable said, saluting. "Report from Inspector Vorn, sir."

"Yes?"

'There are soldiers on the street, sir, advancing toward the Faërie Quarter."

"Soldiers?"

"Yes, sir. Bearing the Ducal Emblem."

"He has outside communication." Hessing stood. "The Duke brought troops in and he didn't tell me."

"The telegraph is down," Cambor reminded him.

"There are other ways," said Hessing. "He could have sent a runner."

"Maybe he did," said Cambor. "Maybe they didn't get through."

"Killed, you mean? All of them?" Hessing shook his head. "I hope not. I've sent out almost twenty myself." He stared into space for a long moment, thinking. Then he banged the table again. "Go back to Vorn," he ordered the corporal. "Tell him to fall back and link up with the soldiers. You too, Inspector, tell everyone you can find. Let the Guard bear the brunt of the fighting. We've done our bit already."

"Yes, sir."

"That's what they're for, after all."

The constable saluted and left. Cambor remained, watching Hessing with a faint frown.

"What is it, Inspector?" Hessing asked.

"Nothing, sir." Cambor turned to leave, but then stopped. "It's just..." He paused. "Is there some reason the Duke wouldn't tell us about the Guard?"

"Of course not, Inspector."

"Very good, sir. Only, you seemed...worried."

"Yes I'm worried! The whole city is falling apart around us!"

Cambor nodded. "I'll make sure everyone retreats as soon as possible," he said. "Get our people out of harm's way."

"Thank you, Inspector."

Hessing scowled at Cambor's back. He was right. Hessing was worried. It was probably nothing, of course. It was chaos out there. More than likely, the Duke's message simply hadn't gotten through. That was all perfectly logical, but doubt still gnawed at him. Suppose the Duke had found out about his dealings with Mr. Nix; or worse, Mr. Tarr. Suppose he was sending troops to arrest him, men he could trust. It was paranoid, but tonight was a good night for paranoia.

*

Lady Olivia could hear the shouting and screams outside. Angry voices were gathering in the street below, shouting slurs and death to her husband. Theodore wasn't there, but she doubted that would stop them. They had come for vengeance. She could see the fire of their torches through the curtains, but she was not afraid. Let the mob batter itself against the walls. She trusted in the house her husband had built. He had done that well, if nothing else. She trusted in faithful, old Lemann with fierceness in his eyes. Then there was her husband's creature, Sergeant Lund, pacing outside the door, armed and determined.

They all seemed so far away, like actors in a play that she was only half-watching. A curious, languid calm had descended on her. Her thoughts were slippery and sluggish. Perhaps Dr. Trefusis had been right after all. Perhaps something was broken inside of her. Even that thought lacked its customary bitterness.

She was keenly aware of Gregor sitting next to her on the bed. His every movement, every breath, loomed large, filling her, until there was nothing else anymore, just her son. Her fingers ached to touch him, to ruffle his hair and hold him close forever, but his hair was greasy and stiff, and his body was poorly knit together and clammy to the touch.

She remembered him as he was—her beautiful boy. She had decorated him in curls and dresses until he was nearly eight, and cared for all his cuts and bruises. He used to tell her all his secrets, and come to her when his father had been cross. That was the Gregor that she wanted back, but she had lost him long before he'd tied the noose.

He hadn't spoken a single word since he'd come home. She wasn't sure that he could. His breaths were torturous sighs that wracked his body and broke her heart. She had barely left his side since his homecoming—every second away tore into her. She was always afraid that the next moment he'd be gone.

The shouting below had picked up in intensity and there was a great pounding on the front door. The walls shook at the force of it. They had built a makeshift battering ram. There were scattered gunshots and shattered glass. She could hear Sergeant Lund outside, stirring and preparing himself.

"It's going to be alright," Lady Olivia whispered softly. Gregor gave no sign that he'd heard.

They sat there together in his old room on his old bed, while the mob raged below them. She had kept the room just as he'd left it, to remind her of him. She stared at his pile of law books, the heap of dirty clothes and handful of old toy soldiers. She looked everywhere and at everything, but not at him. Never at him. She loved the thing that was her son. Loved him completely. But she never turned her head. Not once.

*

Anselm stepped over a fallen harpy that lay bleeding in the street, and raised a plundered rifle aloft.

"Forward," he cried. "Follow me!" The faëries surged around him. After the Guard's sudden appearance, Anselm, Brunet, and, unexpectedly, Covét, had rallied the mob.

The old faun had proved surprisingly useful. Anselm had never doubted his dedication or his spite—in his heart he had always been one of them—but the faun had been vicious in the fighting, almost Droz's equal in ferocity. Anselm could see him now, letting loose a terrible wordless cry as he led a band of ogres, wights, and knockers forward, even as they were raked by gunfire.

Hundreds had fallen, but it didn't matter. There were always more to take their place. On and on they came, seemingly impervious to death, and some, with hides thick enough, truly were impervious to bullets. Even the Guard was giving way before them.

They retreated slowly before the onslaught, but it was a fighting retreat. The front rank fired, then fell back as the second rank fired, and then the third. The Guard was wounded, but still dangerous—spitting fire, and bristling with bayonets.

"Steady, men," Lieutenant Berg said, his voice level. A glance at the men showed him that it had been unnecessary. They were professionals. Even in retreat they were unhurried. There was no panic in their eyes, not even defeat, just confidence, confidence in the Brigadier, confidence in him. That was the most surprising thing of all. He caught Sergeant Rudbeck's eye. The old soldier gave him an encouraging nod. He was doing well in his first command under fire.

From a few streets behind him Berg could hear the screech of wheels, the rumbling of metal, and shouted orders. Kronberger was planning a surprise for the enemy. The faëries did not lack for courage, but their leaders lacked strategy. They would pay for that. He and his men just needed to slow them down a little longer, until Kronberger was ready. He wasn't sure what the Brigadier had prepared, but he had faith. A bugle call echoed in the early morning air. That was the signal.

"Fall back," Berg ordered and the sergeants picked up the call.

"Retreat," Rudbeck shouted. "On the double!" The slow retreat became a rushing stream, but lost none of its discipline.

"They're running!" Anselm cried. "This is our moment!" The faëries charged forward in anticipation. Victory was there at last for the taking.

Waiting for them at the next intersection were two rows of cannon. The faëries stumbled to a startled, frightened halt. The first row was aimed straight for them, and the second was pointed skyward, primed and loaded with grapeshot. The gunners stood at the ready, as Gunnery Captain Reich ran from cannon to cannon checking the sightings. Behind them, Berg and the Guard had reformed their ranks.

Brigadier Kronberger was on horseback, watching the enemy, waiting, judging. The first row of faëries had tried to stop, but they were being pushed forward by the onrush behind. Closer. Closer. They were advancing now in spite of themselves. Advancing into his trap.

Kronberger nodded to Captain Reich. "Fire!" he ordered.

The cannon barrage was tremendous, noise and smoke and death. The faërie line exploded in broken limbs and torn bodies, wavered, but continued forward, trampling the wounded beneath its feet and hooves. High above Droz and his winged cohorts dove down intent of clawing and slashing, but were met with the second volley of cannon fire which burst into thousands of metal balls that mauled wings and shattered stone. The Guard was prepared for them.

"Feed it in!" Captain Reich cried, as his gunners poured more powder down the barrels and readied another barrage. "That's it, boys. Fire!"

Another explosion of sound and death tore through the air. Already the gunners were reloading and firing again and again. Thousands died, and before they could recover, before they even knew what was happening, the artillery tore into them again. Bravery and rage was no match for shot and shell.

Heinrich made for a conspicuous target. A shell struck the troll directly, shattering his knee. He screamed half in shock, then fell. He had never felt such pain. There were few things that could harm a troll. Seeing him collapse, the faërie line splintered. Anselm desperately tried to rally them yet again, as he had so many times that night, but his voice was lost in the confusion, and another explosion sent him sprawling, his whole left side a mangled bleeding mess.

Covét ran to him quickly. Around them the remnants of the mob limped and ran, trying desperately to escape the inferno. The bombardment had not let up. In the distance they could hear Reich exhorting his men to fire again faster and faster.

"We can't lose you," Covét said and lifted the homunculus onto his back. They were never going to make it.

Suddenly Droz swooped down to clutch Covét in his talons, and lifted him into the air. They were gone in a moment. Brunet, having escaped the worst of the attack, struggled to help Heinrich to his feet. The troll was too big to carry, but Brunet could serve as a crutch. They half limped, half crawled behind the others, desperate to escape.

Covét glanced down in horror, his worst fears realized. Everything had changed so quickly.

CHAPTER TWENTY-NINE

Only when the last of the faëries had scurried away did Kronberger give the order to ceasefire. Broad Street was a picture of misery, a scene from some ancient hell—dead and dying monsters lay strewn across the street, blood and limbs were everywhere. Kronberger was unmoved. Slaughter was his business. There was no time for sentimentality in the midst of battle. Already he was planning to press the attack. Only later, when the killing was over, would he stop to mourn.

"Advance," he ordered. "Show no quarter!"

The Guard poured past the cannons, bayonetting the survivors, running after the broken enemy, following them deeper into the city, to the Faërie Quarter if necessary. He stopped Lieutenant Berg.

"Take a detachment," he ordered, "Report to the Duke and

bolster the Mansion's defenses. Inform him that I've broken the mob and am pursuing the enemy to the utmost."

"Yes, sir." Berg saluted.

Brigadier Kronberger turned back to the bloody street. This was a success, but the faëries must be destroyed utterly, or they would rise again. He would run them down, every last one, until even the dream of rebellion was a distant, frightening memory. Anything else would be only half a victory, and he had business with the Commandant.

*

The Countess crept out of an alley onto Broad Street and beheld the devastation. It was sickening. The City sang to her of death and screams, of lives lost, and of dreams slaughtered. It resounded in her mind full of sights and smells and pain. She knew the names of all the dead as well as she knew her own. Their lives and hatreds and fears poured through her. She felt the City's love for each and every one of them, even as her Purpose rejoiced in their deaths, glorified in the ruin of her enemies. The Countess pushed that away, buried the visions and emotions in the deep dungeons of her self, with her doubts and her memories. This was not the time for either. She glanced first one way, then the other.

The fighting had moved on. The faëries were in full flight, and the soldiers had followed, leaving such terrible destruction in their wake. She gestured back at the darkness. All clear. Lady Anne emerged and stared at the sight. Bile rose in her throat. She had never conceived of death on such a scale. She swallowed. There would be time for that later. Survival came first.

"You're almost home," said the Countess. "Just a little farther."

Lady Anne nodded, took a deep breath, and waded into the tangle of death. She slipped once or twice in black blood, and almost tripped over a torso, but she held her nerve. She walked and crawled through the bodies to the far side, toward the Rook Gate, toward home.

*

Police Headquarters was rumbling with activity. Most of the tables in the bullpen had been cleared and thrown together into makeshift hospital beds. The police coroners had been drafted as medics, and were hacking into living people for a change, trying to patch up wounds as best they could, and to remember their surgeon training. Inspectors and constables were shouting orders, shoring up defenses, keeping everyone busy and the panic at bay.

Inspector Vorn and his men had finally streamed in almost an hour ago, his body bruised and dignity battered. He was immediately sequestered in Hessing's office with Cambor and the Commandant. Hessing had interrogated him about Kronberger and the Guard. Went back over and over their brief conversation. He attempted to remain casual, but couldn't hide the intensity in his voice, not entirely. Even hurt and tired, Cambor and Vorn couldn't fail to notice the undertones, in between glaring at each other. Their fight earlier that evening had not been forgotten.

There was a pounding on the outer door. Every head—that was able—turned. The hubbub fell silent. The activity stilled. Even the coroners paused in their bloody work. It had been locked and barred, and chairs had been shored up against it. The pounding on the door intensified.

"It's the Ducal Guard," one of the lookouts called from the window.

Hessing emerged, flanked by Cambor and Vorn, and stood on the observation deck outside his office overlooking the bullpen. A constable by the door glanced up at him, waiting for orders.

Irons in the Fire

Hessing hesitated, then nodded. He had pondered all the angles. There was nothing more he could do. He needed to know one way or the other.

Five constables unbolted the door and it swung open with a protesting shriek. Soldiers poured in immediately, double time. They lined the walls, and took up positions at all the doors and exits. They were dripping wet, but clearly deadly. Cambor and Vorn exchanged worried glances, their enmity briefly forgotten. This had the appearance of an occupation. For his part, Hessing kept his expression level. He had made his choice.

Brigadier Kronberger burst through the doors without any undue fanfare. The soldiers snapped to attention, even as more filed in behind him. He took in his surroundings at a glance. His face revealed nothing, but there was a proprietary air about him. He marched straight up the stairs toward Hessing, who turned his great bulk to greet him. It was a meeting of giants—Hessing the wary boar of a man, and Kronberger the no-nonsense martinet. Every eye was on them. They studied each other warily.

After a moment, Hessing held out his hand. It hung in the air between them. Kronberger looked at the man then down at the hand. He considered. The hand remained outstretched, unwaveringly. Kronberger shook. The whole room seemed to let out a relieved breath, though no one was quite sure why.

"You've done good work tonight," Kronberger said.

Hessing watched the Brigadier for any sign of deceit, any hint of double meanings, and found neither. Kronberger was too straightforward and proud for duplicity. He was safe, for now.

"Thank you," he said. "And I understand many of my men owe you their lives."

"Yes," Kronberger agreed brusquely. Vorn bristled at that, but

Hessing subtly waved him back. Kronberger paid no heed. "Our work isn't done," he continued. "My boys are driving the faëries back into their Quarter, like rats in a trap. I was hoping you might help me close that trap."

Hessing nodded. "My people know the Quarter quite well."

"I have no doubt," said Kronberger. "Furthermore, I shall be setting up my forward command post here for the duration of the crisis. I trust you will have no objections."

Hessing glanced around at the Guards still trouping in below, already starting to make themselves at home. "No," he said, "of course not. It'll be an honor."

Not that he had any choice in the matter. Perhaps he wasn't quite as safe as he had believed.

*

The faëries fell back into the Quarter in droves, streaming in from all directions. Some returned to their homes and cowered behind locked doors, hoping beyond hope that the soldiers would pass them by, but there was no mercy that night. They had been vicious in their anger. The Guard had seen the destruction they had wrought, and the police had experienced it firsthand. They were determined to repay the faëries in kind. Blood for blood.

They leveled whole city blocks and ravaged the inhabitants. The faëries were stronger. They had magic and wonder in their blood, but their force was spent, and the Guard had faced the Wild Faëries of the Borderlands. These urban creatures who had lived for generations under the yoke first of Witchling tyranny and then of human law were only pale shadows. They were beaten and shot without mercy, door by door.

Others retreated deeper into the labyrinth of winding, nameless streets at the heart of the Quarter. They were starting to build barricades—desperate, ramshackle affairs, overturned carts, piled chairs and tables, and any piece of furniture they could get their hands or claws or tentacles on. Ogres, trolls, fauns, satyrs, and gnomes were working feverously. It was their last hope against what was coming.

Covét was among them, handing furniture up the chain to a battle-scarred cyclops, when he saw Brunet and Heinrich limping past. They had been separated in the chaos. He clambered down.

Brunet didn't give him a chance to speak. "Close the barricade!" he cried.

"There are still more coming in," Covét protested.

"And the Guard is right behind them!"

But Brunet could have saved his breath. Covét could see them now through the gaps in the barricade, advancing in ranks.

"Quickly!" he ordered. "Close up the barricade!" The others hurried to obey. Already bullets were whizzing past. They got the final piece of furniture in place at the last second—a misshapen armchair designed for octapedal anatomy.

A pair of crones, elementals and an old forest spirit stepped forward, drawing their symbols, speaking their words, and calling on the souls of murdered trees to defend them. Few of their kind had ventured out into the riots. Perhaps they had foreseen the ruin, or perhaps their place was simply in the Quarter. Magic was concentrated there.

The scent of enchantment was heavy in the air. Covét watched the crones and elementals at their work avidly. He had always possessed an academic interest in their magic. Faun enchantment lay mostly in music and song, but he was tone deaf. That had been his first great bitterness. There was nothing academic about his current interest, however. Their survival rested on the successful spell casting. Overturned furniture would not protect them on its own for long.

Everyone felt the enchantment take root. It was like an onrush of fresh forest air. The barricade didn't look any different, but it felt more solid, almost alive. Even Droz could not escape the notion that one of the chairs was looking at him funny. It wasn't a moment too soon. The Guard was almost upon them.

Covét turned to those gathered around him. "Go!" he said. "Tell the others to get their barricades up and enchanted. This'll be no use if they flank us."

They took off in every direction, running, flying, crawling. One spindle-legged creature climbed the walls and scurried along at breakneck speed. That done, Covét took a moment and rushed to his friend's side with Droz right behind him.

Heinrich was slumped against the barricade, Brunet exhausted beside him. Covét knelt down. The troll's knee was shattered and he was in terrible pain, but his expression was mostly one of confusion. He had never experienced anything like this before in his life. There were few things that could seriously harm a troll, and as a businessman, he had encountered practically none of them. Pain was a strange, alien sensation.

"We've set up a hospital at the Thirsty Goblin," said Covét, patting the troll on the shoulder. Even when Heinrich was sitting, Covét still had to reach up.

"Anselm?" Heinrich managed to ask softly. Brunet looked up at that. The hopes of many rested on the answer. Covét and Droz exchanged glances.

"Not good," said Covét. "The healers and doctors are with him now. If he can be saved by magic or medicine, they will do it." It was not a reassuring answer and they all knew it.

Brunet nodded. He had glimpsed Anselm back on Broad Street. It had not looked promising.

Shouted orders came from the far side of the barricade. The Guard was massing to renew the assault. The alley was narrow and afforded them little room to maneuver, that was why Covét had chosen it, but they would adapt quickly.

"They've brought up their own magicians," a young five-armed boy called down from his perch. Grand Master Undur and his adepts had arrived.

Undur studied the barricade, frowning. He could feel the strength of the enchantment; taste the forest in the air. Crones he could handle easily, but there were elementals at work here, and a forest spirit. Their magic had deep roots to untangle. Not that he doubted himself, but it would take longer than he'd hoped. Still, he couldn't resist the rush of excitement. After a night spent fighting with claws and talons, shot and shell, faërie and human magic would finally be joined. Magic against magic, human against faërie. He had dreamed of this moment.

"Take your positions," he ordered. The adepts moved into position around him, forming a diamond. "Excellent," he said. "Let us begin."

"The Duke must have given them permission," Covét said, peering through the barricade as they began to chant. It had only been a matter of time.

"I didn't think he'd risk a magical war in the city," Droz said.

"We unleashed a Creature from the Depths and tried to kill him," Covét said. "What did you think he'd do?"

Droz shrugged. "I never really thought about it." The Duke had been supposed to die in the attack. Droz still wasn't sure how the

Duke's men had killed the Creature so quickly. He turned back to the increasingly desperate matter at hand.

"We could drive them back," Droz offered with a hint of his former ferocity, but his heart clearly wasn't in it. "Go out in a blaze of glory, not trapped like vermin."

Covét shook his head. He had already thought those thoughts. It was why he'd joined the Dissidents in the first place, but now that it came down to it, he couldn't do it. Things had changed. He had changed.

"No," he said. " We've lost too many already. We need to preserve what we can."

"Preserve?" Droz asked. "For what?"

"For the next time," Covét replied. "I have no intention of going out in a blaze of glory or otherwise. I mean to salvage what I can. I mean to win. It's what Anselm would want." Covét was careful to use the present tense. Droz stared at him as though he had never seen the old faun before, and perhaps he hadn't.

"Next time?" he breathed.

"Yes."

An air spirit floated down the street to Droz, and, following his stunned gaze, turned to Covét. "Anselm is fading," it whispered in the voice of the sky and wind, and the fell silent. Nothing more needed to be said.

Covét nodded grimly. "Can you stay here?" he asked Brunet. "We need someone we can trust to hold the line."

"Yes." Brunet's voice echoed tiredly from his neck.

"Good." Covét and Droz headed deeper into the Quarter, toward the Thirsty Goblin, half dragging Heinrich between them.

*

The tavern was filled with the dead and dying of every

description as faërie doctors, hags, and spirits went up and down the room, tending the wounded as best they could. Anselm was lying on the center table, crippled and probably dying. He was holding on to life by a thin thread of will and magic. A pair of doctors and a sprite were attending to him. Heinrich had been placed in the far corner and was watching Anselm anxiously, even as his own wounds were being bandaged.

The doctors worked desperately, stitching up his mangled body, while the sprite chanted a song of healing. It did not appear to be helping much. The bleeding had slowed, but the homunculus was not built as humans were, or even other faëries. Almost any other creature, certainly the more terrestrial ones, would have died already, but the same uniqueness that had saved him originally was now stymieing further healing efforts. His body was crafted from flesh and spells, and it reacted to medicine and healing magic in unpredictable ways.

Covét and Droz conferred over the body of their dying leader. Anselm had been the center of the movement, the only one that all the factions had trusted. His death could be more devastating than any retreat.

"No one must know," Covét said.

Droz glanced around the crowded tavern. "I think it's too late for that," he said.

Covét reluctantly agreed. "It may not matter, anyway. The barricades won't hold for long. The Guard will break through eventually, especially with the Grand Master himself on hand, and even if we hold out, sooner or later the Imperial Army will become involved. You and Anselm pinned all your hopes on surprise, but we didn't move quickly enough."

Droz rustled his feathers angrily, but he couldn't disagree. The attack on the Ball should have given them enough cover. Even when the Creature died, they had failed more from their own lethargy than any particular action the Duke or Hessing had taken.

"Now that we're out in the open," Covét continued, "we've herded ourselves together, playing by the human's rules. The shadows are where we're strongest, in the hidden places."

"What did you have in mind?" Droz asked.

"We return to our strengths. Get as many as we can into the caves below, Anselm too, if he'll survive the trip."

"Retreat," Droz sneered.

"Yes," said Covét. "And collapse the main entrance behind us."

"They won't show any mercy," Droz said. "The Guard will slaughter all those we leave behind."

"I know," said Covét, "but they'll be avenged."

"You're a cold bastard."

"And he wasn't?" Covét nodded down at Anselm. Droz said nothing to that. He wasn't a paragon of virtue either, but he was a predator. It was his nature. Covét in his shabby, bloodied coat, and spectacles that had miraculously survived the night, was something else entirely.

"Are we agreed?" the faun asked.

"Yes," said Droz. "We're agreed."

"Then there's no time to waste."

*

At the barricade, the crones, elementals and forest spirit were locked in battle with Grand Master Undur and the human magicians. The spirit and the elementals were chanting songs and melodies that vibrated the very strings of the world, while the crones etched symbols in the air. This was faërie magic, the magic of the Word. It was wild and strange and ancient. The air hummed with it. The cobblestones pulsed. The barricade seemed to grow and twist under their power. A number of Guards were already impaled upon it, casualties of the first attempt to break through. A few cannon balls had lodged inside and had become incorporated.

On the far side, Undur and the others had donned their ceremonial robes and were enacting their rites and rituals. They were reciting their formulas and holding aloft their rods and implements. Theirs was the magic of Book and Wand and it met the Word and strove against it, pressing against the barricade.

The magicians looked down upon faërie magic as wild and untamed, but in this they erred, for its great strength lay in its wildness. Faëries in their turn despised human magic as too strict and formulaic, chained behind rules and regulations, but there was power in rites and rituals. The formulas were not so different from the songs, and it was all but an echo of the Deep Magic, written onto the very atoms of creation. In the end, they both miscalculated. As they circled each other on the astral plane, maneuvering spell for spell, they forgot that the barricade in the end was only so much wood and upholstery.

It shattered, splintered into a thousand pieces of shrapnel, flying into both sides, killing or wounding hundreds. Their magic hovered in the air for a moment, groping blindly for the barricade that was no longer there, before fading into nothingness.

The Guard recovered first, fired a volley, then charged with bayonets fixed. Brunet tried to fight them off, but it was no use. He was down to only a handful of faëries and most of them were as exhausted as he was. They fell back, running as quickly as they could. A few gryphons and a centaur even deigned to allow the others to climb on their backs, and sped away. They weren't all fast enough though, and the Guardsmen had good aim.

There was no order to the faërie retreat, only panic and chaos. Brunet ran, desperately trying to escape. A headless man was far from inconspicuous, even in the Quarter, and somehow the Guard had learned of his importance—probably from Vorn. He found the tavern still filled and terrified, but there was no sign of Covét, Anselm or the others. They must have slipped out in the confusion.

An explosion rumbled in the distance, throwing out a cloud of dust, and then another. Everyone looked around uncertainly, but Brunet understood immediately. They had blown up the underground entrance, and set a few more explosions to cover their tracks. It was a good plan, but he was trapped on the wrong side of it.

He ran from the tavern but the soldiers were everywhere. No matter how many twists and turns he took, the Guardsmen were there. He scrambled down a blind alley and came to a halt, trapped. In the end, even he had gotten lost in those labyrinthine streets. He turned. Soldiers were baring down on him, but he wouldn't give up without a fight. He was already dead, after all. Let them come.

CHAPTER THIRTY

Hessing's carriage arrived home in the early morning light. There was an armed policeman sitting up with the coachman, and four more riding alongside. The fighting had mostly subsided. The Dissidents and mobs had slunk back into their homes, but there were still reports of isolated incidents, and caution was the watchword of the day. There were many who would have considered killing Hessing suitable retaliation.

The rain had stopped, but the dark clouds remained looming ominously over the city, mingling with the smoke and ash. Hessing stepped down onto the street, warily. His eyes darted about, searching for anything his men might have missed. Nothing. There was an eerie stillness in the air. Bodies and debris littered the road. The stench was nauseating. Hessing covered his nose and mouth and climbed up the steps to his front door.

There were signs of a struggle. A few of the ground-floor windows had been smashed, but the bars had held. There were faëries lying dead on his front porch—a horned man and a female sphinx among others. The door, reinforced with steel and spell, had also taken a battering, but Hessing had paid good money to turn his home into a fortress, and last night his investment had been rewarded. At least something had gone according to plan.

He felt hedged in from all sides, trapped by his secret involvement in the attack. The walls were closing in around him, and there was no escape that he could see. His position was too precarious. No one had discovered his role, as yet, but it was only a matter of time. Mr. Nix had reasons of his own to keep quiet, but Tarr was a loose cannon. Hobgoblins were dangerously unpredictable by nature, and he was even more so.

Hessing ran his fingers through his hair. It had been a long night and he was bone tired. He barely had the energy left to worry. With a few hours sleep and a clear head, he might be able to find a way out of his predicament. He had fought and schemed his way out of tough spots before, but the Duke had always been on his side. Things would be different this time.

Lemann and the others were waiting for him inside. They seemed to be in good spirits, smiling and nodding. They had escaped the worst of the night's activities. They straightened up when he arrived, but Hessing waved them down and shook hands with Wroe and Waller.

"Thank you, boys," he said. "You've done well. You've done very well. I won't forget this. I promise that your loyalty will be amply rewarded."

"Thank you, sir. Thank you."

He gave them a fond smile, while they bowed and scraped.

They would remember that smile and think well of him. It took more than coin to buy loyalty, but Hessing would make sure they received coin as well.

"Lemann." He turned and nodded to his butler. Lemann nodded back. There was no need for ham-fisted bribery here. Lemann was Lemann, ever-present, ever loyal. That left only one man. He glanced around, but couldn't find him.

"He's upstairs," the butler said. Hessing nodded. Of course he was.

"Get some rest," he said to Wroe and Waller. "You've earned it."

Dismissing them, he began to ascend slowly, his legs wobbling beneath him. Lund was exactly where he expected—still at his post, guarding Gregor's room. He looked even worse than Hessing. He was caked in dried blood, but he was still alert, still on edge. He tensed when he heard someone approach, his hand going to his gun, but relaxed at the sight of Hessing.

"Sir," he said. There was a curious, strangled note in his voice. Hessing couldn't quite place it. For the first time, he felt the faintest stirrings of doubt about Lund.

"Sergeant." They stared at each other for a long moment, each searching for something in the other.

"I understand, sir," Lund said at length. "I understand everything." Whatever he was looking for, he had found it, for better or worse. "I kept them safe."

"Thank you, Sergeant." Hessing breathed a sigh of relief. "You're welcome to sleep here. I'll send someone to fetch the sawbones."

"That's not necessary, sir."

"Yes," said Hessing. "It is. I want you to stay close, just in case." He didn't say in case of what, but it wasn't necessary.

Lund nodded in understanding and limped back toward the stairs. Lemann followed him.

"Try to get some sleep, sir," he said, then disappeared down the hall.

Alone at last, Hessing stood staring at his son's door. He hadn't been inside Gregor's room in months, not since that terrible night. He thought, longingly, of his own bed, but he couldn't wait any longer. Not for this. Summoning what was left of his strength, Hessing knocked and entered. His family was inside, waiting for him.

"Olivia," he said. She was standing behind Gregor protectively.

"Theodore," she replied, her voice trembling slightly. He wasn't sure if it was regret or relief. "You're still alive."

She regarded him for a moment. "You look like hell."

"It's been that kind of night." He offered a half-smile. She did not return it, but he was oddly relieved. There was, at least, one constant left in his world.

"I want to speak to my son," he said. "Alone."

She narrowed her eyes at him. "And if I refuse?"

"I'll make you," he said softly. There was no threat in his voice, just an exhausted certainty.

Her eyes flashed with their old fire. He loved to see her anger, except when it was aimed at him. It was a reassuring sign. She was emerging from her languor. Perhaps she was finally putting her hysteria behind her.

"After everything I've done to bring us all here," he continued, "I have earned that."

"Everything you've done?" She was incredulous.

"Yes." He met her glare unflinchingly.

She sighed and glanced down at her son. After a moment, Gregor nodded at her, but he only had eyes for his father.

"Very well," she said. "But this isn't over."

"No," Hessing agreed. "It isn't."

She brushed past him on her way out and slammed the door behind her.

Once she was gone, Gregor rose slowly, awkwardly to face him. It was a painful shifting of limbs, accompanied by creaking bones, but they stood finally face to face.

"Hello, father," he said. It was a small voice, croaking and broken. It seemed to come from very far away, but it was recognizably his own.

"You can talk," said Hessing.

"Yes," said Gregor. "I can talk."

"It really is you. You're alive!" Hessing couldn't help himself. He grinned. He had risked everything on a hope, but now he knew for certain. It truly was his son beneath the grotesque, misshapen flesh. His son was alive.

Gregor shifted under his father's gaze. He had never seen him smile, not like this. It was disconcerting. It was aggravating.

"You had no right," he said.

"No," Hessing answered. "I suppose I didn't, but I would do it again."

"Why?"

"Why?" Hessing frowned. "Because you're my son."

"That's not a reason."

"It's my reason."

"That's not good enough," said Gregor. There was a long pause. Hessing remained silent, watching. "I've been a failure all my life,"

Gregor continued. "You always thought so. I could never measure up to the great Commandant. Now I've failed even at death, and it's all your fault."

"I'm not sorry for that," said Hessing. "Everything else, but not that."

Gregor wilted. "I know," he said. "And that's what makes it worse."

He looked so miserable, so small, but Hessing couldn't help but feel a giddy sense of joy. He was talking to his son. It didn't matter if they argued. It didn't matter if Gregor hated him. He was alive again, and they were talking. He would always have that. Whatever happened now, it would all be worth it. No matter what.

*

Auberon Square was bristling with armed soldiers when Raske arrived at the Ducal Mansion. He had wanted to leave Evá at their apartment. It had been a strategic move as much as anything else. He needed to appear competent in his own right. Rumors about his 'muse' had already begun to circulate. But she had insisted. They would be safer together, and it was hard to argue when they passed countless burnt and bombed-out houses.

The last time Raske had been here, he had been attempting to undermine the Duke's support. The speech seemed like it had been years ago instead of days. Living in the city, it was easy to think of Lord Edward as just another politician, another faction. Gazing at the martial display, Raske was reminded for the first time just how powerful the Duke truly was. It was a sobering thought, but it only made his errand more imperative. The past week had been a series of disasters, but today was an opportunity.

"Halt!" A pair of soldiers approached, brandishing their rifles. "No one's allowed in the Square."

Raske raised his hands high and fought to keep his voice level. "My name is Charles Raske," he said. "And this is my wife." She gave them a wan smile. "I need to speak to the Duke. Immediately."

The soldiers, a lieutenant and a private, exchanged glances. "The Duke doesn't have time to meet with civilians," the lieutenant said. "Take your wife home and lock yourselves inside. The streets aren't safe yet."

"Thank you," said Raske. "What's your name?"

"Berg," the lieutenant answered. Raske reached into his pocket slowly, careful not to startle them.

"Well, Lieutenant Berg," he said, handing him a photograph from the file Evá had found, "just show that to the Duke. He'll see me then."

Berg glanced down at the photograph, then back up at Raske. The man seemed very sure of himself. Behind him, the woman met his gaze unblinkingly. Berg shrugged. "We'll see about that."

*

The Duke was in the telegraph room, hovering over the map of the city. He was surrounded by a number of tired-looking men detailing the situation on the ground. An officer approached and stood to the side, diffidently. The Duke glanced over. He didn't recognize him. The Mansion was filled with unfamiliar faces now.

"Your grace," the officer said.

"Yes? What is it, Lieutenant?"

"There's a man outside. He says his name is Raske."

"Raske?" The Duke frowned. "Send him away. I don't have time for that man's nonsense."

"Yes, your grace." The lieutenant shifted slightly.

"Was there anything else?"

"He said to show you this." Lieutenant Berg handed over the photograph.

The Duke pulled out his glasses and studied the picture for a long moment. He didn't say anything for almost a minute—then he pocketed the photograph.

"I need to see Raske," he said. "Bring him to me. Immediately."

*

Lady Anne half stumbled down the familiar halls. She and the Countess had finally reached the Ducal Mansion and safety. The guards had almost not recognized her. Dirt-stained and bloody, she and her companion had been ushered in by the chief steward. It had been a long, grueling night. They had spent most of the time hiding in gutters. She had thought they were dead or worse half a dozen times, but she was home now.

It had been less than a day since she'd last been here, but the Mansion with its smooth marble and opulent furniture now seemed like another world. The Countess trailed behind her, gazing around with the same shell-shocked expression. Lady Anne had lived here for the better part of sixty years. Sometimes it was difficult to remember that first awe-inspiring impression. It had been built as a witch's palace, after all.

Lady Anne did find it reassuring that the Countess could be awed. Indeed, she seemed more overwhelmed by the Mansion than she had by the riots. They had spent the past few hours together running for their lives, and the younger woman had been relentlessly calm under pressure. She had saved Lady Anne's life multiple times, often seemingly effortlessly. The nonchalance had been impressive, if intimidating.

They reached Lady Anne's sitting room and collapsed gratefully onto the settee. They were trailing blood and muck, but carpets could be replaced, furniture could be reupholstered. Lady Anne gave a sigh of relief, the Countess not far behind. A servant moved to pour them a drink.

"The Duke is on his way," the steward announced.

"Thank you," said Lady Anne. Beside her, the Countess sat up straight.

"Should I leave, my lady?" she asked.

"Call me Anne," the Duchess said. "You've earned that right. And no, stay where you are. We've come through hell together. I owe you my life. The Duke should know that."

The Countess opened her mouth to protest, but Lady Anne sent her a quelling look. "As you wish," the Countess said, and they fell into an exhausted, companionable silence.

The Duke came running in moments later. He could be surprisingly spry when motivated. He came to a halt and stared.

"Anne," he said. "I feared you were dead." He reached down and embraced her tightly.

"I nearly was," Lady Anne said. "More than once, but I survived thanks to the Countess here."

The Duke turned to the other woman and schooled his expression. "Forgive me," he said. "I did not mean to be rude."

"Please." The Countess waved that away. "There's no need to apologize."

"Edward," said Lady Anne, "this is Countess Antoinette Wyman-Straus."

"Charmed," said the Duke with a bow. "And the Count is your...?"

"Husband," the Countess answered. "He was my husband."

"I see." The Duke grunted, studying her curiously. "Well, it appears that my wife and I owe you a great debt."

"I was merely trying to survive." The Countess shrugged modestly.

"You succeeded," said the Duke, "and we are all very grateful for that." He hid a frown. Something about the gesture had felt far too practiced. She was clearly an intelligent and resourceful young woman, but he had never heard of her.

A pair of servants arrived and announced that the ladies' baths were ready. The Duke blinked and held up his hand, pondering. "No," he said leaning forward. "Not yet. You two are perfect exactly the way you are."

The Countess frowned, but Lady Anne sighed. She knew exactly how her husband's mind worked. "Is that really necessary?" she asked.

"Yes," he said. "I'm afraid so."

"Very well."

The Countess glanced back and forth. "Is what really necessary?" she asked.

"He wants to have our photographs taken as we are," said Lady Anne.

"As we are?" The Countess glanced down at her tattered, stained clothing.

"Yes," said the Duke. "The story is going to break, and we need to get out in front of it. The world needs to know what those animals did to you, to two ladies of noble rank. It is imperative that the faëries not garner any sympathy. Your pictures would be most useful. I understand if you are reluctant…"

"No, I understand perfectly," she interrupted. "Anything I can do to help."

"Then I must thank you again," he said.

The Countess looked the Duke in the eye and felt the Purpose, the glorious, terrible Purpose inside her sing with vicious joy. The Countess shivered with a pleasure that was not entirely her own, and she smiled.

"Rejoice," the Purpose seemed to say. "There is the enemy. At long last, there is the enemy."

Epilogue

They had retreated to the caves just in time. The underground chamber was filled with goblins and minotaurs, trolls and fauns, sprites, ghouls, and other creatures, most of them injured. Where before this had been a storeroom, a staging area full of hope and anger, and busy with plots and sorcery, now it was filled with the wails of the dying, populated by long, disheartened faces. Even Droz, whose hatred had helped stoke the movement, and had been its burning predatory soul, was dimmed.

Anselm had survived the journey in the dark, through the sewers and hidden places of the under city, but only just. Droz and Heinrich were gathered around him, mourning him even before he drew his last breath, mourning the dream that had been lost. Mr. Tarr had reappeared from wherever he had vanished, and had managed to slip in with the others.

Sitting apart from them, however, Covét was lost in his own thoughts. He had not been part of the Dissidents' plans. He had not known about the box or the thing inside, had not spent days in this very cavern hatching schemes and sharing dreams. He had not been wedded to their grand design, and so he had learned a different lesson tonight. Anselm and the others had miscalculated

Epilogue

human resistance and faërie ferocity alike. Subtle and tricky, but ultimately small in his thinking, Anselm had dreams of faërie equality, of a stronghold and a sanctuary, but on the other side of his vision there had only been emptiness.

Where the others saw only failure, Covét saw possibilities. They had come close tonight, so close. He could feel it, had glimpsed it in his mind's eye. The others had lost sight of that. Tonight had been a beginning. The Duke and his men hoped to stamp out resistance, but Covét could turn their violence into a rallying cry, make every dead faërie into a martyr. The others were fighters, but he was a writer, an academic, and a rhetorician. Words were his weapon. There would be other nights—he would make certain of that.

*

The Countess was alone at last. She headed immediately for the washroom and started running the water for a bath. She was dirty, grimy, and so very tired, but there was one last task to perform before she could sleep. The water gushed out of the taps and she sat almost in a daze, watching the water level rise higher and higher, preparing herself.

The Duke and Duchess had insisted that she stay in the Mansion. The city wasn't safe, after all. She had allowed herself to be persuaded after sitting for the photographs and letting a reporter ply her with questions, but she was secretly triumphant. Nothing had proceeded according to plan, but she was here nonetheless. She had penetrated into the heart of the city, into the so-called Ducal Mansion itself and it was glorious. She had heard the stories, of course, felt it from a distance, but it was nothing like being there, seeing with her own eyes, hearing the City whisper

Epilogue

the secrets of its construction, and feeling her Purpose purr inside her, as it never had before.

She turned the tap off and let her clothes sink to the floor. The dress was ruined, but the Countess had never cared about such things. She had never had the chance. She dipped her toe into the water, then sank in with a satisfied sigh. It was burning hot, but she preferred it scalding. That was necessary.

The water felt heavenly. She could feel the filth of the night's events washing away, but she was not there to bathe. The Countess took a deep breath, closed her eyes, and then immersed herself entirely beneath the surface. The Countess lay motionless at the bottom of the tub. The water pounded in her ears. She was in another world. Everything seemed so far away. There was only her, the heat, and the water.

It came from the great river of Talis by way of pipes and cisterns. The river flowed down from in the north and had its origins high in the mountains in a hot spring, where the Witches-in-Exile had made their home. The Countess followed the river hundreds and hundreds of miles upstream, past fish and boats, until she reached the spring.

"Hello," she said, and the water rippled with her speaking, and then was still. It was an unwieldy form of communication, but magic mirrors could be blocked, and astral projections could be intercepted.

After a moment, she felt another presence enter the water—old and encrusted in bitterness. It was Aenora, the Elder of the First Witchling Tribe.

"You're late, child," Aenora said.

"I was delayed, Great Aunt," said the Countess.

Epilogue

"Apparently so." Aenora oozed displeasure. The water throbbed with it. "Report!"

"I had made progress with the Dissidents before the riots started, but I don't know who survived. We will have to see where we stand in the weeks to come."

"Yes," said Aenora. "The riots were unfortunate."

"I did manage to save the Duchess' life," the Countess said. "She and the Duke are now in my debt. They have offered me a suite in the Ducal Mansion."

"The Palace," Aenora corrected. "Well, that's something at least. And what of the one they call Nix?"

"I have arranged for his neutrality."

"And in return?"

"A favour to be named later," the Countess said.

"I see." Aenora's voice was harsh and cold. "I suppose you've done the best you could in the circumstances."

"Thank you, Great Aunt," the Countess said. She hesitated, and then pressed onward. "I know," she said.

"What are you talking about, child?" Aenora asked sharply.

"I know about your plan and your secret orders to Elise and Jules."

The water went deadly still. "Are you accusing me, Leonora?"

The name struck her like a physical blow. The Countess had carefully wrapped herself in layers of identity, but they were all torn away by the force of the Naming, and at the core of her there was only Leonora.

The water shook and throbbed in her ears. She could feel the bath churning around her, splashing onto the floor. It was an unexpected and risky slap to the face. Water carried secrets well, but water sometimes spilled.

Epilogue

"No," she said with as much dignity as she could muster. "I'm not accusing you." Then without another word she opened her eyes and emerged from the bath in a cascade of water.

Leonora had always felt small in her great aunt's presence. Aenora had never made any secret of the fact that she believed she was better suited to carrying out their glorious Purpose. She was the mightiest of the Five Elders. Her presence vibrated through the water, but Leonora was not the same Witchling she was even the day before. She had survived the Merging with the City and seen a Creature from the Depths with her own eyes, had felt reality twist around it. Leonora was not openly accusing her great aunt, not yet. But she would remember. She had discovered depths in herself that she had never imagined. Her time had come at last.

Leonora was home.

*

The Duke sat hunched over his desk. His forehead was heavily bandaged, and he was nursing his drink distractedly. From down below he could hear the sounds of shouted orders and the crunch of booted feet echoing through Auberon Square. The police and their treacherous master could no longer be trusted. For thirty years he and Hessing had stood shoulder-to-shoulder, keeping order, keeping the peace, or the nearest equivalent. He had showered Hessing with titles and wealth, more than amply rewarded the man's service. The sheer ingratitude!

He banged his hand on the table and winced. His head hurt. His body ached, but the betrayal was worse, far worse. He knew Hessing was venial and corrupt, but had tolerated his faults, because above all Hessing had remained loyal, until now. He glanced over at the file spilled open on his desk. The evidence was damning and irrefutable. Extortion and bribery was one thing, even consorting with body snatchers, necromancers, and known agitators could be tolerated, but he had aided and abetted the faëries, let them into the Victory Ball, and helped unleash the Creature. The Duke sighed.

"Long day?"

The Duke jumped up in surprise. Mr. Nix was seated calmly across from him. His legs crossed and fingers knitted together. "How did you..." the Duke trailed off into silence. He knew from long experience that it was useless to ask. There were few powers that could prevent Mr. Nix from going where he pleased, and the Ducal Guard wasn't one of them.

"Very long day," the Duke agreed. "Have you come to commiserate? These days it seems as though you only ever show up during a crisis."

"As I recall it was you who strongly discouraged my social calls. Something about keeping me a secret weapon, I believe."

"You heard, then?"

"I was there, your grace."

"Of course you were." The Duke forced a smile. "You'd never miss a Victory Ball."

"That would be very unpatriotic of me."

"I still can't believe that Theodore would do this. I was expecting trouble from the Faërie Quarter. I tried so hard to build a long-term solution, to give them what I could, when I could, but they couldn't see that. They were too impatient. I can understand that, but Theodore is another matter. If the humans won't stand with me, then where are we?"

"Are you sure the Commandant really was involved?" Mr. Nix asked innocently.

Epilogue

"There's no doubt. Young Raske has proved unexpectedly resourceful. See for yourself." He gestured angrily at the file.

"No need," said Nix. "If you're convinced, then I'm convinced. But Hessing won't be easy to deal with, and at least half the police force will remain loyal to him. He pays them too well."

"I don't care how many thugs and spies he's got," the Duke snarled. "I have an army."

"Yes," said Mr. Nix, "but where is he?"

"I don't know," the Duke said. "Home, perhaps. Kronberger let him walk right out of Police Headquarters."

"How was he to know?"

"That's not the point." The Duke glowered. "But it doesn't matter, I'll find him. I'll burn him out of whatever hole he's crawled into. Then I'll line up every last one of his men and have them shot. Even the blasted faëries would enjoy watching that." The Duke stormed to his feet. "As for Theodore Hessing, I'll strip his Barony and run him through the courts. Raske could do that for me. He is supposed to be a lawyer, after all, and I'll need to find a use for him." The Duke paused. The room was starting to spin. He was exhausted.

"Sit down, your grace," Mr. Nix said. "You need rest."

"What I need is to be free of my enemies," the Duke said, but he sat down willingly enough. "Instead they're multiplying. What do you know of this Countess Wyman-Straus?"

"Not much," Mr. Nix replied. "Why?"

"My wife's newest friend," said the Duke. "They survived the riots together. We owe her everything. She's even willing to have her picture taken and to do an interview to help steer public opinion."

"Very kind of her," said Mr. Nix.

Epilogue

"Yes," the Duke agreed.

"And yet?" Mr. Nix prompted.

The Duke sighed. "It's probably paranoia. I did just learn that my oldest and closest friend has betrayed me, after all, but I find it odd that this Countess arrived just as all hell broke loose, and she's oddly determined to attach herself to my wife, with an introduction from Hessing, of all people."

"Yes," Mr. Nix agreed. "That does seem suspicious."

"And there's something about the name, Wyman-Straus. I feel as though I've overlooked something obvious."

"You're tired."

"Exhausted."

Mr. Nix paused. "There's something else about her," he said.

"Oh?"

"She has a Mark upon her."

"A Mark? You mean the Mark of a Witch?"

Mr. Nix frowned. "Yes, a familiar one, too, but I can't quite place it."

"A voluntary one?"

"That I cannot say."

The Duke glanced down thoughtfully. "I'm not sure if it's relevant," he said, "but apparently the Emperor has heard rumors about the Witchling Heir to the Throne of Talis."

"Interesting."

"Is that even possible? My father always said that the whole line was destroyed."

"That is what we have always believed."

"Then perhaps I need you more than I thought," the Duke said. "Your fate is bound with that of my family."

"This is true," said Mr. Nix.

Epilogue

The Duke rubbed his forehead, tiredly. "I'm considering consulting the Oracle," he said tentatively.

"I see." Mr. Nix leaned forward. He seemed briefly discomforted.

"I know the risks," said the Duke. "But I'm under siege. I need all the help I can get."

"If you prefer," Mr. Nix offered, "I can consult her on your behalf."

The Duke studied him questioningly for a moment, and then sighed. "I appreciate that," he said. Mr. Nix nodded.

"So, will you look into this matter for me?" the Duke asked. "Help me as you once helped my father, as you once helped my ancestor?"

"Well," said Mr. Nix, "I am always happy to help an old friend. For a price."

"What did you have in mind?"

"I'm sure something will present itself," Mr. Nix said and smiled his most crooked of smiles. "Something always does."

About the Author

A New Yorker born and bred, Antonio Urias is a speculative fiction writer and a lifelong storyteller with a history of rooting for the villains and a love of the dark, the weird, and the cursed. When he was nine years old, he planned out an epic twelve book series about knights and dragons, before deciding that was too ambitious and downscaling to eight. This may explain a lot. He is also the author of *The Nightmare Man*.

https://antoniourias.wordpress.com

Made in the USA
Las Vegas, NV
30 April 2023